The

Ghost Hawk

a novel

DONALD GRECO

Jan-Carol
Publishing, Inc

"every story needs a book"

The Ghost Hawk
Donald Greco
Published August 2024
Little Creek Books
Imprint of Jan-Carol Publishing, Inc.
All rights reserved
Copyright © 2024 Donald Greco
Front Cover Desgin: Tara Sizemore
Front Cover Photograph: © Adrenalinapura/Adobe Stock

ISBN: 978-1-962561-39-6
Library of Congress Control Number: 2024946490

You may contact the publisher:
Jan-Carol Publishing, Inc.
PO Box 701
Johnson City, TN 37605
publisher@jancarolpublishing.com
www.jancarolpublishing.com

To Angie,
my dream of love

Book I

The Golden Bear

THE AUTUMN MOON HUNG beige and low on the horizon. Soon it would be high and bright, lighting the steps of the little band to rest and comfort, their journey almost done. A lean, powerfully-built young man hauled a sled behind him, laden with the carcasses of two deer and two turkeys. Three other young men followed him, each bearing another load of deer and turkeys, and a few beavers. The men were weary and cold yet sweating in the autumn twilight.

The leader wore a cougar skin over his head, the tail trailing down over his shoulder. Each of the other men wore cat skins, either of wildcat or cougar that abounded in the forest. They were the hunters of the Salt Springs tribe, a part of the Erierhonon, the Cat Nation that lived far south of the great lake.

"Do you think we can get there tonight, Dark Moon?" one man said to the leader.

"I do not know," he answered. "I am tired. How are you?"

"Tired. This load is heavy. But if the Huron are close by..."

"Well, some of the load must go as gifts to the Huron, but it will be well worth it. Elk Calf is an old friend. He has fed me many times when I was young and hungry...taught me much about hunting in these woods."

"Well? Should we go forward then?

"Can you still pull your sled?"

"I think so," said Wind as the others nodded in agreement.

"The tribe lives in the valley of the Cuyahoga. Beyond these hills, the woods will clear, and at the far end of the clearing will be the Huron."

"And they will feed us and grant us rest?" asked another of the men.

"I know they will, my friend," said Dark Moon.

Within an hour, the small band came upon the clearing where the meadow sloped gently away from them. One man clucked in relief when he realized that their racks would slide easier down the hill.

The men, though tired, breathed sighs of satisfaction as they headed across the field. They had done a good job, and their own Salt Springs tribe would honor them for the abundance they brought home for the winter months; a job well done. The air was cool, and sleep would come easily that night.

But as they neared the midpoint of the meadow, Dark Moon sensed something strange. "What is it, Moon?" asked Wind, his own unease drawn more from what he sensed in his leader than what he himself was aware of.

Dark Moon stood still, listening to the sounds of the meadow. "Hsst! Wind, do you hear that?"

"Only sounds of the meadow," Wind answered, curious.

Dark Moon seemed to be speaking only to himself. "Did I hear a hawk call? What would bring a hawk to this meadow at night?" No one else heard. "Again! You hear, Wind? A hawk?"

"But could they just be geese looking for a resting place?" said one of the other men.

Dark Moon shut his eyes and took a deep breath. "Let us hurry before we are all mad from weariness," he said, "hearing strange sounds when our bellies are empty."

"Moon," said Wind, interrupting him, now troubled by his own senses. "Why is there so little smoke from the campfires of the Huron? On such a cold night?"

Dark Moon surveyed the edge of the clearing. "Just so, Wind. Why are their fires so small?"

Suddenly their anxiety impelled them to move faster. "Again, the hawk," whispered Dark Moon to himself. "Why come upon this meadow at dark?" He craned his neck to follow the sound as he heard the hawk circle over the entire meadow.

Dark Moon was perplexed. "But there... Hear his call? He cannot only be hunting," he said as he scanned the sky for the hawk.

As they turned back to the woods, they saw the path worn through the trees that led to the camp of the Huron. Dark Moon signaled to the men to wait for him off the path. He threw his catskin headdress to Wind as he proceeded. He was more at home in the forest than any man of the Erierhonon. He moved through the trees silently. He was part cat, the great hunter of the Salt Springs, who came upon his prey so silently that they would seldom escape his arrows.

Farther into the woods, Dark Moon came upon another clearing, not as large as the meadow they had just traveled, but large enough to hold the lodges of Elk Calf's tribe. Silently, in a crouch, Dark Moon waited and watched. No sound, no movement, only a few smoldering fires on the outside and yet no smoke from the lodges. No fires—even on this clear autumn night? Suddenly, again, the hawk screeched a strange and echoing sound that chilled Dark Moon's spine. *There is something to fear here*, he thought.

Suddenly, he started, thinking he had heard the hawk again, but he wasn't sure. He listened again. A cry. A child's cry. He surveyed the campsite. There was no sign of life. Would a small child be left in the camp alone? He waited, as still and quiet as he could be. There was no life here. Strange. No sound from the clearing—only night noises of the forest and the meadow behind him.

Slowly, he backed away from the clearing into the darkness of the forest. When he returned to the meadow, the others greeted him anxiously.

"What have you seen, Moon?" asked Wind in a hushed, anxious tone.

Dark Moon shook his head. "Everything is quiet but..." He hesitated. "I think I heard a baby cry. But only smoldering campfires are around...some stew still steaming in a bowl. I could smell it from the forest. If they are gone, they left in haste."

"But who would leave a small child alone?" said one of the young men.

Dark Moon shrugged. "We must go to the camp, just to know what awaits us there."

Wind approached Dark Moon as he pulled his sled, and the others lagged out of earshot. "What do you make of this, Moon? This silence?"

"I have faced bears and bison before, Wind, but this one scares me more than ever."

As they approached the clearing on the path, Dark Moon had his bow and arrow poised to shoot. The others also had axes or spears ready. Dark Moon turned and motioned to the others for silence and then pointed to the environs of the clearing, meaning that they should all spread out and encircle the camp. Dark Moon could hear the wings flapping before he heard the cry of the hawk overhead. "Again, the hawk," he whispered to himself as he moved forward, waving his arms to the others to continue onward.

Overhead, the hawk was watching the men as they entered the camp. Then, it landed in a tall pine as it watched. These men seemed different from the others, though they had dragged the dead carcasses of other animals on their long journey. The anguish the hawk felt seared its heart and made it restless, never able to stop or have peace. Once again it flew upward, in great circles and banking its wings against the wind, watching the leader of the band of hunters, who wore a catskin on his head. It screamed in anguish and called again.

Dark Moon shivered. He could hear the others call to each other in whispers, while moving on. Suddenly, behind one of the smaller lodges, he came upon a form on the ground. He couldn't see it clearly. Dark Moon looked around, careful for a sign of danger. Then, he approached the form, the man whose large frame he knew. Elk Calf stared with lifeless, glazed eyes into the night.

There was a spear in his neck, and his genitals had been cut off with the crude swing of some large weapon. Behind his head was a pool of blood, and his stomach had been ripped open. Dark Moon shuddered. He reached behind Elk Calf's head and gasped as his hand felt only softness and no bone. His friend's head had been shattered open. Hesitating first, then removing Elk Calf's headdress, he turned his head over slightly, so he could see what had been done to his old friend. Elk Calf's brain was gone.

Dark Moon muttered curses to himself, whispering his outrage as much to calm himself as to show his anger.

Suddenly, he saw Lame Deer, one of his young disciples, a boy of fifteen winters, coming toward him. "There is no one, Dark Moon...All who are here are dead."

"No one?" said Dark Moon. "Not even in the lodges?"

"No one. Small children, even babies, all dead." He paused a moment, seeming to swoon.

"Give me your hand," said Dark Moon, trying to steel his young friend against the nausea he felt.

"I only saw that lodge over there," the boy said, pointing to another smaller one. He paused again. "Dark Moon...All the male children, even the babies, have their roots torn out—every one."

"Are the woman all dead?"

Lame Deer nodded. Just then, they both heard a small cry. Instinctively, both men grasped their weapons. Then, they saw Wind coming toward them. "I have something to show you," he said, "over behind the big lodge."

After several paces, Wind stopped. "Dark Moon, look over here, where Two Birds is standing."

Dark Moon looked at him questioningly but stepped forward. Before him was a baby, genitals torn and barely alive, uttering soft, anguished whimpers. He could see the heart throbbing in his chest, slowly and spasmodically. His eyes were vacant and unseeing, insensitive to anything but pain. "What will we do? We can't let him suffer so," said Wind.

Dark Moon crouched down, touched the child's head, grimacing in horror as he touched the brow, now damp and cold. "Give me your spear, Wind," he said as he stood erect.

Wind uneasily handed him the spear. "He will not live. No medicine can cure this affliction."

Moon nodded in agreement. Then, with one quick movement Dark Moon plunge the spear into the chest of the child as the fevered breathing stopped, and the pulsing in the veins of the neck stopped. Both men breathed deeply. Dark Moon fell into a crouch and supported himself with one outstretched arm against the ground.

"There is another sight," said Wind, motioning to a table a few paces from them. As they moved toward it, the cries of a hawk echoed through the clearing, calling desperately in a cascade of anguish and anger.

"Now I hear it," said Wind. "He has been watching us, but until now, only you alone have heard him. You have heard the Ghost Hawk." On a table were some shards of pottery, and in the center, a young hawk was still alive but dying in agony. The bird's wings were bound together, making it unable to fly. For an instant, as Dark Moon looked at the hawk, the animal seemed to sense that he was not an enforcer of torture. There was a moment of communication. Dark Moon saw that the bird had resigned himself to death. He saw, in the meeting of their eyes, acceptance for what he was compelled to do.

Both the bird's wings had been broken, but rather snapped cleanly, with one stroke. The injury was not quickly fatal. It was meant to cause agony—slow death—to one who would be crazed with suffering. As the moment of death neared, one bone had worked its way through the skin and protruded through a bloody tear in the flesh.

Dark Moon looked for the hawk overhead but did not see him. He looked at Wind, who was silent. He turned back to the dying hawk, drew a flintstone knife from the cincture on his waist and plunged the knife into the breast of the bird, killing it instantly.

Then, the torrent of cries fell upon the meadow. The hawk was aloft, crying shrilly as it flew overhead, seeming to feel release now for what the men had done.

"Who would do this, Dark Moon?" said Wind softly. "Who would slaughter these good men, and defile these women? Who would torment the Sky God with such horrible suffering?"

Dark Moon didn't answer. The other men searched the camp further, each time calling grimly to one another at the sight of more mutilated bodies and dead children. For several quiet minutes, neither man spoke. Finally, Dark Moon shook his head. "Never have I seen such carnage as this—without sense, without cause. Elk Calf was not a warrior; he was just a gentle hunter, someone who always gave food and shelter to a traveler."

Dark Moon listened to the hawk calling again. He looked at Wind, who stared silently back at him.

"We must burn this place, Wind," said Dark Moon.

"Moon, do you remember the stories the Grandmother often told us about the Ghost Hawk? You have been hearing the Ghost Hawk all this night."

Dark Moon shook his head. "I am not sure of what I have been hearing… It may only be waking dreams at seeing this slaughter."

"But you heard it before we came upon this slaughter, did you not?" asked Wind. "Before this discovery… and none of us ever heard it. You surely have heard the Ghost Hawk." He looked directly into the eyes of his best friend.

"Then, what does it mean, Wind? Why me and not you?"

"I know not, but the Manitou does...and you must have a calling to avenge these murders. It must be the way of the Manitou whenever good men and babies are mutilated, and when innocent women are torn asunder by marauding killers. Perhaps when the dust of these people is restored to the earth, their spirits will be whole again."

"I have no skills to be an avenger, Wind. I am only a hunter, just as you are."

All through the night, the men gathered bodies and put them in a makeshift funeral pyre. They were too amazed to rest, and too horrified to leave. They could only continue the grim work they had started.

The fires burned in eerie darkness. The smell of burning bodies sickened the men, but they continued their gathering of the dead. By dawn, their horrible work was done. The fires blazed, and later smoldered. The lodges and the bodies were all gone by morning. The sickening smell of burning flesh still lingered but was less strong than it had been.

Wearily, Dark Moon and his men rested in the morning light. Their awful task, and their leader's fond memories of Elk Calf, had left the small hunting party drained of life's energy. They slept upwind of the fire until the afternoon sun was high in the sky.

"I must tell this to Chief Big Hand...and to no one else," Dark Moon said to the men. "We must keep this awful story to ourselves, and let the tribe think only of the bounty we have returned to them. There will be time later that Big Hand will tell the Cat people how to prepare for such danger as we have seen in this forest." He gestured over his shoulder. "Our own people, even the warriors, would otherwise be as trusting and unaware as these poor creatures."

The Grandmother

DARK MOON SAW WIND in the morning as he walked toward the creek. Wind gestured to him, as if he had something to say. Dark Moon approached and said, "Did you sleep well last night?"

"Yes. Moon, the Grandmother wants to see you."

Dark Moon nodded. "It has been two suns since our return. I should have seen her before now."

"She told my sister to tell me, so that I might remind you," Wind said. "Perhaps she feels that you must be punished for your evil life," he finished, smiling.

Dark Moon laughed softly and gently jostled his old friend. "With friends like you, I have no need of enemies. I will go as soon as I bathe in the creek."

"Fear not, Moon," said Wind. "You deserve to hear some good news."

Sometime later, after he had bathed, Dark Moon approached the entry of the Grandmother's small lodge. Dark Moon called through the deerskin entrance. She called back to him and told him to enter.

Inside, she said, "Hail, tardy one," and gestured to a place on a mat beside her own. He squatted and sat cross-legged, intent upon her face, curious about what she would say to him. "You have been here two days and have not yet come to see me."

"I was intent on unpacking and skinning animals and preparing skins for the women to tan...but I should have come sooner. Are you angry with me?"

She smiled. "You are not a child that needs to be forgiven."

"In the past, you have gently forgiven my misdeeds and made my heart always light and hopeful. Can you not find one more pardon for an errant hunter?"

"I will always forgive you, my son," she said. "But is there not something you would ask of me this day?"

"You said you would tell me my future when I returned from the hunt."

"I have dreamt some of it for you...but there is still much I do not know," she said.

"Can you tell me what you know?" he asked softly.

When she sighed and shook her head, his mood darkened. "Only that you will not be chief of the Salt Springs, nor the Great One."

Dark Moon swallowed hard and was silent. She studied him. "Do you know why?" he asked.

"I do not, except that it is not your life. But you will live to be an old man."

"Will I marry?"

"Yes, but I know her not...and there will be some trouble in your life."

The Grandmother was silent for several minutes, staring at him, and trying to reconcile her dreams and what she knew about him. *He is strange*, she thought, *really much like a cat.*

There was a quality about him that drew some people toward him, and yet drove others away. He was cordial with most members of the tribe, but he had only one true friend, Wind. He was honorable and warm, yet private. He came to the Salt Springs as a stranger, a small boy whose parents had been killed. His rescuer, Wise Apple, the man who saved his life, had become his adoptive father. And because of his father's status in the tribe, and Dark Moon's obliging behavior, most people accepted and grew to respect him. That acceptance was also sustained because of his seemingly unnatural skill as a bowman and hunter. It was said that he could hear voices in the forest that others could not hear and was able to walk the land in darkness…as does a cat. And he also did not have the brash and willing personality of Red Eagle. Dark Moon was thoughtful, while Red Eagle was flamboyant. He was exactly what the tribe of the Salt Springs would need as chief.

The Grandmother always felt sorry for him as he grew up without a mother's tender touch that would make his spirit feel the happiness of childhood. "Dark Moon, I have dreamed these many nights, and I have learned that I will soon be with the Great Spirit."

"Grandmother, you know I will keep you warm and nourished during the great cold. You must live to tell me truths as you always have. You will be the wise one of the Cats for many more winters, and I will be much favored for it."

"It will not be from loss of warmth or food that will make me die," she said softly, turning toward him. "I am old, and it is my time. And that is why the Manitou has revealed these troubling images to me."

"And these things will bring sorrow into my life?" he asked.

She shook her head, as though unsure about her words. "Sorrow and pain…and yet joy."

"But these are more riddles than revelations," he muttered.

"Perhaps. But not all of it has been foretold to me. And I know not why."

Dark Moon looked at her silently for a few minutes. "What part of the story can you tell me, Grandmother?"

"You will be a stranger to the Erierhonon, my son."

"But there are those out here," he waved his arm, gesturing to the entry, "that, to this day, call me a stranger. My father found me alone in the forest and brought me to live among the Salt Springs. And I feel that I have always been untrusted by some who see me only as an intruder no matter how much food I bring from the forest."

"But you also know that there are those who would see you as chief of the Cats."

"But yet there are those who would only want a warrior as chief, are there not?" he asked.

"Red Eagle?" she asked.

"Indeed, Red Eagle. Is it not said that he should be chief because he is a great fighter who protects the Salt Springs from intrusion?" Dark Moon snorted softly, but kept silent, just shaking his head.

"But," the Grandmother continued, "the Erierhonon will rue the day that you are not their chief."

"So, now I am to be a stranger to them?"

"Yes. There will be another tribe that will welcome you and give you their hearts."

He shook his head. "Have you ever been wrong before, Grandmother?"

"Not when the Manitou has taken the shroud from my face. And not when he has given me his final message in this life."

"Do you know much of my life? Who will I marry? Will I have children?"

"Only what the Great Spirit wishes me to see…The Manitou was angry with me for the false and foolish talk I made as a young woman, for the one time I betrayed my husband."

He frowned. "You do not have to tell me this," he said. "I am unworthy to hear stories of your disgrace."

"Yet the Manitou knew I would tell you my dreams."

"Why me? Why not Red Eagle, who will be chief?"

"The Manitou does not favor Red Eagle."

"But he will be chief, will he not?"

"Yes, not just of the Salt Springs, but of all the Erierhonon."

Dark Moon huffed. "The Great One," he muttered. Then, he was quiet again for several minutes, turning from the old woman and staring into the fire at the center of the lodge. "Who will be his wife?" he asked finally. "Do you know?"

"Yes."

"Who?"

"You know in your heart who it will be."

"Calling Dove?"

"Yes."

"Will they have children?"

"Yes. One woman and one man."

He snorted again. "And this is not finding favor in the eyes of the Manitou?"

"You would not barter your life for his," she said.

"He will be the Great One and have a lovely, spirited wife, and fine children, and I am to be a stranger to the Erierhonon, and yet I would not trade my life for his?"

"He will be powerful and great, yet there is a dark shadow that will haunt him and bring grief into his life." She stopped for several minutes, moaning softly and rocking her body back and forth. She turned her face to Dark Moon's, and he saw tears streaming down her cheeks.

He knelt down in front of her. "Grandmother..."

"The tears are not for Red Eagle, nor for you, my dear son...but for the Erierhonon."

"No tears for a stranger who must leave the Salt Springs and the fields and forests that he loves, the people that he loves?"

"No tears for you are needed. Your life will bring some suffering and loss, but there will always be the blessing of the Manitou in your life."

"Will I take a wife and have children?"

"Yes, you will have three daughters, and like their mother, they will all be creatures of strange hair."

"Strange hair? What does that mean?" he asked.

"It will have a mark. I know not what the mark is."

"Strange marks on their hair?"

"Yes. I know not where they are from or where their journey began, but you will be happy with them."

"And no sons?"

"No."

He shook his head. "Grandmother, these dreams are too much. You speak only of daughters, but no sons to carry on my spirit, a wife who is not the woman I have dreamed of all these winters, and blessings, though I will be turned away from this bountiful land of the Salt Springs."

"Dark Moon, I know little of your future except what I have told you. I know you will have suffering and sorrows, but they will turn to happiness if you wait. Most of my worst dreams were of the Cats."

"Dreams of Cats and Red Eagle," he muttered.

"Listen to me, my son. The shadow that fell on the dreams of Red Eagle also fell on my dreams of you. But when the shadow touched your face, it glowed. When it touched the face of Red Eagle, I saw only darkness."

"What is the nature of this shadow?"

"It is the death shroud of the Erierhonon."

"Of all the Cats?"

"When I was a child, my own Grandmother could also see the future. She told me of the death shroud. And now I have had the same dream. The Erierhonon will be delivered from the land of the Salt Springs by its own weakness and evil."

Dark Moon was silent as he stared somberly into the fire. "Have you told anyone of this?" he asked.

"Only you."

"Will you not tell Big Hand?"

"He was not in the dream, and he is right with the Manitou."

"But you must tell someone so that we might prepare for the shroud."

"There will be no preparation. The shroud will fall on many, but not all. And the honorable ones among us will leave."

"When will this happen?"

"Many winters hence…long after I am gone from this valley."

"And where will I be?"

"I do not know."

"Do you know when I will become a stranger?"

"It will be when I am gone. But it will begin in the time of a yellow bear."

"Yellow bear? Can you jest of this? Is this mockery?"

She made a long sigh. "All I know is that a yellow bear came to look on the death of the Erierhonon. I am sorry to bring you terrible stories of your future, your pained and hurtful life. All I know, in truth, is that in the end you will find happiness."

They both remained silent for several minutes, trying to sort their notions of what they had considered. "There is something more we must think of," the Grandmother said softly.

"What is that?"

"There will come a great cold this winter and the next, and some of our people will die of it."

"People of the Salt Springs?

"People from everywhere…from far to the great lake to the mountains of the morning. And there will be other great colds in near winters to come."

Dark Moon sighed and bowed his head in acknowledgement. "I was told by a man from the north, a Wenro, that a great cold was coming, as though the Manitou was punishing us."

"I think not," she said. "My grandfather told me when I was a child that he knew of many great colds in his life. They come and go. He lost some of his brothers and sisters, and even his mother."

"Then we must prepare for the one coming to the Salt Springs. I will tell Big Hand of this."

"He may know of it already. And he will call a council of elders in two suns. They must send out more hunters than your group to gather meat from the forest. You and Wind will lead hunters in groups. But be careful, my son. You are a great hunter, but I sense the forest will bring you danger."

"Have I not always heeded your warnings in the past? You know I will be careful."

The Grandmother wailed softly and embraced him as she often did when he was a small child. "Remember me."

"How can I forget you?" he said. "I will return to protect and feed you during the winter."

Calling Dove

CALLING DOVE WAITED FOR Dark Moon as she watched her sister approach him and whisper a discreet message. Tonight, there would be feasting and songs and dancing in celebration of the harvest and the hunt. There would also be roasted salted meats, chestnuts, boiled roots, and nuts, sweets, and honey. And there would be commotion with brawls and games and noise. The hunt had been good; the winter would not be grim and miserable, but rather would be easier to keep warm and to forget hunger.

Soon, Dark Moon approached her. She smiled as he came toward her. "Does the great hunter stoop to talk to a lowly maiden of the Salt Springs?" she asked mockingly.

"You are anything but lowly," he said.

"Then why have we not even spoken greetings in more than two moons? When we were children, we would talk into the night...and be kindred spirits. But now, has the great hunter forgotten the friends of his youth?"

"You mock me," Dark Moon said, looking troubled by her teasing. "You want play and banter, and I do not do that well."

She grew more careful, and more serious. "I do not mock you when I speak the truth—that you do not talk to me."

"I do not talk to you because you are bespoken," Dark Moon said.

"I am not bespoken," she said emphatically. "Red Eagle has no claim upon me."

Dark Moon stared into her eyes at that moment as she looked back at him defiantly.

"I did not mention the name of Red Eagle," he said quietly, making his point and watching her flush in embarrassment. Suddenly, her expression changed, her eyes showing vulnerability. He relented, content to say nothing more, and to let her speak in her own justification.

"You and I have grown apart these winters," she said. "Do you remember those times when we talked long hours even after the fire had gone out?"

"Yes, I remember." He nodded slightly. "I will never forget those days."

"Then why have you avoided me for almost a whole winter?" she asked plaintively. "No one has ever understood that. Do you know how many times I was asked what had come between us?"

"You changed."

"What?" she said, now showing some anger. "Was it not you, the great hunter, who lived for the adulation of all the Erierhonon? Did you not savor the talk that you would be chief, that perhaps one day you would be the Great One? I am just a maiden who would only be valued for my hips and my breasts to bring forth strong sons. How was I to change?"

"As your beauty grew, and your stature and your body changed, you became—"

"Became what? Say it!"

"You became foolish and fickle as the squirrels that play in the forest."

She glared at him again, hating him for what he said, yet strangely captivated by his presence. There was something so elemental about him, something hidden and mysterious, that unraveled all her best laid plans. Maybe the great presence of Red Eagle had clouded her eyes. This was a man, calm yet reserved, but never obviously proud or arrogant, that somehow had ties to her heart. He wasn't the kind—at least she told herself—that would make her weak and flushed as he held her in his arms as Red Eagle would. But yet, she knew she could not love Red Eagle in her age as she would love this man.

She spoke softly to him, cooly containing her anger. "Other men do not find me so fickle," she said softly. "If our friendship was so fine, should you not have wanted to change me?"

He shook his head. "I did not know how."

"But did you want to? When your exploits made you the objects of songs and chants? When your skill made you as respected as our old chief? Come, great hunter, my own vanity was not enough to drive you away, was it?"

He turned away from her, watching some children play near the great fire in the center of the camp, as though she were not there beside him. Both were silent until their closeness made them uncomfortable. Finally, she moved slightly, breaking the stillness of the moment.

And as she stepped sideways, he spoke, "It was not your vanity, for I was vain also." He stopped for a moment longer. "But I was also afraid... that I would say the wrong things to you...and be embarrassed. You seemed suddenly bespoken, as though my fate was never to have you."

"To whom was I bespoken?" she asked.

"At first, to many in my imaginings, but later, only one."

"Whose name I have mentioned once tonight," she sighed, finishing his thought. "But I have also said that there is no one to whom I am pledged. Do you believe me?"

"I will," he answered, "if you say it is so."

"But am I to choose as my own spouse a man who does not seek my heart? Who stands aloof and watches me as though in his heart there is cold water and not warm blood? Someone whose passions I could not stir?"

"Do not say it," he said, interrupting her. "For it was never so."

"Then why have so many moons passed since you have barely spoken to me?"

He shook his head, as though to himself. Finally, he said, looking directly at her, "I wanted to speak, but I was…timid."

"A man who kills wolves and bears and great cats is too timid to talk to a maiden who he has known all his life?" she asked doubtfully.

"If the maiden would have wished for my company, she had but to ask me…only to speak. But I believed that you had grown too proud, or that you had found another."

"There has been no other," she said firmly.

He huffed and shook his head. "But yet there has been one…"

She made a disconcerted grimace. "Yes, I have heard that he wishes to marry."

"And so, are you not thus bespoken?"

"I am bespoken only by my consent," she said firmly.

"Red Eagle is a great man," Dark Moon said. "You will be the wife of the chief of the Salt Springs and perhaps someday the Great One. Your dreams will all come true."

"There are rumors that you will be chief," Calling Dove said.

"I cannot match the glorious deeds of a warrior. A few carcasses of deer do not stir the hearts of the Salt Springs as the tokens of battle grandly taken from a foe."

"So, you will not ask me because you fear that you will not be chief?" she said, not concealing her disdain for his reasoning.

"And you would consent to be the wife of a hunter—someone often away many suns, an ordinary man—someone who would not be chief?"

"Would the hunter cherish me and look only to me as his wife?"

"The hunter would have cherished you as none have ever been cherished," Dark Moon said.

Calling Dove paused a few moments before answering him.

"I..." she stammered. "I must find a way to separate my dreams."

Dark Moon looked silently at her. "Your choice will make his chance to be chief all the more certain. But is that not what you want? To be the wife of the chief?"

"But what if you are chosen?"

"No. I will never be chief."

"And how are you so convinced?"

"I just know."

She huffed. "You, who know so little of what people think, are suddenly so certain that you will not be chosen chief?"

"Why do you say that I know little of what people think?"

"You know nothing of what I think."

"You are different. I have learned not to trust in what you think...but to only trust my own eyes. They have seen you do what I never would believe."

"And what terrible thing have I done to you?" Calling Dove asked.

He didn't answer. Instead, he knelt down to tie a bundle of arrows that he had unraveled.

"Tell me!" she said angrily.

Dark Moon was also angry. The bitterness he felt that winter had never left him, though he tried to suppress it. But Calling Dove had unwittingly given him assent to let loose the bitterness and turn it upon the very person who had caused him such pain. Finally, he stood up again and gazed into her eyes.

"In the autumn past, when you knew my feelings for you, feelings you knew I was unready to speak, whose blanket did you sleep under on the night of the yellow moon? Who felt your nakedness in the darkness?"

Calling Dove looked back at him silently, unable to answer because she never realized that he had known of her night with Red Eagle. Dark

Moon's voice then grew softer. "And yet, when you talked to me, you pretended that it never happened…And you expected me to come courting you as though Red Eagle and I were on equal footing? As though I did not know what you had done?"

She lowered her voice. "It happened only one time," she said softly.

He snorted. "Do you expect me to believe that?"

"No," she said inaudibly, as though to herself. "So, you have carried this hatred and anger in your heart all these moons?"

"Did you expect me to consider it a trifle when you knew how I felt about you…after all the times we spent together as innocent children? That your sleeping under his blanket would be the same in my heart as your sleeping under mine?"

"I have known other girls who have found you under their blankets."

"Yes. And it all happened after your sleep on the yellow moon with Red Eagle. And they were not you."

She had tears in her eyes. "So, you have hated me all this time?"

"I have hated your lies."

"And you hate me now?"

"I have never hated you."

"And what is this you are speaking, if it is not hatred?"

"I have spoken only of what will be. You will be the wife of Red Eagle, and I will not be chief."

"So, have you never wanted me?"

"I have wanted you every day of my life before that yellow moon. But you showed me that what I dreamed was only the fond hope of a boy… and yet you expected me to play the fool."

"You must know it meant nothing. What one does on the yellow moon surely does not mean what one will always do."

"But what you did on the yellow moon was the beginning of your lies to me."

"And for that you can never forgive me?"

"I can never forgive the future," he snapped. "I cannot forgive what you could have said to me but did not. The secrets of your heart were a test by which you would choose between me and Red Eagle. But those lies were only an omen for my own misery."

"Please…" she said softly. "When you return from the hunt, will you let me explain my foolish actions? Please talk to me, even if you can never love me?"

"But when I return from the hunt, I will still not be chief."

"You do not know that."

Dark Moon huffed. "You have longed to be the wife of the chief, and when the hunt is over, you will…and I wish you good fortune." He stooped to grasp a load of arrows. They looked at each other one last time, and then Dark Moon turned and walked away into the morning mist.

Red Eagle and His Father

As RED EAGLE ENTERED his father's lodge, he could see that they would be alone. Starving Wolf motioned for his son to squat on the mat nearest his place by the fire. The old man spoke in a low voice meant only to be heard by his son.

"Big Hand will choose Dark Moon...and he will sway many others by his vote."

"How do you know this?" asked Red Eagle anxiously.

"I know everything," huffed his father.

"But what of my exploits? What of my conquests? Does Big Hand think that peace comes to this valley only by chance? Have I not driven away all but the Cat Nation from the Salt Springs?"

"There was a story told in council of the slaughter of the small Huron tribe that lived under the great lake. Dark Moon has told the chief of their mutilation and death. And the chief has told us to prepare to be wary of strangers who pose as peaceful travelers, and who then may rise up against us."

Red Eagle looked troubled. "They were strangers in our land," he said. "I once warned Elk Calf that his tribe should not hunt near the Salt Springs. But he said that he was just a simple hunter and planter who had lived near us many winters in peace. And he said that his tribe hunters would only take a few deer or beavers or turkeys for the winter." Red Eagle hesitated. "But again, I told him that this was the land of the Cat people, and that he was not welcome among us."

"And so he did not depart?" asked Starving Wolf.

"At first. But then some of his hunters returned. And now he has atoned for his arrogance."

"Did you do these mutilations?" asked Starving Wolf.

"My father, my men are warriors. When they are aroused—or challenged—they fight and capture the orenda of those they vanquish."

"Fah!" said his father contemptuously. "Do you think you can act like some tribes of the Iroquois nation? Are you eaters of the flesh? Do you not know that our people see that as an abomination? Have you heard the grandmothers tell stories of the flesh eaters? Fah!"

"It is done, my father," said Red Eagle, surprised and ashamed at his father's reaction. "If I would tell our tribe of this, what good would come of it? I would be outcast by Big Hand. And Dark Moon…"

"Dark Moon would be chief," his father said, finishing his sentence.

"And Dark Moon would be chief," said Red Eagle somberly.

"But, as their leader, could you not have stopped them, even in the heat of battle?" asked Starving Wolf.

"How could I have stopped them? This Elk Calf…"

"Elk Calf's tribe was renowned, even though he was a Huron, for his friendship with the Cat people. This will displease the great spirit."

Starving Wolf hesitated for a moment, looking anguished.

"Did my son eat the flesh of the Huron?" he asked softly.

Red Eagle hesitated a moment, avoiding his father's gaze. Finally, he said, "I am a warrior…and I have captured the orenda from Elk Calf's Hurons."

There was a cup of salt near the fire where Starving Wolf sat. He took some out and sprinkled it around him and his son. Red Eagle watched in amazement as his father did the same mysterious ritual that he had seen his grandmother do long ago. Starving Wolf stopped his movement and grew silent. Finally, he spoke.

"You must never tell of this abomination, Red Eagle. Your band of warriors must be silent forever, never to tell of what was done to the Huron. I believe Big Hand will call a council someday soon to choose a new chief. You will not then be chosen as chief unless you hold your silence."

"But others might be chosen...Perhaps Wind."

"There will be no other. But the spirit of Dark Moon has moved among the people of the Salt Springs. Unless there is a change, Dark Moon—"

"Is there nothing I can do?" Red Eagle interrupted.

"You must do something. If the orenda of the vanquished has made you strong, now you must grow wise. The Salt Springs people must be taught to fear the five nations, especially the Seneca. And they must be convinced that they need a great warrior as a leader to save them. Choose your best opportunity to speak of war when you can. Do not seem to be someone who welcomes war, but only show yourself as a great leader. The people must believe that you will be their savior and protector."

"And who should they hear these words from? If I am to be the one they pick, would it not be unseemly for me to talk of these things?"

"I will talk much of war," said Starving Wolf. "When you speak, you will only have to agree that war is coming." Starving Wolf hesitated for a moment. "My son, you know Calling Dove will marry whoever is chief. She will want to beget sons of the chief, one of whom may himself be the Great One of the Erierhonon."

Red Eagle was troubled by his father's words, but he understood their meaning and intent. "I will make her my wife, my father."

"She will make you happy. Your lodge would be one of sweet sleep. I would see strong grandsons..." He paused for a moment, looking directly into the fire. "But if the talk in our tribe is only of Dark Moon becoming chief, then he will have her as his wife."

"I tell you, Father, she will be my wife," said Red Eagle. This time, he spoke in a soft voice, but there was no doubt of his conviction.

"Then, we must act, my son. When all return from this great hunt, we must make the Salt Springs fear the Seneca and think only of war...war in which only you will bring victory and peace."

The Old Chief

THE OLD MAN STOOD alone, looking across the Mahoning as pale mist rose from the land bordering the river. He had been waiting there several minutes. Suddenly, he sensed someone approach from behind his back. The figure stopped beside him, also looking out into the mist, and waited.

"I knew you would come to me soon," he said to Dark Moon as he continued looking straight ahead.

"I have some stories to tell you, my chief."

"I am listening," said Big Hand. "And you are troubled, are you not?"

"Yes, I am full of foreboding," said Dark Moon.

This time, the old man turned his face to Dark Moon. "Is that why you have delayed coming to see me for three suns?"

Dark Moon shrugged his shoulders. "My story is unlike anything I have ever known."

Big Hand had known Dark Moon since he was a small child—found by the man who became his foster father—when he found the boy wandering, alone and starving, in the woods. "Come," said the chief, "let us speak in my lodge."

Inside, Starving Wolf threw another log into the fire that was still smoldering from the morning burn. Then, he sat down cross-legged near the fire and gestured to Dark Moon to sit beside him. As Dark

Moon sat down, the old chief nodded. "Continue, my son."

"You recall Elk Calf, the tall Huron I introduced you to some winters passed?"

Big Hand nodded.

"Well..." Dark Moon sighed and paused again. "A few suns ago, my hunters and I were feeling content and weary on our way home to the Salt Springs after a plentiful hunt. I knew that Elk Calf would feed and comfort us if we stopped at his camp, for he was an old friend and mentor who would always grant me rest and peace in the night. And he was always grateful whenever I offered him, as tribute, some parts of my hunt. And...there were times, lately, that he would send me a young woman to bring warmth to my night as I rested safely."

Suddenly, Dark Moon stopped, his voice barely a whisper, and his eyes ran with tears. He lowered his head to his chest.

Big Hand clutched his forearm and held it firmly. "My son, I know you bring a terrible story. But I have seen the Ghost Hawk, and I know my days are but few in number. I will be with the Manitou before the next Thunder Moon. But until then, I will help you mend this affliction that you carry in your heart." He gestured with his hand for Dark Moon to continue.

"Well...as we drew near his camp, Wind noticed that there were no fires and little smoke. So, we stepped carefully as we approached." He stopped again, looking at the old chief. "All had been slaughtered as though they were animals. Not one was left alive but a horribly wounded child and a young hawk that was tortured as though to spite the Ghost Hawk."

"For the men, their heads were destroyed, and their brains removed... seemingly to capture their orendas," Dark Moon continued. "All their roots, even of all the male children, were gone."

"But, my son, did you see the Ghost Hawk?" Big Hand asked anxiously.

"No," said Dark Moon. "I heard him many times, but I was the only one. Wind and I heard it together once, but none of the others ever heard it. I thought I was going mad."

"But you did not see it?" asked Big Hand.

"No, do you not believe me? I speak the truth."

Big Hand was as animated as he seldom was. "I believe you, Dark Moon. But I am thankful that you have only heard him. For if you saw him, then your suns upon this earth would be few in number, and you would soon be with the Manitou. When you heard the hawk while no one else could, it means that you may have great travail, but that later you will still breathe as you do now."

Dark Moon looked at him questioningly. "I have heard the tale only once before, as a boy, but I have never had great trust in the legend, thinking it was the prattle of old women."

Big Hand was quiet for a few minutes but then said, "I have heard it in my life before, with my own father...And now, since I have seen the Ghost Hawk, I bear great trust in the legend."

After a few thoughtful moments, Big Hand asked Dark Moon if he had any idea of who could have done the massacre of Elk Calf's tribe.

But Dark Moon shook his head. "I have never known of anyone in the Ohio who would do such evil upon innocents—everyone dead, all the women defiled, small children destroyed. Never." He stopped for a moment, looking into the fire as though thinking out loud, and said, "They must have come upon them as friends, for there were no signs of struggle, no evidence of wounded left among the killers. Perhaps Elk Calf's people were killed as they slept."

"I have been told long ago that some few tribes across the mountains of the morning were capable of such brutality, but I, too, have never seen or heard of such acts near the Ohio."

"So what are we to do?" Dark Moon said. "Surely we must be ready... and not trust wanderers who come upon us with more than a few men."

"I will tell our elders in the council a few suns away," Big Hand said. "Meanwhile, we must lay by sustenance for the Cats this winter."

Dark Moon didn't speak for a few minutes. Then, he said, "Grandfather, there is something more I must tell you."

Big Hand looked at him almost fearfully. "Is there more, my son?"

"No, no more of marauding killers, but there is something else we must also prepare for."

The old man looked troubled as Dark Moon spoke: "Do you know of one of the young boys who is among my hunters? The one called River Bend?"

"Yes. His grandfather and I are friends from our youth."

"Well, he and Lame Deer are both of sixteen winters, and we are all good friends. Wind also likes them and thinks they are among the finest hunters in all the Erierhonon."

"And so?"

Dark Moon sighed, as if to fortify himself for telling a strange story to Big Hand that might not be believed. "One moon ago, they came upon some other young men near the great lake of the Ohio. And they told me a strange story, the same one that my father also told when I was a small boy."

"And this story? Do you believe in its truth?"

"Yes, Grandfather."

"Well, then, tell me. I will listen."

"My father, before he was called by the Manitou, told me a story about the lands above the great lake of the north. It is said that strange creatures live there that are different than those of the Ohio. There are large wolves of many colors, all gray or black or white, great large owls that are white in the winter and dark in the summer, giant weasels that can kill a deer, and pale bears that are almost white, and some that are brown and gold as the summer sun."

"Your foster father was a great man who would have been chief of the Cats, had he lived," Big Hand replied. "Wise Apple was a friend of my youth who was as true a man who was ever in the Cat tribe. It was an act of mercy that the Great Spirit made him find you in the forest and bring you back to be one of us. To our people, you were a gift of the Manitou. Even today, there are voices that you should soon be chief of the Salt Springs."

Dark Moon shook his head. "I will not be chief," he said softly, almost to himself.

Big Hand didn't argue with his comment, but instead said, "Go on, my son. Finish your story."

"River Bend and Lame Deer were gathering nuts, far from the Salt Springs, up where the Wenro live. And they heard from among them stories of the same creatures of the north who now have come into the hills—giant weasels, huge white owls, and sunny brown bears. They are now in the forests near the camps of the hill people."

"Do you believe these stories?"

"I believe my young friends…but the story also seems easy to believe if I trust my own reason. We have all heard legends of bitterly cold winters. The world does indeed seem to change from time to time. And if we sometimes see warm winters, why should we not believe in very cold winters? And if the small creatures that are the main food of the wolves and bears and other large animals all die in the great cold, would not those strange, large creatures from the north come to our valleys to feed, where many of the small creatures still abound?"

Big Hand nodded. "You have wisdom, my son. And we will begin tomorrow to gather food. We will also send out many hunting parties before the cold comes. And we will store in our underground cellars as many nuts and berries and vegetables as we can find, and the women must make more coats and moccasins and boots and leggings for everyone, lest the cold turn their fingers and their feet to black. I will tell them that we should begin storing food and making clothes quickly. The council will determine the hunting parties, each one led by one of your finest hunters."

The chief was quiet for a few moments, then said, "Dark Moon, my son, I know there is much talk of you in our camp. Many say that you would be chief."

Dark Moon snorted in disbelief again. "Red Eagle will be chief," he said somberly.

Big Hand was surprised, turning toward him. "Red Eagle troubles people. He is a man of war."

"Yet such men instill fire into the hearts of many in our tribe," said Dark Moon.

"But you inspire respect. They would follow you. Hear me, Dark Moon: many in this tribe are like children. They may be happy when their bellies are full, but the foolish ones still harbor dreams of conquest in battle. They will heed the war cries of a man like Red Eagle unable to imagine that such men might bring suffering and death into this wondrous valley."

Dark Moon shook his head. "All of the Erierhonon have heard of Red Eagle's bravery. Everyone knows that he throws his axe like a thunderbolt, and struts and dances by the campfire." But as Dark Moon spoke, a strange thought troubled him for a fleeting moment. *A great fighter, who gives no quarter to an adversary, who is a warrior who kills for glory.*

Suddenly, Dark Moon stopped speaking and paused, listening to his own thoughts. "My chief, when did Red Eagle's band return to camp last?"

The old chief turned toward him suddenly. "Why do you ask this?"

"Was there blood on their skins? Or their faces? Where did they get their wounds? And who did they vanquish?"

"Hush, Dark Moon. Say no more of this. Would you say such things of a brother?"

"I am a brother to no one, my chief. And to some, I will always be a stranger. So must I now not speak of the carnage of Elk Calf's tribe?"

The chief paused and was thoughtful. "If you would be chief, you must wait. Elk Calf walked alone. He may have enemies we know nothing of. The Great Spirit must choose to avenge Elk Calf."

Dark Moon shook his head. "I've seen the blood of so many innocent ones, and it cries out for vengeance. Yet, I will not be the chief to avenge them."

The Elders

The smoke was pale gray and thick, as if waiting for the arrival of the tribesmen before filtering slowly out into the wind. The pine needles that formed a thick mat on the floor crackled underfoot as men and women of the Salt Springs tribe filed singly through the deerskin entry. They all sat cross-legged on mats until the chief's lodge had a full complement of elders.

Soon, one woman nodded to a man whose robe had skins and furs of several cats and other creatures long since hunted down and skinned by the old chief. The meeting commenced as he lifted a crooked arm slowly. The pain in his shoulder brought a fleeting grimace as he held up an outstretched hand, gnarled both by injury and old age.

"I have heard words these last few suns," he began, "that should give us much to think about. Of the Iroquois coming into the valley of the Mahoning from far upriver. And that in a few winters, they may be coming into the hunting range of the Salt Springs. The Wenro, the eaters of fish, have been to the five nations, and there are, among them, men with white faces who came from the endless lake across the mountains of the morning—in great canoes larger than even two lodges of any families of the Erierhonon."

There were murmurs among the crowd for several minutes until he continued. "It is also said that animals are acting strangely. Such behavior of animals that sense a great cold coming upon them, not seen in the regions of the north near the great lake since the winters of our grandfathers."

"So what must we do?" said one woman.

"We must prepare for two things: the great cold that may come upon us in a short time, and then we must be ready to protect our camp if strange tribes come here seeking to take possession of the Salt Springs."

More murmurs followed. "So, do the Wenro fear these white ghosts?" asked one man. "Have their planting fields been destroyed? Is there war among them?"

"The Wenro shaman said that the white ghosts have brought war among each of the Onondaga, Cayuga, and the Oneida. They kill easily."

"But have not these tribes been at war among themselves since the winters of our grandfathers? So, why do they never come to this valley of the Cat people?" asked another man.

"I have heard tales of the white ghosts who have thunderbolts in their quivers," said one woman impatiently. "And even if the ghosts do not come themselves, they will drive the Iroquois into our valley."

Another man spoke, "But now there is talk of a pact among the five nations. And if the five great nations ever become one, surely, we, the Erierhonon, will be their next war. And that war will not be across the mountains of the morning, but it will be here." He gestured with his arm over his shoulder. "In these planting fields that border the Salt Springs."

"But have we not made peace with the Seneca? And they are part of the five nations. Would they make war on us now?" asked a woman.

"But among the five nations are the Iroquois, and all they do is fight," an old man responded. "Have they not destroyed the mighty Algonquin nation?"

"But then, to make all of this ready, must we not have a chief?" asked another.

A woman stood up to speak, and said, "In the present, we are at peace. And a dark winter is coming upon us...either this one or the one over the next horizon. And we must provide for what will surely come now, rather than for what may come later. I say Dark Moon is the one to lead us."

Another woman stood up to speak. "I have fed Dark Moon from our fires since he was a small child. He has never known a mother, so he would depend on my fires and the fires of others that are in this lodge tonight." She gestured to the group. "And as he became a man, he grew wise and respectful. And more...There is no one in all the Erierhonon who can shoot an arrow as truly as he, even among our warriors. Have we not been fed during past winters by the deer, elk, bison, and turkeys that he and Wind have delivered to us in preparation for the cold? So, if we are to endure a terrible winter soon, should he not be the chief who will lead us through this torment?"

A man stood up to say, "All the food animals in the forest will do us no good if we are destroyed by an enemy from the mountains. I speak for Red Eagle, a warrior who will drive the invaders away from the Salt Springs."

This time, a tall, elderly man spoke. "Peace is not the time of Red Eagle. I, who am a friend of Starving Wolf, his father, must say these words that are in my heart. Dark Moon is a man for the peaceful times. He is a man who listens. He knows the ways of nature and knows the ways of men. With Dark Moon as chief, the tribe will flourish. We will prepare for these terrible winters. We will live in peace with the Iroquois and will make peace with the Ottawa."

Big Hand, the old chief, raised his hand. "Starving Wolf, do you wish to speak of your son before this council?"

"My friend, Little Dog, speaks from his heart," said Starving Wolf, somewhat bitterly. "But he knows that there are many tribes who would make war with us. We all know that someday the Iroquois will surely desire this abundant land in which we live. There is fresh, clean water here, never drought as the people of the deserts often experience. There are deer, elk, bison, turkeys, beavers, bears, every kind of animal for our food and clothing. And the Salt Springs have made it easy for us to season and preserve our meat. And the soil is good. When we plant seeds, they grow in abundance. Do you think all the tribes of the east will let us live in this verdant land and not wish to take it from us? They surely must know of the plentifulness of our region. If the white ghosts come like bees to a hive, when they bring their bitter medicine to the Five Nations, will not some of the Five, perhaps the Seneca or the Onondaga, look to us here at the Salt Springs and want its beauty and plenty for themselves?"

He paused, wanting to be sure he had the attention of all the council. They were listening intently to his argument. Starving Wolf went on, "And who will save this land for the Cat people? Hunters?"

He stood silent for a few moments, then with a grave face said, "My son is a brave and fierce warrior, as you all know. But no one asks a warrior for wisdom. Is it not his courage and his will to defend us that should matter when we are in danger of losing our valley? Does not a warrior dance and walk proud to put fire into the hearts of his followers? But it does not mean that he is only a strutting turkey. So, I tell all this council: There will be war someday. The white ghosts will drive the Five Nations into our valley. We can no longer pretend that the stories of the white ghosts are just fanciful tales to scare our children. If the stories are false, then there is no danger, and we will thrive as we always have. But if we are wrong and the Five Nations descend upon us, they will fight like wounded mother bears, for their future is at stake. They will have nothing to lose and everything to gain. Will the chief you choose be the one to force any of the Five Nations to make peace or die trying? Will we send hunters into the forests to fight a desperate enemy, fighting to save their children and their history? Or will we be weeping bitter tears for our senseless neglect in not having a warrior chief to protect us?"

"Are we all forgetting about a man who has helped us through many past winters?" asked one of the elder women. "Dark Moon and Wind and a few of his young followers have saved us from being starved in our lodges."

"Besides," said another, "Dark Moon is patient; he has the heart of a chief. He will grow wiser in his age. Our people will never starve. He will learn of the Seneca *before* they come to our valley—as a cat who sees things, even in the dark. Who better to be chief of the Cat tribe than a man who is part cat himself."

Another woman spoke, "When you say he is part cat, you speak unknowingly. For his parts are unknown to us. We do not know who his mother and father were. We do not know if he is even of the Cat nation. Bah!"

Big Hand, the chief, raised his hand again and spoke to the entire group, "We have heard many words this night. Does another wish to speak?"

No one stirred, so he continued.

"I have told you that there are choices that must be made to preserve our home in the Salt Springs." He paused for a moment, his head bowed down and facing the ground. "Here are my words. If a great cold comes upon us this winter, we must make ready now, or most of our people will die, especially the children. Therefore, all members of the Salt Springs, even warriors, must do the work that is before us. We need not fear invasion now, for no tribe will attack us through the winter. They, themselves, must guard against starvation and death if they have traveled far from their homelands. So, the task before us now is not the preparation for war, but for keeping hunger and death away from the Salt Springs.

"As grave as the belief is that we will be attacked by the Algonquin or the Iroquois, the cold will surely bring death and sickness upon us more swiftly than any tribes from the endless mountains. Therefore, we will band together into hunting parties. And they must go into the forests, perhaps farther distant ones than we now hunt, and bring back meat for the winter. Those who cannot hunt, that remain here, will bring wood from the forest for our campfires and lodge fires so the fires can be kept alight both day and night. We surely know that we must all have firewood, food, and clothing to sustain us.

"Thus, I have spoken. Tomorrow, all will begin. Make ready, for we will regret our tardiness if we have not prepared enough. When this council meets next, when the winter is gone, then we will choose our chief. And though he will be ours, he may also someday be the Great One of all the Erierhonon. Ponder these words and be wise."

Calling Dove's Choice

CALLING DOVE WAS SLEEPING fitfully, if at all. Each time she awoke, she was tormented by the same decision that always faced her. Either of the two men where hers for the choosing. Yet the very choice that seemed so clear and fixed yesterday would now seem lost amid new feelings and dreams that she had once sorted out but were now back again calling confusion into her sleep.

Dark Moon...Why was he like he was? Why was there a struggle between her heart and his? Why couldn't she just surrender to the passions of Red Eagle? Why did this strange and remote hunter confound her peaceful dreams of a life as the wife of a chief, and perhaps of the Great One of the Erierhonon?

She was always a light sleeper, but now these nights were endless as she awakened to small sounds that drove away her rest. And what if Dark Moon, despite his belief, becomes chief of the Salt Springs? Would he want her always in the bed beside him? Would he be like Red Eagle and begin to want others? Would he ever be one with her, or would part of his heart always be somewhere else? Somewhere in the forest? Somewhere in a place that she will never know? And yet, how could she choose Red Eagle? How could she live her life with Red Eagle and not think of the mystery of what she had forsaken? But who then would she choose?

Her mind seemed to be telling her that Dark Moon was her choice, but her heart still yearned for the passion she felt in the embrace of Red Eagle on the night of the yellow moon. Her heart or her mind. But would she ever know if Dark Moon would thrill her as Red Eagle did? She had to choose.

Outside, all eyes are always on Red Eagle, his look of immoderate confidence as he walks and dances and talks; the slight, presumptuous smile as he speaks; the look in his eyes that told all maidens of the tribe that to sleep on his mat would be a night to remember all their lives.

And Calling Dove wanted it. She wanted the thrill of being with a man who could make her scream and sweat in his arms. She wanted the envy of all other women who would see her that next morning. She wanted them to have the feeling that she and Red Eagle were a mating forged by the Manitou.

But still there was Dark Moon. With him, she was troubled. With him, she wondered if she would ever have the same thrill as she would with Red Eagle. But he was also a great man. And he, too, was renowned and cherished by the tribe. He was also different. He was a man who thinks when he looks at her. He was a hunter, quiet and patient, at home in the forest, fearless and quietly proud, but he was also a man who had mysteries about him. He dances, but not like Red Eagle. Yet unlike Red Eagle, he does not strut.

Dark Moon is kind to people, and he has great strength. Yet he also has silence. He would never boast of his love for her. If she chose Dark Moon, she would be uncertain. He was not as open as Red Eagle. He was cooler in spirit, a watcher—someone who thinks before he acts. A cat.

"Red Eagle will be chief," Calling Dove's sister told her. "It is said he will also be the Great One. Who will you choose?"

She shook her head. Could she choose complexity and mystery and uncertainty? Or would she give her heart to a man who brings excitement and glory to the Salt Springs? Dark Moon was a man who dreams of other things. But Red Eagle's spirit is easy to know, to understand. And greatness will be his.

Besides, Red Eagle wants her. She would be his totem, the same as a feather in his headdress or another lion's tail on his cloak. Dark Moon has said little, though he led her to understand his thoughts. Who would she live her life with—the quiet, mysterious stranger who was found in the woods as a child, or Red Eagle, the proud warrior who is bedecked with totems of a life of conquest?

"But Red Eagle will be chief," her sister said again.

"Yes, Red Eagle will be chief," Calling Dove said.

The Great Cold

THE NEXT DAY, THE camp bustled with life. Big Hand reminded all the elders about the great cold that would possibly come their way within a moon's passing. He also repeated the tale of large, exotic creatures that were seen north of the Salt Springs and south of the great lake. And the elders accepted the reasoning that these animals were coming south because their homelands were overcome by bitter winters in the past that killed many of the prey species that sustained the lives of the larger animals. Everyone was again made aware of the death that could await them if they were not prepared.

Big Hand did not tell the tribe about the possibility of a band of killers that might come through the forest someday and descend upon the Salt Springs. That story was for another day—after the Cats were sure that they would not starve in the coming winter. Then, groups of hunters were organized and led by members of Dark Moon's hunting team. In all, there were six chosen: Dark Moon and five others, who would lead a band of men who were not ordinarily hunters. Even the warriors, including Red Eagle, were impressed into one of the individual hunting parties. They had only one or possibly two moons to gather stores to last the winter.

Everyone, even children, had tasks to do. Honey was found and stored. Meats were butchered, and pemmican was smoked constantly and stored in large wooden boxes. Pots for melting snow were fashioned from the clay in the streams, and then were dried and glazed and waxed.

The next morning, on a cool autumn day, the Salt Springs people assembled to ask the Manitou for his guidance and favor for the hunt to be successful. Each young man stood silently in his appointed party as the people invoked blessings upon the hunt. After the ceremony, the final work began. The night before they set out, the tools for rack making, the ropes for binding, and the weapons for hunting were being assembled. Red Eagle approached Dark Moon.

"How are you, old friend?" he asked.

Dark Moon was surprised at the cordial tone of his old comrade but greeted him with a warm smile and outstretched hand.

"So, tomorrow, we go out once again, hunting together, just as we did as boys," Red Eagle said. "How many winters has it been since you and I were in the same hunting party?"

"More than I can count," answered Dark Moon. "But would that it had not been so long."

"Do your arrows fly straight as ever? And as far as ever?"

"I do not know. Perhaps I am growing old, and my aim is not as true as it was."

Red Eagle grinned. "You are overly modest, my friend. Your partners in the hunt have said that your shafts fly more true and long as ever."

"Those are just campfire boasts and tall tales."

"Modesty again? I think Wind has told your story faithfully."

"Perhaps he owes me a knife or a skin," Dark Moon snorted as he chuckled.

"Perhaps," said Red Eagle, pausing a few seconds to change the subject. "But here we are, once again girding for a great hunt."

Dark Moon grimaced. "If we can hunt well enough to keep the wolves from our camp, we will still be almost dead from weariness when we return."

"True enough, my friend. This is more serious than our playful hunts when we were young, when we hunted the great cats for our headdresses and the beavers for our coats."

"They were good days, were they not?" asked Dark Moon wistfully. "I wish we had more of them again."

"I, too, regret that we have not been as close in recent winters as we were as boys. What happened to make it so?"

Dark Moon sighed. "I do not know. I suppose we just got older and went in different directions—you as a warrior, and I as a hunter."

"But yet we have remained friends, have we not?" asked Red Eagle.

"I have always believed it," said Dark Moon.

Calling Dove and Dark Moon

THE NEXT DAY, BARELY past dawn, all the scouts were preparing for the great hunt. It was cold, and the breaths of everyone showed clouds of vapor from their noses and their mouths.

Dark Moon stored axes, arrows, knives, and especially ropes of leather in small bundles. It was easier to carry shared burdens among the hunters. Not everyone was yet ready, so he worked alone on the side of his lodge, quietly going in and out as he gathered and sorted his tools.

Suddenly, he heard someone approach behind him. The footfalls seemed familiar as he turned, expecting to see Wind coming to wish him well.

"You work quietly," Calling Dove said.

Dark Moon didn't answer but stared at her in surprise. "Why are you out so early in this cold?"

She seemed hurt but let the expression pass quickly. "I have come to wish you a safe hunt," she said.

Dark Moon stared at her quietly for several seconds—troubled, as usual, when he spoke to her.

"Thank you," he muttered.

"Where will you go?"

"Toward the great lake. Then, toward the setting sun."

"Is it true that you go with Red Eagle?"

"You know it is," he muttered.

"If you have a good hunt, it will be said that he is not only a warrior but also a great hunter."

Dark Moon only looked silently at her in response.

"Will it not make his chance to be chosen as chief all the greater?" she continued.

"But is that not what you want? To be the wife of the chief?"

"Does it not bother you that he might be chief?" Calling Dove asked.

"No. I know I will never be chief."

"But why are you so sure you will not?"

"I just know."

Suddenly, he was silent, looking away as though seeing something she could not see.

"Dark Moon?" Calling Dove said softly. "Did you just hear a call in the distance?"

"I heard something," Dark Moon said. "Did you also hear it?"

"Yes. Of late, I have been hearing that sound. What do you think it is?"

"It is a hawk." He was thoughtful for a moment, then said, "Have you ever seen it?"

"No. I only hear the cry. What do you think it means?"

He shook his head. "You have never seen it?" he asked again.

"No, only its cry, and it seems forlorn," she said. "Dark Moon, I know you are angry with me, but when you return, will you talk to me? I do not want you to hate me. I just want our words to show faith in each other...always."

Dark Moon closed his eyes and took a deep breath. They both sensed, at that moment, the pain that she had caused him. It was the first big dream in his young life that had been shattered. He tried to banish the thoughts. Then, he said, "I had dreams." He stopped and looked at her, then shook his head to himself. "But you must have dreams also, and I do not want to shatter your dreams." He nodded. "We will talk."

"May the Manitou keep you safe," Calling Dove said, "and bring you back to talk to me."

Wind Warns Dark Moon

Later that night, Wind came to the lodge of Dark Moon. "How was your meeting with Red Eagle?" he asked.

Dark Moon shrugged. "Just two old friends talking," he said absently.

Wind snorted. "Do you not find it strange that suddenly, on the eve of a great hunt, he has tried to rekindle the friendship of your youth? He who is consumed with ambition, who never shrinks from talk of his being chosen as chief?"

"How can talking to me further his interest in being chief? I have nothing to say about that."

"I do not know. Perhaps he wishes to persuade you that you are not fit to be chief. That, in modesty, you should defer to his desires to be chosen."

"He made no mention of such a thing as we talked."

"This may not be the place for such talk now. Perhaps he would prefer to persuade you when you are alone together in the forest, where no one else would hear."

"He must know me well enough to understand that I will not be persuaded by such entreaties."

Wind was quiet for a few minutes. Finally, he said, "Moon, did you know that Red Eagle's band returned to the Salt Springs only a few nights before we, ourselves, returned?"

"Yes, I had heard so," responded Dark Moon.

"Was there blood on their skins? Or their faces? What wounds or injuries did they have from their travels? Has anyone questioned what they did in their travels?"

Dark Moon realized what Wind was thinking, as he had already thought it himself, but he shook his head. "Wind, Red Eagle and I are old friends. When I was brought to the Salt Springs, his family welcomed me into their lodges and fed me often from their own fires."

"Yet your father did not like Starving Wolf, is that not so? Would he trust their family now...if he were here today?"

"Wind, are you truly thinking that Red Eagle had some part in those killings?" asked Dark Moon. "Could someone of the Salt Springs be so evil as to do what we saw? Could the people who sit around these campfires, and sing and dance to these songs, do such violence to a peaceful group as that of Elk Calf?"

Wind shook his head. "I do not know, Moon," he whispered. "But I am troubled, for sometimes I can, indeed, think that it could happen. And yet...we will never know the truth. Is that not so?"

Dark Moon put his hands on Wind's shoulders. "You are my best friend, and you have become a great hunter. And someday, you and I will be able to make the hungers of winter be only a memory for the Salt Springs. Leave these thoughts, for they will only bring discord into our lives. Let us rather look forward to a happy future."

Wind took a deep breath and shook his head, not comforted by Dark Moon's trust. "Look out for him, Moon. His tongue is that of a serpent. Do not trust him."

Dark Moon stood up. "You are a cherished friend, Wind, but you worry too much."

"And you worry too little," Wind muttered.

The Hunt

THE NEXT DAY, DARK Moon's party was already far from camp. They had run at a steady pace, tireless in the warm weather. They had traveled into the Western land, and already it was beginning to be more flat in many places. But the hunting was not good.

"Where shall we go?" asked a young man called Curly Hair, who Dark Moon had befriended because he was a quick learner and a hard worker and had gone a few times with him on smaller hunts. "Do you think we will find bears in this forest?"

"Perhaps. If the cold is coming, they may be trying to catch deer before they must sleep for the winter."

"Do you think it is too late to find them?"

"I am not sure. This cold may make them do strange things. They may sense that the deer will be their only food now."

After an hour rest, the party began to move again, heading north. They ran at a steady, ground-gaining pace. Some of the warriors were beginning to show fatigue at the relentless pace being set. They seldom had to cover as much ground as the hunters did, and the steady, constant run was wearing them down.

Dark Moon sensed the strain on the men who were not used to the exhausting run and began looking for a place to camp for the night. He had a feel for a good place on higher ground, with some cover along one side to shield from the wind.

Finally, he found a spot in a valley near a small creek. He remembered having camped there in winters past, after a hunt. There was always some danger from wolves and from cats lurking about in search of food, but this night, Dark Moon sensed that the region would be safe enough.

As they set up the camp, Red Eagle approached him. He asked, "Is this the place where we may find animals?"

"I am not certain," Dark Moon said. "But the men are tired, and I have seen bear tracks since the sun went behind the clouds...old tracks. There are also wolf tracks on this path, so there must be larger animals for them to eat."

"Have you been following tracks all day?" said Red Eagle.

"Yes, but remember, they may be two days old."

During the night, the party could hear wolves howling in the distance. Dark Moon had fitful sleep drawn from his responsibility to the Salt Springs to bring back large carcasses for the winter.

The two separated for a time, but then Dark Moon began walking around the camp until he encountered Curly Hair. "Did you hear a hawk?" he asked the boy.

"In the dark?" Curly Hair responded.

Dark Moon shook his head and snorted. "Perhaps my ears are playing tricks on me again," he said, not wanting the boy to think he was troubled.

"I know you are much troubled by the hunt, but we will be all right," said the boy. "When have you ever come back to the Salt Springs with your arms empty of food?"

Dark Moon huffed softly. "You are right. I was just thinking..."

Suddenly, he turned toward the sound again, straining his ears. He paused a moment and turned back to Curly Hair, who was silent.

After a few seconds, the boy spoke again, trying to reassure his mentor.

"I have heard nothing."

Dark Moon nodded and put his hand on the boy's shoulder and walked away.

⊷•⊷

The next morning, Red Eagle joined Dark Moon at the lead of the hunt, leaving his own group to proceed by themselves. Dark Moon was still uneasy at Red Eagle's behavior. The words of Wind still haunted his memory, that no good would come from Red Eagle's attentions.

"Do you think we will find the game today?" asked Red Eagle.

Dark Moon nodded. "More than I did yesterday. The tracks of cats and wolves are growing fresher."

"And the bear?"

"They too are a day fresher."

"Then, soon, we should find something to hunt, should we not?"

"I think so. We surely are ready for it."

Throughout the morning, Red Eagle stayed with Dark Moon, watching his every move, trying to learn the ways of Dark Moon as he tracked the animals. He asked questions often. He studied his friend who walked so comfortably through the forest, always seeming at home in his surroundings.

But he was also chagrined by the things he, himself, could not do. Dark Moon was indeed like a cat. He heard everything. He knew when to hesitate and when to go. Every sound he heard seemed to add more to his sense of place and understanding of his quarry.

Red Eagle realized suddenly that he was trying to fathom instinct, with behaviors and skills that made Dark Moon who he really was. Success enjoyed as a hunter was not all from learned behavior. He was indeed a cat, born with certain instincts, comfortable with the hunt, with tracking prey, with pitting his skills and physical gifts against those of his quarries, and always being smarter than the creatures being stalked.

Red Eagle was pained by his revelation. The man was gifted, and gifted men are usually chosen as chief among the Erierhonon. And beneath all the turmoil in his soul, Red Eagle realized that what he had were not the same gifts that Dark Moon had. Red Eagle had leadership, great skill as a fighter, and confidence born of leading men and inspiring them to be fighters. He was indeed a great leader. But he sensed that his own traits were more abilities than gifts. As good as he was in his own way, he was not as good as Dark Moon was in his.

In a fight, he would surely be the victor over Dark Moon. But that knowledge did not console him. Mainly because Dark Moon's gifts were somehow appreciated instinctively by the elders of the tribe. His own were obvious to all, easily seen, easily appreciated. But Dark Moon's gifts were insidious, entering the consciousness of all who knew him in a way that set him apart in their minds from all the others. And those insidious revelations seem to thrive in their minds, giving Dark Moon the aura of inevitability. He would not only be chosen chief of the Salt Springs, but he would probably become the Great One of all the Erierhonon.

Dark Moon hunted through the morning as he usually did, at the lead of his small party, quietly communing with himself as he made his way through the forest. He was aware that Red Eagle had faded into the pack, as he heard his voice several times talking to others around him.

As the day went on, Dark Moon noticed a change in the tracks. It looked as though two bears were in the region, perhaps a huge male and a female. He walked back to the pack and told them that soon they would come upon one or two bears, and even perhaps a deer that the bears were stalking.

They all rested a few minutes and shared some pemmican and honey cakes. Dark Moon saw Red Eagle out of the corner of his eye several times, bantering easily with other hunters, and enjoying their adulation. It was inconsequential. Dark Moon had a job to do, and Red Eagle's recent incongruous behavior soon lost its fascination.

But it did seem strange not to hunt for every kind of game; wild turkey, and others like beaver, were all ignored. Dark Moon's task was only to find large game. The great racks they were lugging through the forest had only one purpose: bringing meat to the Salt Springs. Even deer were to be taken only if a bear or elk or bison had eluded them.

It was soon decided that the party would break down into smaller groups of two or three. Dark Moon told them of a rendezvous place where they would meet two suns ahead. There was a great plain along the edge of the swamp. The river ran through the plain that sloped downward and splashed into a large pool below. Beyond that was a small oak forest on the other side of the plain. That was their rendezvous place. There, they would cut trees and solidify the racks that were needed to bring their catches back to the Salt Springs. And there they could bleed and butcher the game and then distribute it to the racks. They would hang their quarries on long cords from high trees so that the wolves and cats could not reach them during the night.

Each small hunting party was to take many ropes and thongs of leather. Everyone had a set of bows and arrows. One man even had an atlatl that could bring down large quarries if the hunter was a skilled enough marksman. All had two day's supply of pemmican and cakes. All had knives and axes.

Dark Moon gave them instructions the next morning before their departure. Each party was led by the oldest warrior or hunter. Red Eagle wanted some of the youngest men—a curious request, but one that Dark Moon honored by letting his friend choose young men from their small group. They would all be excellent marksmen with the bow and would probably someday become warriors under his authority.

Then, they all dispersed, knowing that when night came, each group would be able to see or smell each other's campfires from a distance. Dark Moon instinctively felt that at least one of the quarries would somehow be near them in the woods.

He thought he saw the hoofprints of a wood bison earlier in the day. If there was one, there might be another, and they would be fine catches that would bring much sustenance to the Salt Springs. But he had to be careful. The creatures were so huge and dangerous that they could easily kill a hunter who was not an experienced marksman. And he surely wanted everyone in the groups to return to the Salt Springs alive.

Dark Moon's little group strode stealthily through the darkened woods. Perhaps it was instinct, or perhaps it was an accumulation of small skills that he had acquired in his lifetime, but there was something about him when he was on a hunt that made him alert to any quarry that was nearby. Perhaps it was hearing, the sensibility to noise from the woodland, like the sounds of large animals walking slowly through the forest, little knowing that they were being hunted.

He signaled to the others in his group to stop suddenly. They found themselves spread out behind him, watching Dark Moon as much as they looked for prey. They all watched as he crouched motionless for minutes at a time, the pulse in his neck barely showing. He stopped again, motionless and alert. Then, he moved to the right, then slightly forward again.

Dark Moon motioned to them for silence and no movement. He waited several minutes, then suddenly he crouched down low. Quietly, his right hand shed the bow from his shoulder. He drew an arrow from his quiver and mounted it, turning his gaze upward as though hearing something. He was still as he listened, then turned slowly back to his quarry.

He heard a faint sound. Slowly, he settled onto one knee, remaining still. After a few minutes, he set the arrow on the bowstring, slowly pulling it backwards, and held it for several seconds. Then, with no movement but the fingers of his right hand, he let the shaft fly.

In a second, there was a great bellowing roar and movement crashing forward. Dark Moon sprang from his crouch and ran into the shadows. As the others followed after him, they could hear another bellowing sound that lasted for several more seconds.

They finally came to a small clearing where they saw Dark Moon standing, watching intently the sight of the huge beast on the far side of the field. The bison was standing unsteadily, faltering on his front legs. Then, suddenly, he fell over on his side.

Several of the hunters let out a whoop and ran up to Dark Moon. He cautioned them not to approach the bison yet, for there was still danger in coming upon any wounded animal, especially one this large.

"Where did the arrow strike?" asked one of the younger men.

"The neck, I think," said Dark Moon as they advanced cautiously toward the bison.

"Careful," Dark Moon whispered, as he had a spear ready to plunge into the beast if it suddenly turned on them. But there was no steam coming from its nostrils, and its opened eyes were vacant and lifeless. As they advanced toward the creature, they could see that the arrow had gone through the bison's neck and advanced near its brain.

"What kind of arrow is that?" said one of the younger hunters, amazed at the thickness and length of it.

"It is for large creatures such as this one," said Dark Moon. "I only carry a few. The rest of my arrows are just as yours."

"It is the bow that does it," said one of the older boys. "See the length of it and the strength it takes to let these arrows fly."

"May I see your bow?" asked the same young hunter.

Dark Moon handed it to him. "Draw it," he said. The young man tried to pull it with all his strength, but he could not. "You must practice. Then, someday, you will be able to do it."

The rest of the day was spent bleeding and butchering the bison into parts. Then, they would be loaded in sections onto the three racks in the morning after the parts were hung for bleeding through the night. They talked about the burden they would each have the next day, since they never expected to find a catch of this size and weight.

The next day, Dark Moon split the burden of the carcass over three sleds. He told all the young men to take their loads back to the Salt Spring as quickly as they could in order to keep the meat from spoiling. After telling them details of how best to travel, he bid them farewell. He would remain to help Red Eagle's party get their quota of meat.

Dark Moon and Red Eagle

Dark Moon trotted at a steady pace for several hours as he searched for Red Eagle's party. He was getting close to them. They were going north into the hill country, something he had advised them not to do. The hills were treacherous and had sheer drops into narrow ravines that awaited any errant traveler who ventured after game among the hills.

He knew where they had camped the night before. The blood on the grass meant that they had caught some small animals, probably turkeys, and had sent at least one of the parties home to the Salt Springs. Later he could smell the smoke and see the campfires of Red Eagle's party. Stealthily, he approached the camp.

He watched and listened for a few minutes. Where was Red Eagle? Had he gone home? With only a few young animals on a rack? He called into the camp so they would not be startled. In a few moments, they were all around him.

"Where is Red Eagle?" was his first question.

Stonehouse was the spokesman for the group. He was a scout and a warrior, and he and Dark Moon had been friends for many years. He was one of the older boys who was kind to Dark Moon when he was brought into the tribe as an orphan.

"He said he found the trail of a bison," said the now older man, "and that, since we have had good hunting, we should return to the Salt Springs with our bounty."

"Did he see the tracks of a bison?"

"No...nor did we. But he insisted that the bison was there and that he would kill it."

Dark Moon shook his head. "Does he know this country?"

Stonehouse shook his head. "No. In the past, he has gone mostly east or south of the Mahoning. We have all traveled together to the great Ohio in the land of the tall ones. But I know he is strange to this country."

"Did you not tell him my words about these hills, how death can come so easily in this region?"

Stonehouse nodded. "We have all told him your words, and also that we will not go into these hills. He grew angry and said he would go alone—that the bison awaits him, and he will kill it. And that the timid of the tribe will never be remembered as great men of the Erierhonon."

Dark Moon shook his head. "He is in danger and does not know it. And even if he kills a bison, how would he bring it home?"

"I do not know," said Stonehouse.

"My friend," said Dark Moon, "our groups have already sent two deer, a young bear, and a bison on the way to the Salt Springs. And we will find much smaller game of beaver, geese, and turkeys on our way home. It is growing cold, and I am afraid the bitter weather will be upon us soon."

"Do you think, then, that we should return?"

"Yes. I am sure that we will have food enough. And we know that Wind is a fine hunter. His men will have done much good also."

"And you?"

Dark Moon shook his head in frustration. "I will try to track Red Eagle. There is danger in these hills, both in the cliffs and ravines, but also with animals. There may be bears, or even great cats that could easily stalk a single hunter and kill him. I must find him before the cold comes."

———————●·•||•●·———————

Dark Moon followed Red Eagle's tracks. *The whole day is a wasted effort*, he thought to himself as he pursued his old comrade. Often, he would find the trail meandering and then circling backwards. Once, he saw a partially eaten goose killed by arrows and left to rot in the woods. Some other animals had already taken most of the carcass.

The next day, he pushed farther into the woods, tracking Red Eagle, who seemed to be more purposeful now, traveling in a straight northern path. Suddenly, he stopped and listened. Birds and other small creatures? He listened again. Was he being watched... or followed?

Dark Moon continued on the trail. Soon, he would be near the ravines. But how would Red Eagle know enough to avoid the dangers on his way?

It was getting dark, so Dark Moon rested by a fire and ate some pemmican and nuts and berries. He knew that there was a huge valley ahead with many cliffs and ravines leading down to a swiftly flowing river. Red Eagle, with his lead of at least a day, would almost surely be on the other side, at the top of a huge cliff with many substrate shelves jutting out from its surface. Red Eagle might not be an experienced hunter, but he was a fine warrior, strong and nimble and well-conditioned. He surely would be safe on the other side.

Dark Moon dozed a short time but soon awakened to something that he heard. That same noise, that same call in the air from across the valley. But what was it? He listened again. This time, he knew he was hearing the cry of a hawk. And why does he hear the creature that no one else can? And why does it sound as mournful as it did when they discovered Elk Calf's devastation? Was the hawk following him? Could it be the same one that Calling Dove heard also?

He stood up and walked around the light of the fire. *What am I doing?*

he thought to himself. *Why am I chasing a man who was too proud to be just a hunter, a man who puts himself in danger in a foolish pursuit of glory? Just because he wants to be the chief of the Salt Springs?*

Dark Moon put out his fire and began traveling toward the sound. Daylight would soon come, and perhaps there would be more strange noises. But...

He hesitated and sniffed the air as he always did before pursuing a quarry. He could smell the odor of burning wood. It had to be Red Eagle's fire. He grew excited. Maybe he would find Red Eagle and convince him to head back with him to the Salt Springs where he would surely become chief of the tribe.

Dark Moon gathered his bow and quiver, bound his blankets up, secured his food in a sack, and was ready to move on, just as the sun was shining faint rays over the horizon. He trotted steadily through the sloping meadow that led to the trees. They were on the edge of the huge ravine between the woodlands on the other side.

Slowly, he began to descend the hill, releasing one branch after securing another with an outstretched arm. There was water seeping out of clay deposits on the hillside. Once he fell a short way and barely hung onto a small branch to save himself.

Now the sun was well over the horizon, and he was already cold and tired. When he fell that short distance, he had torn his leather sack and lost most of the pemmican that he carried. He dared not go back up because he had to be careful not to destroy his bow or damage his arrows. His ax and knife were still bound to his side. The fall had not dislodged them.

It took Dark Moon most of the morning to get to the valley floor. Then, he had to make a crude raft to get himself across the river. He found several pieces of dry wood and bound them with thongs to travel across. Somewhere between where he landed and some rock formations upstream was the trail of Red Eagle. He was sure of it.

The crossing was wet and dangerous. As Dark Moon made his way upstream, he looked carefully for features he had memorized from the other side. He then judged about how far down Red Eagle could have landed in his crossing. It took some time to find his trail, but when he found it, he knew it would lead to Red Eagle.

He could tell that the trail was made swiftly with not much stopping or hesitation. *He must have been following something,* Dark Moon thought. But there was no evidence of a large animal anywhere—no bear, no bison. Very quickly the hillside grew sheer and steep. He started the long climb up the cliff. Climbing down on the other side was tiring enough, but now the river crossing had brought him near to exhaustion. If he made it to the top of the hill, he would barely be able to make camp.

On his way, not far from the riverbank, Dark Moon heard the sound again, louder this time, more easily recognized as a hawk's scream. He peered back over his shoulder but saw no hawk in the sky. Perhaps it was his imagination, always confusing him when he was tired.

But through the trek, he had the uneasy sense that he was not alone. He knew that one is never alone in the forest; animals are always there to watch, as any intruder must be watched and feared.

He looked for shelves that could support one lone man, and he was careful. One misstep could bring a fall far below onto the rocks on the riverbank.

Once more, he heard the hawk cry again. And, again, there was no hawk that he could see. This time, he increased his effort to climb. Soon he was at the top of the hill. He looked around. There was nothing between him and the tree line, about fifty yards away.

He gazed ahead, looking for paths Red Eagle may have made, but there were none. He sank to his knees, exhausted from his climb, and huffed in frustration. He would have to search in the tall grass all along the edge of the tree line until he found the trail.

He looked to the north. Perhaps he could start his search there and use the morning sun to guide his way. Then he paused, holding his breath. Did he hear something? He listened. The hawk? No. This sound was different. The sound of a man? It did not come from the north, but over his shoulder to the south. He turned back. It seemed faint and muffled. All he knew was that it was not one of the forest sounds he was accustomed to.

He clutched his bow as he leaned on it to stand erect. He was tired, but he knew the trail of Red Eagle would be colder each moment he tarried, and he had to find him before darkness came.

He headed south to the high grass that grew up to his waist. There was no sign of Red Eagle's trail. He moved slowly and deliberately using his bow to move the leaves and twigs that were scattered through the grass. And as he walked through the grass, he could cast sideways glances at the tree line to see if there were any unusual combinations of leaves and branches that were signs of a man foraging through the brush. But there were no signs.

He stopped, gazing intently at the tree line. There was something wrong. He called to Red Eagle. No answer. He stopped breathing and listened for a few seconds. Nothing. Sometimes, he could hear the rushing water of the river far below in faint splashing echoes. He huffed disgustedly to himself for hearing noises no one else could hear, or imagining spirits that leave no paths in the woods.

All this was taking too much time. The cold would soon come in, and Dark Moon would be trapped in a strange region with no food and no safe place to rest for the night.

Suddenly, he called out Red Eagle's name and listened. Nothing. The wind was beginning to howl through the trees and the grass. He stopped and tried to listen again, and from time to time he would call Red Eagle's name as it echoed throughout the hills surrounding the valley. The sun was behind the clouds, and it looked like first snow might be coming that night.

Unconsciously, he began walking faster. Then, he heard something again.

He began to move forward, calling for Red Eagle, and each time listening. He was angry with himself. Was he going mad? Is this what madmen do as they approach death? And why was this happening to him now? One day his life was normal, and he was a hunter caring for his tribe. Then, without any strange sickness or injuries, he was doing things that no one would ever believe.

It was growing colder, so he walked faster, still calling time after time. Then, suddenly, he heard a response—the voice of a man, faint and distant, up ahead of his search. But now that he had heard a call, he scurried through the grass, pausing occasionally to listen. His pulse quickened. Red Eagle must be hunting nearby.

The responses began to be more frequent. But the sound was strange. They were not from the woods. Instead, they seemed to come from the valley. He was breathing heavily as he paused to rest and listen momentarily.

As he neared the sound, he knew it came only from the valley. It was the voice of Red Eagle. He was sure of it.

"Eagle," he called, "where are you?"

"Dark Moon? Down here!" The call came from the north wall of the valley, on the hillside.

Finally, Dark Moon looked down the steep cliff. "Call out so I can find you, Red Eagle!"

"Here! I cannot move."

"Where?" Dark Moon asked.

"On this ledge. Can you see me?"

Suddenly he saw Red Eagle lying on his back, perched on a small outcropping ledge half his body width, holding fast to the roots of a bush that grew out of the hillside.

"If I move, I will fall, Moon," Red Eagle said. "I feel the ledge beneath me crumbling."

"Are you hurt?"

"No, not badly. But I cannot move to find out."

Dark Moon drew near to the rim, peering into the abyss. "Hold fast, my friend. I will lower a cord."

Dark Moon laid down his bow and quiver and unraveled the leather cord in his shoulder bag. He drew the cord and looked to bind it to a nearby tree, but there was none close by.

Dark Moon cursed in frustration. "Red Eagle, I am lowering a rope. When it touches you, wrap it around your arms first, then your chest. Careful that you do not fall."

Dark Moon looped and knotted it securely to his waist. He called to Red Eagle, "I will slowly cast this cord toward you! If you can loop it around yourself securely, you will be safe."

"Hurry, Moon," said Red Eagle, his voice quavering and fearful.

Dark Moon threw the rope out away from the hillside beyond the level of Red Eagle. "Do you see it, Eagle?"

"Yes. But it is not near my arms or legs. I cannot move, Moon. One slip and I will be lost."

"All right. I will throw it again." Dark Moon pulled up the rope and threw it again. This time, it was near Red Eagle's grasp.

"I have it," said Red Eagle.

Suddenly, as Dark Moon drew the rope up, he heard the hawk call. It was loud and nearby. Dark Moon stopped.

"What is wrong, Moon? Is it stuck?" Red Eagle asked.

"No, the sound of the hawk startled me. I will bring you up slowly."

"There is no hawk. Are you all right, Moon?"

For a few seconds he didn't answer. *There is no hawk?* But he heard it clearly as it rang through the valley. *There is no hawk?*

"Dark Moon?" Eagle asked.

"Yes, Red Eagle, I am pulling slowly," said Dark Moon after several seconds.

This time, he drew the rope upward, and Red Eagle caught it around his outstretched arm. "I have it," he said.

"Secure it, and I will pull you up slowly. But be careful; there is nothing to attach the cord to, so I must pull you to the top myself."

"All right," said Red Eagle. "It is around my chest. I will help you when I can."

"Just do not work against my efforts."

Dark Moon had never been a warrior. He was a hunter whose strength was always tested as he made his way through woods carrying heavy carcasses or pulling racks of kills. Throughout his life, he grew ever stronger as years passed. His body was powerful, just the opposite of the tall and slender Red Eagle. But this time, the powerful body of Dark Moon was the answer to the task of getting his friend up the hillside.

Gradually, he pulled Red Eagle upward. He was exhausted, but he pulled relentlessly. Red Eagle braced himself against the hillside.

"Eagle, do not pull," said Dark Moon. "Let me get you up farther. Maybe then you can help."

Dark Moon was beginning to feel lightheaded from his efforts, but he continued.

"I can see the top, Dark Moon," said Red Eagle. "I am almost there. We cannot fall now...after all this."

A few more pulls, and Red Eagle reached the rim. At the top of the hillside, he lay motionless. Dark Moon touched his shoulder, and Red Eagle seemed confused, looking at his rescuer as though not knowing who he was.

Dark Moon pulled him away from the edge slowly and carefully. When they were several paces apart, Dark Moon paused for a moment and sank to his knees. Then, he fell forward, his hands barely bracing his body as it collapsed against the earth. He was motionless, almost too tired to breathe.

For several minutes, both men seemed to be unconscious. Then, Red Eagle awakened and stirred slightly. He lay motionless, trying to imagine himself safe and alive. He listened as he lay, seemingly unaware of the presence of his companion. He saw Dark Moon and called out to him. Dark Moon stirred and raised his head and let it fall back to the ground.

Red Eagle paused for the moment. He heard something. He lay his head back down on the ground for a minute. Both men were quiet. Then he heard it again. A strange animal sound, low and threatening. He heard it from the nearby underbrush, then the roar, nearer to them on the edge of the cliff.

Dark Moon, however, knew the noise; it was that of an angry bear. He lifted his head and turned toward the sound. Instinctively, he called out, "Beware, Red Eagle!"

But the bear was intent on attack, and Dark Moon was nearest to him. As the bear drew near, Dark Moon yelled to Red Eagle, "My bow and arrows… there on the ground!"

But Red Eagle seemed paralyzed. He was on all fours as he watched the bear come upon Dark Moon. The bear was huge and gold, much larger than any black bear he had ever seen. Dark Moon scrambled up, trying to run from the bear, but the bear caught him from behind, biting his thigh and tossing him through the air with a sharp jerk of his neck.

Dark Moon screamed again, "My bow! You can kill him!"

Once again, the bear attacked, clubbing Dark Moon and hurling him several feet away. His leg burned with pain. The bear had torn some of the sinews on his thigh and had crushed part of his knee.

All the while Dark Moon fought for his life, Red Eagle stood silently, watching the bear begin to kill his companion.

"Eagle? Why do you wait? Kill him… Kill him!" Dark Moon yelled.

The bear struck Dark Moon with his paw, tearing his flesh and throwing him several feet away again. *What am I going to do?* Dark Moon thought in the split-second he had to avoid another attack.

His leg gave out as he tried to avoid the next lunge. But this time, he grabbed a handful of sand and threw it in the bear's face. It stopped and snorted and turned away for a few seconds. "Eagle!" Dark Moon yelled.

He saw Red Eagle pick up his bow and quiver and calmly watch the bear attack again. This time, it bit Dark Moon's arm, as Dark Moon pounded the bear's muzzle with his other hand, and the bear lost his grip.

Suddenly, in that moment, Dark Moon understood. Red Eagle was waiting to see him die. This terrible creature would deliver him of a rival as chief of the Erierhonon. As the bear turned toward Red Eagle for a brief glance, Dark Moon shouted again, "Kill him! Kill him!"

But those words only made the bear turn his attention back to his closest prey, Dark Moon. With that, Red Eagle gathered Dark Moon's bow and arrows and quiver, stood erect, and scampered away into the woods.

Dark Moon, knowing he was about to die, drew a long flint knife that was strapped to his waist. There was not much chance the weapon would hurt the bear, but it was all he had. He felt blood on his chest. The bear had clawed his chest as Dark Moon was trying to avoid him.

The bear advanced again, knowing that he would have a fresh kill in a moment. With his last bit of strength, Dark Moon held the knife firmly, and as the bear lunged, Dark Moon, barely standing on one good leg, slashed at the bear's neck as he lumbered past and dodged the bear's advance. The bear let out a howl as the knife slashed into its neck. It was disoriented and pained for the few seconds it turned away, and Dark Moon, with almost no strength left, plunged the knife with all his strength upward toward the back of the neck, just beneath the skull, and thrust the knife into the bear's brain.

Dark Moon dropped to his knees and fell forward on his face. He was finished. But the bear now lay on top of him, motionless and dying. And suddenly, pain and weakness overcame Dark Moon as he fainted.

Red Eagle was now far into the forest, on his way south, back to the Mahoning and the people of the Salt Springs.

Cricket and Snake

THE GIRL WAS EXHAUSTED as she climbed the short, north cliff of the great valley. Her brother was below her, pushing himself up to the top of the rim. He looked for his sister but could not see her. He called softly. Then he called again. She responded faintly, and he headed toward her voice. When he saw her, she was kneeling near a huge bear. He ran frantically toward her, unsure that the bear was dead. When he drew near her, he could see that she was holding the upper body of a man in her arms.

"Is he dead?" the young man of nineteen winters asked.

"No, but he is gravely hurt," the girl said.

The boy knelt down and touched the bear.

"The bear has kept him warm," the girl said.

"How did this huge creature die?" he asked.

"Look at his head," she said, pointing to the head that was facing away from them.

The young man pursed his lips and blew his breath. "He must have killed the bear himself," he said. "That is his knife. Are you certain he is not dead?"

"No, I can feel his heart beating," the girl said, still cradling his head in her arms. "He is not a large man, but he must have great strength...to kill so huge a creature."

"Have you ever known a man who alone can kill a bear like this one with only a knife?" the young man asked.

"No...and we never will unless he lives."

"We must be careful. I can see blood beneath the bear. It may be his own and not the bear's. Hold his head, Cricket. I will try to move the bear without harming him."

The young man strained to pull the bear off Dark Moon. He pulled and shoved, straining his legs for further leverage. Finally, they had Dark Moon free.

The girl gasped as she finally was able to see the extent of his injuries. "We must bind these wounds, or he will bleed and die," she said.

The two of them worked on Dark Moon for more than an hour.

"Is he still alive?" the young man would say often as they worked feverishly.

"Yes, but hurry," was always the reply. "We must bring him to Mother."

Finally, they had the wounds bound. The worst of them was on his leg. It was slashed and torn by bites and claws. The skin and muscles were damaged, but the bones seemed to be intact. His knee was slashed, and his other thigh was slashed and torn also.

Slowly, they assembled a rack on which to carry him. When they were done, they carefully dragged the rack for several hours back to their camp. An old woman stood up as she spotted their approach in the distance.

The camp was unusual for the region. There was no lodge. Instead, there were two wigwams, one large and another smaller. Behind the old woman, tethered to a stump in the ground, were two brown horses. Their ears pricked forward as they saw the young woman and her brother come nearer to the camp. One snorted and tossed his head in expectation, but after a few moments, resumed grazing.

When they finally drew near enough, the old woman walked out to them to help pull the rack. She could see that both her children were exhausted.

"We can finish this, Mother," said Snake.

But Snow Flower knew better and quickly grabbed her daughter's ropes and helped her drag her load the last few yards toward the tent. "How are you, Cricket?" she asked.

The young girl responded with a smile and touched her shoulder. "I'm glad this work is done...and we are home."

Only then did the older woman notice that it was not a slain animal that they returned. "Who is this man?" she asked anxiously.

"We found him near the great valley," said Snake from the River. "He was mauled by a huge bear of golden color. But he killed the bear with only a knife. Now we must see if we can make him live. A man who can kill a bear as he did has much courage. We must try to save him, Mother."

"Where are his worst wounds?" asked Snow Flower.

"Here, and here, and there," said Cricket, pointing at the bandages. "We bound the wounds as best we could, lest he die."

"Take him to the small house," said the mother.

Inside, they undressed Dark Moon and carefully unwrapped the bandages around his wounds. Cricket knew from long practice what she should do. She went to the side of the wigwam and drew a dark leather sack of medicines and bandages and liniments that her mother used to treat the wounded of their now abandoned tribe. She opened the sack and began to set out the various medications her mother might use.

"He is not bleeding, and that is good. We must be careful not to reopen any of these wounds again," Snow Flower said. Carefully, she cut off the bandages one by one. Snake brought water from the nearby lake and set it to boil on the fire outside. Cricket helped her mother wash and clean the wounds.

As they cleaned, they saw large slashes and cuts. In some places, the wounds were so large that Snow Flower had to sew the flesh closed. It was an ancient method of caring for such wounds: wash and clean the wounds carefully, stop the blood flow, smear them with ointments that would help the wounds stay clean and stave off infection, and sew together gaping wounds that would not heal unless they were closed by stitching.

Finally, the old woman said to Cricket by way of instruction to an apprentice, "All that's left for us to do is rejoin the parts of his leg where it is broken."

The young girl did as she was told while Snow Flower watched.

"Here," said Cricket, "something is loose here." She pointed to the right knee.

Snow Flower watched as Cricket moved the leg. "Feel here," Snow Flower said, pointing to Dark Moon's hip. Cricket slowly moved the leg at the hip. Then she stopped.

"Hold the other leg, Snake," said the mother. The young man held the leg. "Now, feel here, Cricket," she said, pointing to the right hip. Snow Flower nodded to Snake to move the leg slowly as she felt Dark Moon's right hip. "Does it feel the same?"

"No, it is different from the other leg."

Finally, Snow Flower herself tested both hips. She shook her head. "Put the leg back where it was," she said as she nodded to Snake. "This leg has been torn here." She pointed to Dark Moon's right hip. "We must place it as it was, as best we can, near its proper place. Cricket, grab this with me. Snake, when we tell you to hold the leg off the floor, do so gently so we can move this bone properly."

When they had the leg in both their hands, Snow Flower nodded to Snake. "Now, daughter, we must move this slowly. We will know when to stop...when we feel it rest in its place."

Cricket hesitated, but her mother urged her onward. Finally, she began to move the leg at the hip. She looked at her mother doubtfully, but Snow Flower nodded encouragement.

"Slowly, slowly," the older woman said. "Hold it steady, Snake. Slowly."

Finally, they all heard a snap, and the hip could be moved no farther.

Snake was sweating nervously, and Cricket was drawing deep breaths.

"Now, we must sew the leg wound shut," said Snow Flower. "Are you ready, Cricket?"

She didn't answer, so her mother continued, "Do you think you can do this?"

"Yes, I think I can," the girl sighed.

"Even after all we have done, if any of these wounds begin to stink, or if he cannot live through the sweats and the fever, then he will die," said the old woman. "You must know that."

"Yes, I know. I will care for him, and clean and bandage his wounds every day—whenever it is needed."

"All right," said Snow Flower. "You must sew the wound carefully. Your hands are smaller than mine, so you can do it better than I. Then we can let him rest. If he lives through the sweats, then we can hope he will be well."

"Mother, what medicine do we need?" asked Snake. "I will help you make it."

Red Eagle Returns

THE COLD CAME SUDDENLY upon the Salt Springs and turned the Mahoning to ice. Red Eagle was weary and cold, his feet bleeding from the chafing and dampness in his moccasins. He made the remaining half-day journey slowly and carefully, stopping to rest and rub his feet so they would not turn black. He had found some nuts as he traveled. And the wondrous bow of Dark Moon enabled him to shoot rabbits at two different times on his way back home. He marveled at the bow. It was balanced as no other he had ever seen. If one drew on the cord, the wood gave just enough to send the arrow truly into a prey. It was light and beautiful.

A few more hours, and he would be home. It would be a relief to smell the air around the Salt Springs, to hear the Mahoning's ice crack in the cold. He knew that the tribe would welcome him. He also knew that the tribal hunt was successful and that the Salt Springs would survive the cold because of the hunting of Dark Moon and Wind. And the ultimate pleasure would come when he heard the roar of the tribe proclaiming him as their new chief. It was the dream that had kept him alive through his long journey homeward.

He wearily crossed the frozen creek and trudged over the two hills that led to the northwest end of the Salt Springs. He took a deep breath.

He knew he could not make the trip over the hills without rest. But he also couldn't tarry long because the cold would probably kill him in his weakened condition. He shook his head. How strange it would be to die from the cold, almost within arrow shot of the Salt Springs, just when fortune had cleared his path to becoming chief.

Red Eagle had convinced himself that the great gold bear was sent by the Manitou to remove the one man who would be his rival as chief of the Salt Springs. And that the Manitou had sent Dark Moon to rescue him from certain death along the cliff. It was easy to believe.

Now, he had it all in his heart: the Manitou wanted a warrior, not a hunter, to be chosen. And he would be the husband of Calling Dove. And he would be the father of a chief and, eventually, the grandfather of a chief. Yes, it was easy to believe.

After the slow and arduous journey over the two hills, he stumbled through the meadow that bordered the Mahoning. An old man was the first to see Red Eagle in the distance, and he ran through the camp shouting his name so that everyone could come out to greet the warrior who they thought was lost. Even in the bitter cold, the tribe would always welcome one of their great men. Red Eagle slowly stumbled into the camp as others supported his weight and led him to the lodge of chief Big Hand.

Inside, in the warmth and quiet of his lodge, the chief greeted Red Eagle. "How are you, my son?"

"Weary," Red Eagle whispered.

The old man put his hands on Red Eagle's shoulders. "You will rest tonight at home in your own bed. When you are whole again, you will tell me your story."

"I am grateful, my chief," said Red Eagle softly.

"And Dark Moon? Do you know when he will return?"

Red Eagle tried to show anguish, but instead, he could only manage discomfort. But it was emotion enough. "He will not return, my chief. He is with the Manitou."

"And this is the story you would tell us?"

Red Eagle nodded.

<hr />

The next day, as Red Eagle rested, people would come to his lodge and bring food and blankets and fresh water. He was exhausted still, so everyone tried to be polite. They would visit, leave a gift, say a few consoling words, and depart. Red Eagle's father made sure his mother and younger sisters cared for him constantly. Not a moment of his sleep was unguarded by some member of the family.

Two days later, Red Eagle met Big Hand again.

"Are you rested, my son?" asked the old chief.

"Yes, Grandfather, the rest has done me much good."

"And your story?"

"I can tell you now," said Red Eagle, looking troubled and imaging an impression of regret to the old man.

"Begin."

Red Eagle took a deep breath. "Are all the others back?"

"All but one," Big Hand said. "We now have enough food for the winter, even with a great cold."

"Then we have done our work."

"Yes."

Red Eagle sensed that the chief was anxious to hear his story, especially about Dark Moon, so he began, "The great hunter, after killing a bison, sent it home with the others of his band. But for some reason—I know not why—he wanted more. So, he set out for another hunt. But I was thinking, surely, he must have known that finding another bison in the forest would seldom happen. And yet he went on.

"I also knew that my men had caught enough deer, so I told them to return home the next day, since I realized that the cold was coming and the slain animals had to be preserved. So, they started back home, intending perhaps to meet the others on their way. There is a great Valley in the north. Do you know of it?"

The chief nodded. "I have heard others talk of such a place, near the great lake of the north."

"It is a place like no other," Red Eagle said. "The earth is cleaved into a valley so that, on each side of the water, narrow cliffs arise to the heavens. The cliffs are such that a man could easily fall from them into a chasm that would bring certain death upon the rocks below. For reason known only to Dark Moon, he tried to climb the sheer mountainside at its highest part. I crossed the valley from one side to the other and discovered his tracks left as he climbed. It took a great part of the day for me to climb without falling to my death."

Big Hand nodded appreciatively at Red Eagle as a sign that he should continue.

"Dark Moon must have been on the north side of the valley, weary of climbing such a steep hill. And he must have been injured, for I could see the blood droppings as I followed his path. I know not how long he tarried, but for some reason, he had set his bow aside and was wandering without any protection but a knife. He may have been weak—or in a dream trance—but I know he was not aware of the presence of the bear."

"This is a golden bear that I have heard stories of?" said the chief.

"Yes."

"What kind of animal was this? Was it sunlight brown but the size of two of our blacks? This is what I have been told by some travelers in the past."

"The stories of such a bear—though we believed them as fables—are true, because I have seen it and have killed one."

"You have done this?"

"Yes. I came upon the edge of the cliffs from the north side." Red Eagle stopped and looked away from the chief, seemingly overcome with grief.

After several seconds, Big Hand said, "You must tell your story, my son. The Salt Springs must know how the great hunter died."

Then, Red Eagle took a deep breath, playing the role of hesitant hero.

"I came upon the bear and was amazed at the strange color and the great size, the likes of which I have never seen. I had come quietly downwind of the creature who did not know I was nearby. Then, I saw..."

Again, Red Eagle stopped, turned away from the chief, and remained silent.

This time, Big Hand waited several minutes without speaking. Red Eagle finally looked up at him. The old man nodded. Red Eagle took a deep breath, made a grimace and then continued, "As I came upon the bear, he was eating his fill." He stopped again, swaying his head side to side, and peered right into the eyes of the old chief. "The bear had eaten Dark Moon. Most of his body was gone. All that was left were his legs and his head."

Red Eagle stopped and held his head in his hands.

"What did you do, my son?" Big Hand said softly.

"I destroyed the bear with three arrows. At first it looked away from Dark Moon. It was then that I made the deadliest wound. Then, as it came toward me, I put another wound in its neck and then into its heart. When he took two steps toward me to kill, he fell and then rolled over the edge. But he was dead before he fell, I am sure."

"And were you injured?"

"No. All I did was burn the body of Dark Moon so he could be one with the great spirit. The bear will never live again. All I could think was to return to my family in the Salt Springs."

Both men were silent for several minutes. Then, the old chief spoke,

"My son, tell no one of the bear eating Dark Moon. The Erierhonon must not have such unseemly memories of him. Let it be known that the great hunter of the Salt Springs was attacked by the bear and fought him bravely. You acted with honor...All you could have done. You killed the great beast that murdered your friend, and you sent the smoke from his ashes to the attention of the Manitou. Now, go rest and make yourself well. Soon you will have other service for the Salt Springs."

"Thank you, my chief," said Red Eagle, certain that the old man accepted his story unquestioningly.

There was another silence between them. Then, Big Hand spoke again. "When this winter cold is gone, I will ride into the night to meet the Manitou."

"Do not say such things, my chief."

"It is all I can do, my duty. I am old and sick. No medicine man can make me young again."

Red Eagle shook his head.

The old man continued, "Red Eagle will be chief of the Salt Springs. And perhaps even the Great One of all the Erierhonon. Think of the future. I am certain you will have a wife that will stand at your side as you lead our people. You will be proud, courageous, and honorable. And may the Manitou be at your back as you lead the Cats."

Wind and Shadow Cat

WIND HAD ALWAYS LIKED her. She was funny, beautiful, quietly intelligent, and afraid of no one. How was it that this girl who was so special and exciting to him seemed unnoticed by most of the other young men of the tribe? All they talked about were Calling Dove and her friends. What was there about this girl that they could not see?

She was small, unlike the sleek and comely beauties who were friends of Calling Dove. Yet she was strong and lean, and darker than any other girl of the Salt Springs. It occurred to him that she had to be appreciated up close, because to Wind, she seemed bright and alive. And lately, he could walk past Calling Dove and her friends and not dream of one of them naked in his bed. But when he saw Shadow Cat, he did dream and wonder what it would be like to touch her, to be the object of her attention, to be the object of her love.

He loved looking at her legs as she came out of the river just after having washed clothes. And when she was wet, her breasts were small and perfect against the wet clothing she wore as she worked, revealing the tops of each breast that hinted at what they would look like if she were naked, and her body showed its dark, creamy brown color.

She was like her name: Shadow Cat. To almost everyone, she was a quiet mystery. One day, Wind was watching her at the far end of the village washing clothes in the river. She was a pleasure to watch. She moved easily and gracefully and was wholly self-possessed.

He walked toward her as she gathered her clothes to wring them out to dry. She saw him approach and wondered what he was thinking. She knew he noticed her, and she was glad. Of all the young men in the tribe, he had caught her eye. He was not proud or brash or haughty, as some of the warriors were. He was intelligent and serious. And now, without Dark Moon, he was the finest hunter in the Salt Springs.

After the death of Dark Moon, everyone realized how skilled he really was. They realized he had learned his lessons well from his legendary mentor.

"May I help you with your clothes?" Wind said by way of greeting.

She smiled. "Do you not fear the taunts of other men if they see you doing a woman's work?"

"Merely because I help you carry clothes?" he asked.

"Carrying wet clothes is the work of women, is it not?"

Wind smiled. "You seem to mock me as I try to help?"

Shadow Cat smiled back and stepped a few paces closer to him. "But why would you not ask the other women of the tribe, the beautiful ones?"

"I am asking a beautiful one," he said, "who mocks me and turns my offer of help back in my face."

For a split second, she hesitated, thinking that she had teased him too much. But he didn't seem angry as he spoke.

"You think I am beautiful?" she asked.

"Yes, but you are also different."

"From other girls of the tribe?" she asked.

"From anyone I have ever known," he said.

"Is this difference good or bad?"

Wind stepped closer to her so that their faces were but a few inches apart. He looked at her silently.

"Is it good or bad?" Shadow Cat repeated softly.

At that, he moved forward to kiss her. For a moment, she was startled and stiff. But then she yielded and returned the kiss, pressing herself against him as he enfolded his arms around her.

When they moved apart after a few seconds, they stared each other almost in disbelief.

He smiled, shaking his head, and said, "Who are we, who would do this?"

"Perhaps wanderers who have been searching for neighbors we never knew we had?" she answered.

"Wanderers who have found the other parts of our spirits?"

Then, Wind kissed her again. Afterward, she stepped away and stared back at him.

"What?" he said.

"I never thought I would ever find you," Shadow Cat said.

"Nor I. But what does it matter if we have done so now?"

"Will it matter for your whole life?" she said. "That is the only way I can be part of you."

He smiled. "It is my way. It is the reason why I can walk through a crowd of all the women of the Erierhonon and still look for the face of the only one who matters. The Manitou must have known I always would."

Dark Moon Awakens

When Dark Moon hovered near death, Snow Flower and Cricket would administer to his wounds and watch carefully for infections and decay of his injuries. In the weeks that followed, he slept almost constantly—and endured the pain and secondary infection that accompanied his wounds.

Each day, as the two women would bathe him, he would often speak out at random dreams, calling names of friends, warning them to be careful of imagined predators or other dangers that confronted them. Snake would come every night to move his limbs carefully, turn his legs and arms, and move his head and neck backward and forward. And always, no matter who cared for him, they would wet his lips with water and whatever nourishment Dark Moon could swallow.

One day, Cricket came into the wigwam with warm water from the fire outside. She knelt beside Dark Moon and slowly examined him. Carefully, she would work on each wound, and then apply fresh liniment from her mother's bag. It was hard work, and when she concentrated so much, she would sweat, even in the chill of winter. And she would worry also. Though weeks had gone by, and he seemed to be better, she still had a dread of what she would find whenever she cleansed his wounds. The fear of a stench or a sweat was always with her.

Her mother would counsel her and ask her to explain if she had worries. Snow Flower would smile and examine him herself, and Cricket would breathe a sigh of relief if her worries were unfounded.

Cricket had never, in her eighteen winters, been a caregiver as she was now, for one man alone. She had learned at the side of her mother, the medicine woman, and had become skilled and knowledgeable with bandages, washing and dressing wounds, and setting bones. But she never had the task of caring for someone so close to death, and yet someone who always seemed to fight for his life. In the weeks that went by, through his long dark sleep, through the fever, and now to the slow healing, the one part of her day that she thought of most was when she was in the wigwam taking care of Dark Moon.

Sometimes, in his delirium, he would speak, but the words seemed to be from disjointed fantasies. He called out names: Calling Dove, Red Eagle, Wind, Grandmother. But none of them had any meaning to the girl, as though they were spirits from another world.

One day, Snake came into the tent as he did almost every night.

"You have worked hard today," Cricket said.

"No more than you," he responded. "How is he?"

"He still talks of the people in his life. He calls out to Red Eagle sharply. Yet he talks softly of Calling Dove, Wind, and the Grandmother. Sometimes, there is anguish in his voice. And..." She hesitated.

"Yesternight, after you left here, there were tears flowing from his eyes."

"Will he live, sister?"

She hesitated, thinking before she spoke. "Yes, I think he will. He is strong...and I feel he wants to live."

"Anyone with the courage to kill a bear must surely want to live. Do you think he will tell us his story?"

"I wish it so," she said softly. "Help me turn him, Snake. Hold his leg so that I can anoint the wounds on his back."

Carefully, they turned him, with Snake holding the leg and Cricket turning his torso so that her brother could make the leg go up with the turn and not bend. Then, Cricket carefully bathed the wounds and applied ointments before putting new bandages over the slashes made by the claws of the bear.

When she was done, they turned him over again, and as he settled on his back, Dark Moon's eyes opened.

As Dark Moon stared, they both gazed back at him silently. At first, he was confused, seeming not to know where he was. For several minutes, he stared at Snake. The young man smiled and stared back at him and ruffled his hair playfully. Dark Moon snorted and smiled slightly. Then, he turned to Cricket. He seemed confused again.

"He must think you are a servant from the Manitou," said Snake to his sister.

The girl didn't move or change her gaze. This was the first time in weeks that his eyes seemed to focus and really see her. Finally, Cricket said, softly, "How are you?"

Dark Moon nodded and gave a weak smile, then closed his eyes. For the first time since he was attacked by the bear, he was sensate. He could feel something; he could actually wonder.

———◆◈◆———

As the weeks progressed, Dark Moon seemed to have a firmer grasp on reality. He remembered the bear and was aware that strangers found him and brought him to the place where he now was. He became constantly aware of the visits his benefactors would make each morning, afternoon, and evening. He was able to take bigger sips of the soups and water that they brought to his lips. Even his urine and bowel movements, when he became conscious of them, were cleared quickly and his body parts washed.

So as the weeks went on, each day he became more aware of his surroundings, and the three people who saved his life. Now, he smiled at them and responded to their questions, at first with nods and head shakes, then with one-word responses.

The pain he endured in his recovery was soothed as much by the sight of his caregivers as the medicines that he was given. Each day he looked forward to one of them bringing tea or broth in the morning, and then in the evening, the quieter time for their attentions. But none of the movement and stretching or stroking of his limbs seemed endurable unless the beautiful young girl came to feed or clean him and dress his wounds.

One night, when she came into his tent, bearing tea and biscuits, he felt strong enough to speak. "What is your name?" he asked her.

She was startled for a few seconds, not expecting him to speak after so many moons of silence. "I am known as Cricket," she said.

He smiled, and she reacted quickly, continuing, "Do you think my name is improper?"

"No," he said. "But now that you say it, I cannot think of a name better for you."

He was smiling, and she was glad to see it, but she was also aroused in a combative sense of play. "Does my name bring humor to you?"

"No," he said. "Somehow, as I know you, I think it is perfect." He was smiling, and she softened to his cheerful demeanor.

"How do you feel? You must be better if you are able to talk so."

"Did I offend you?" he said. "I meant no disrespect. I am thankful, for I should be dead, but for your kindness and care."

"You were helpful in responding to our care."

"But you must have other duties you perform? And do I not make your day's work harder?"

"All days are filled with work and sleep," she said.

"But if you did not have the burden of my care, would not your day's tasks be easier?"

"There is always work enough to fill a day," she said.

"Well, I thank you…for I owe you and your family my life. And I will be grateful forever."

"We are just doing the bidding of the Manitou to help those who are afflicted. Is that not the honorable way?"

"Yes, it is, but all people do not act with such honor," he said, thinking of Red Eagle's treachery.

"But in life, do not trials often also come with blessings?"

"Yes…both. You have not only saved my life, but you all have showed me acts of honor that I will never forget."

"Then, someday, perhaps you will do good works for others," she said.

They were both quiet for a few minutes, just looking at each other. Then, Cricket asked, "Is there anything you need before I depart?"

Dark Moon shook his head, thinking quietly to himself, *It is so easy to talk to her. She makes me glad to be alive when I see her.*

As Cricket turned to leave, he said one last thing: "May your dream be of health and happiness."

She nodded and left the tent.

Dark Moon and Snow Flower

S NOW FLOWER CAME INTO his tent quietly and walked over to him and squatted down. Dark Moon had just awakened, but still his eyes were closed. Suddenly, he felt her hand lie gently against his forehead and linger for a few moments.

His eyes opened and he watched her. Neither of them spoke for several minutes. Then, he said, "I did not thank you for saving my life. I have never known anyone whose medicine was so great, and you will have my thanks forever."

Snow Flower shrugged. "The medicine was in your strong, young body. You have great strength, and your health is good. Such things make all medicine better." She paused and looked away from him, then turned back. "The claw marks of the bear, the teeth marks, and the scars will grow smaller in time." She smiled. "You will now be known as the great warrior and bear killer."

He snorted. "All my life I have been a hunter because it was what I did best. I was never thought of as a warrior."

"Anyone who fights a bear, kills it with a knife, and then lives, has shown that he is a great warrior."

"Perhaps in days gone by, but no more. My leg..."

"Your leg was torn in two places," Snow Flower said. "I have tried to make it straight, but it would not be. You will limp always, but yet you will walk. And you may still go quietly in the forest, but that you must teach yourself again."

"I must learn to be a cat again," Dark Moon said, and Snow Flower looked at him curiously. "I was a hunter among the Erierhonon, the Cat People. Hereafter, I will be the cat with the crooked leg."

She smiled in return. "Then I will call you Crooked Leg."

He chuckled softly. "I will be your Dark Moon, or Crooked Leg."

"But remember now, you must first teach the crooked leg to move with stealth through the forest."

"How long will you stay in this place?" Dark Moon asked, changing the subject.

"Since we were driven from our tribe, we have trusted the Manitou to tell us when to leave. We have had no sign to tell us, so we stayed, waiting. That is when Cricket and Snake found you…as the Manitou wished."

"You believe such things?" he asked.

"Yes. There is a reason for all things. There is a reason why you were in the forest; there is a reason why you alone killed a bear; there is a reason why Cricket and Snake found you when they were looking for nuts and berries; and there is a reason why you are here with us and will live again, Crooked Leg."

"I have had no signs to tell me where to go," he said.

"Perhaps because the Manitou does not want you to go," she said, looking directly at him.

"Do you mean that I could stay with all of you?"

"Unless you are called somewhere else…back to the land of the Erierhonon."

"But with you? You would permit me?" Dark Moon asked.

"Yes. I would treat you as a son," Snow Flower said.

"You think I would fit into your life?"

"Yes, or I would not have been able to save you. You would help Snake become a man, something I cannot do, and with Cricket you..." She paused and shook her head.

"What does the Manitou want for Cricket?" Dark Moon asked softly.

"I cannot answer that. All I know is that she and her brother went into the woods to find mushrooms and berries, and they found you."

"Would Cricket want me to stay?" he asked.

"You must ask her that yourself," said Snow Flower, though she knew her daughter would say yes.

The little family had been wanderers since their small tribe was destroyed. They were good children. They helped her through the terrible dark times after their father was killed, and they showed love and respect for each other. They also worked hard and never complained. Yet their wandering existence seemed to leave a void in their lives. Suddenly, there was no place to be comfortable, no place for them to know rivers and streams, hills and valleys, the places where nuts and berries and mushrooms always grew. Snow Flower knew there was something missing in their lives, even if her children did not.

Dark Moon was quiet for a few minutes as Snow Flower tidied up wigwam.

Finally, Dark Moon said, "Tomorrow I would like to go outside. Do you think I can?"

"I think you can. But you must have help. Cricket and Snake will lend you support. But if your leg is weak, you must not walk on it without their help."

He nodded and smiled slightly in appreciation. "I long for the day that I can draw my bow and..." He stopped for a second and shook his head. "But I forgot. My bow is lost, and I do not know if I will have its like again. There were great trees in the forest around the Mahoning that I have seen nowhere else. They made the finest of bows."

"Someday, you will find such a bow again. It is not only a tree that makes good bows," Snow Flower said.

———————

One night, Snake came into Dark Moon's tent, as usual, bearing two cups of tea. Dark Moon thanked him and motioned for him to rest beside him. The two men had grown to like each other and enjoyed conversing over long visits in the evening. After a few opening remarks were exchanged, Dark Moon sensed that Snake wished to ask him something.

"Do you have a question for me?" he asked Snake.

Snake nodded. "I was wondering why you were in that forest by yourself."

"I was looking for an important man of our hunting party," Dark Moon explained. "We had been divided into many small groups, each led by a hunter, because we were told that a great cold would come upon us this winter, and we would need more meat, lest our camp starve in the cold. So, our chief sent us out to the forest in small groups to gather the meat we needed to survive."

"And did you find enough?" asked Snake.

"Yes. There was good hunting in the forests, and we found much that would sustain us, though we all traveled to regions far from the places that we would often hunt."

"So why did your team not come and find you?"

"We had captured much game, and my own group had all the meat we could carry. So, I sent my small band to return home to the Salt Springs so the meat from our bison would not spoil and could be salted and stored for the winter."

"And that is why you were alone?"

Dark Moon nodded his head. "One of our tribe, a warrior, could not stand to be bested, so he abandoned his own men and sent them to return home. But then he foolishly set out alone to find a bison. He did not want it said that only I found a bison in our hunt. And besides, he harbored dreams of being chief of the Salt Springs. But our warriors who were made to join the hunting groups for fear of starvation this winter had not much experience of hunting carefully through the forest. Most of the men in the Salt Springs were either warriors or in a much smaller group as hunters.

"But he was going into a region that he did not know, and I believed that he was in danger because he was not a climber of hills and a traveler through the forest—not an experienced hunter."

"So, you never found him?" Snake asked. "And how, if you are an experienced hunter, could you be attacked by a bear?"

Dark Moon sighed. "The story is long. I will tell you on another night. Do you trust that I will?"

Snake nodded and took some tea.

Dark Moon sighed and changed the subject. "Once in my travels, I was hunting near the great lake. And I met two good men from the Wenro tribe, and we camped the night. They told me stories of strange men with white faces."

"White faces?" said Snake. "Did you ever see such?"

"I have never seen them. But these men seemed not fools, but men of honesty, and they said that they had seen them on a sojourn across the mountains of the morning. They told tales of their coming across the endless waters in great canoes, larger than two of our lodges — amazing stories of sticks made of hard dark substance that is not wood, a kind of atlatl that hurls small arrows great distances and that shows great smoke when they shoot. And they told stories of huge creatures, the kind no one has ever seen…as though giant dogs and bison in one. They told of the white eyes riding on the backs of these animals."

"And you believe the stories?"

Dark Moon shrugged. "I trusted the words of those two good men."

"I must tell you, my friend, that I know the stories of the great beasts. They are called elk dogs," said Snake.

Dark Moon showed surprise. "You have seen these creatures?"

"You may see them yourself on the morrow."

"Where?"

"We have some elk dogs here with us," he said as he gestured over his shoulder.

Dark Moon was amazed at Snake's casual attitude. "In truth? You are not jesting?"

"No jest...Tomorrow. Our father, who is now gone to the Manitou, was given some of them after he and my mother helped save the life of the son of a great chieftain of the Seneca. The boy had been attacked by a young cougar and was badly injured."

Dark Moon shook his head and smiled. "When I wake tomorrow, I hope that what you're telling me was not part of my dreams."

Dark Moon and Cricket

A FEW DAYS LATER, Cricket came into the tent with some of Snow Flower's tea. Nowadays, she would smile as she entered, knowing well that Dark Moon would be awake enough to welcome her.

"How do you feel today?" she asked, squatting down beside him.

"I am fine...getting stronger every day. Your mother said I might walk outside today."

"She said you could—if you had help."

"Maybe I can find someone who will help me," Dark Moon said, smiling as he looked at her directly. "Perhaps it will be Snake."

"You will need more than Snake, Crooked Leg." Now, Cricket was teasing him in return.

"I wonder if he knows someone who would help, someone strong and kind."

"He knows only his sister and must be content with her help."

"But will his sister give her help willingly? To a man from a strange land, a Cat?"

"The sister is kind enough to help a proud man who cannot walk, who has a crooked leg."

"And how long will she help him?" Dark Moon asked.

She looked directly at him. "As long as he needs...or until he decides to leave us."

"But what if he will not leave? Would he be welcome into this little tribe of a girl and a boy and a mother?"

Again, Cricket studied his face. "Why would he want to stay here and not leave?"

He took a deep breath. "There is this girl, who, if he did not see her come to his tent in the morning, his day would be lonely and dark."

"So, she would be a nursemaid? And come to see you from some other place?"

"I do not know. I do not know if she would sleep in my tent. Do you think she would?"

Cricket was silent for a few moments. Then, without looking at him, she said softly, "She would sleep in your tent."

Dark Moon felt his flesh tingle as he heard her words, but still he hesitated. He had to know how she felt beyond a doubt. "How long would she sleep in his tent if he walked like a baby bear...and if he were always crooked?" He still did not make eye contact with her.

"She would stay forever, as long as he wished...as long as he wanted her."

Dark Moon reached out his hand and touched her chin, turning her face toward his. "And if I told you that his days would be ever filled with happiness because he thought of her as his true gift from the Manitou?"

Cricket stared back at him, her eyes searching his, as if to know exactly what was in his heart. "Would you want me for wife?" she asked softly. "Would you forsake the Salt Springs, and someone named Calling Dove, and remain with me even if we were to journey into the northern lands?"

"Yes. I would...but only if I could always be with you."

She snorted softly as though not believing what she had heard. "You would love me?"

"I have loved you ever since I awoke from my injuries. But I could never have a wife who does not love me in return, as I love her."

Cricket leaned over to him slowly, her face coming near his. But this time, unlike all the others, she kept coming and kissed his lips slowly and softly.

"I have loved you ever since I saw you under the bear, Crooked Leg."

Cricket and Her Family

THE DAY AFTER DARK Moon and Cricket pledged their love to each other, Cricket came upon her brother as he was cutting wood for their fires. She handed him a cup of cold water that he drank down completely.

"Thank you," Snake said.

She responded with a nod and was quiet for a few seconds.

"What is it?" he asked, sensing that she had something to say but seemed uneasy about speaking.

"Sister?" he asked, by way of showing that he was open to her thoughts.

For the first time in his memory, Cricket seemed uneasy about speaking. He nodded to her in encouragement.

"Would you...would you accept..." Cricket shook her head, annoyed with herself for seeming so inarticulate. "You see...Dark Moon has told me—"

"That he loves you," Snake said, interrupting her.

Cricket nodded in relief. "Yes. But how do you know this?" she asked in frustration. "Did he tell you?"

"He did not have to tell me. Any fool can see that he awaits each day for you to go to him—that you bring light and joy to his life."

"But if he did not tell you, how can you be certain enough to say these things? He may be merely reacting to the care I give him for his wounds."

"Do you not marvel at the recovery he has made from his terrible injuries? Do you think all men so injured would survive, no matter how much medicine our dear mother prepared? When you are near him, I see sunshine on his face.

"You spend each day thinking of ways to comfort and heal him. You bathe and feed him, you anoint him and bring him tea, and sometimes talk with him long into the night. He is not a small child that needs such loving care. Yet that is just what you give him."

Snake opened his arms toward her as an invitation to come to him. She ran into his arms tearfully and kissed him, and when she did, Snake said, "You and he are the Manitou's gifts to each other."

"But he wishes to marry me. Do you approve?"

"Of course, little fool. He has become a brother to me, and I cherish his love and friendship. And he, in turn, has mine. And you, little Cricket, have my blessing along with the Manitou's."

———————

Later that day, Cricket approached her mother, who was forming leather into winter moccasins for Dark Moon and Snake. Her mother, in barely a glance at her suddenly timorous daughter, sensed what she was about to tell her.

"Mother, Dark Moon and I have had a long talk."

"And he wishes to marry," Snow Flower said.

Cricket shook her head in wonder and amazement. "But how does everyone know of these things before I even tell them?" she said in exasperation.

"Because it is easy to see as the sun or the moon," Snow Flower said. "How could anyone not see the glow in your face as you come to his tent, and not see the regret he tries to conceal whenever you leave him?"

"He said he loves me, even though I know he has dreamed of someone named Calling Dove."

"Do you believe him when he says he loves you?" Snow Flower asked.

Cricket was quiet for a few moments, then she sighed. "I do believe him. He tells the truth always, but the girl from the Salt Springs seems to haunt his dreams."

"Child, he does not have to dream of you. You stand before him so that he can reach out and touch you." Snow Flower paused a few seconds. "Do you not believe that the love he has for you can make him forget his feelings for that other girl? Daughter, he himself is a gift—not only to all of us, but especially to you. You know of his courage when he fought the bear. I tell you this: men such as he do not have false hearts."

"We have only kissed once...last night."

"And how did you feel?"

"Like I was in the camp of the Manitou. Like my heart would beat out of my chest."

"What did he say to you?"

"He says I have brought him happiness he has never known...and that he wants me for wife."

"And do you wish to be his wife?"

"Yes, more than any wish I have ever had, or anything I could dream of."

"Dear one, you have been blessed by the love of a fine man, of someone who has never known anyone as wonderful as you. Do you think you can make him happy?"

She looked toward the top of the wigwam. "Yes. Do you know that sometimes we play, seeming as though we were children?"

"And does your heart sing as you play?"

"Yes...like something I have never known."

"Then, that is the Manitou's way of telling you that you belong in Dark Moon's bed."

"He asked me if I would wait, perhaps a moon, until he is able to stand near me as a man should. Then, he would, before all of us, ask the Manitou to bless our union."

"Then, my daughter, for the joyous time I see before you, tell him that you both have my blessing."

Dark Moon Stands

SNAKE CAME INTO THE small tent as usual the next morning with a hot cup of tea. Dark Moon looked up at him as he entered and said, "You must labor early to get so much water to boil."

"It is one of my best skills, Crooked Leg, of which I have many. Oh, I forget. My instructions are to henceforth call you by your old fantasy name, Dark Moon." Snake smirked. "I am told by Mother that I must indulge your pride and call you by your old name and not by your true ones, Crooked Leg or Mushroom."

Dark Moon threw a small wrap of leather at him, which he dodged. "Perhaps I will choose my own name for you. I know... I will call you Dark Leg or Crooked Moon. How does that feel to you, in your new nature?"

Dark Moon was quiet for a few seconds, caught off guard by the impishness of the man he had grown to regard as a friend on par with his lost friend, Wind. He snorted and smiled, shaking his head. "You must have eaten some strange berries from the forest this morning. Is this the tea that you have brought to poison me or make me as crazy as you are?"

"I will leave the poisoning to my sister when you make her angry," Snake said. "The Manitou has given me the task of teaching you to walk again."

"I already know how to walk. I do not need a braggart who tries to poison me when I take his sister to my bed."

"I have tried to keep my sister from believing your 'Cat' tales, but she will not listen, and now she tells me that you wish to marry her...to take her to wife?"

Dark Moon was quiet, then he slowly nodded, expecting Snake to say something disparaging in jest. But instead, Snake knelt down beside him, and suddenly seemed to show a different persona, someone very serious.

"You know, if you have my sister, that we will henceforth be brothers?" Snake said.

Dark Moon nodded slightly again.

"Most men cannot choose their brothers, Crooked Leg," Snake continued. "But it seems that the sister that I love, who was born a year later than I, has made a choice for me." He paused and put a hand on Dark Moon's shoulder. "And she has delivered to me someone who has made me proud and happy. And I thank the Manitou for his wisdom, for Cricket has made the choice that I would have made for her myself. And I am blessed to have a fine friend as a new brother."

Dark Moon nodded in appreciation. "You are the friend of my lifetime," he responded.

Snake was thoughtful for a few minutes. "Do you ever wonder how all of this could have happened? How did Cricket and I find ourselves in that forest...and then find you beside the great bear? How you lived through your terrible injuries? How you and my sister found love? Does it not seem hard to believe?"

"Only if the Manitou has desires that we all be happy," said Dark Moon. "I would not have survived if he did not want our family to be together. Your mother and your sister brought their magic into my life, and also a brother, who I must teach how to hunt properly."

"Just because you have the love and respect of my mother and sister does not mean that you are forgiven the arrogance of you 'Cat' people. Come now, arise from your slumber for I must teach you to walk again."

Snake extended his hand, and Dark Moon grabbed it as Snake pulled him erect. "Remember, you must learn one step at a time. Be patient, Crooked Leg, and we will show these women that men can accomplish much if they work together."

Snake held out both arms toward Dark Moon. "Come here now, only one step," he said.

Dark Moon, without thinking, took a step on his left leg and almost stumbled. Snake grabbed his arm to steady him. They waited a few more seconds. "Now, the other," Snake said, still holding out both hands to catch his friend if he faltered. "Steady."

But as soon as Dark Moon tried to move his right leg, he felt a horrible pain at the turn of his hip. He blinked his eyes and then reopened them as involuntary tears flowed down his cheeks.

For a moment, it seemed that he would collapse, but Snake grabbed his shoulders to steady him. "Pull it forward," he said softly.

Dark Moon hesitantly dragged the right leg across from his left.

"Enough," said Snake as he grabbed a small stool for Dark Moon to sit on. "Your work is done for this morning. We will do it again tonight."

"But—" said Dark Moon, weakly.

"Tonight, you will be more ready, for your girl will soon be here with your morning porridge."

"Will you not stay to join us?" asked Dark Moon.

"Not this day. I have more wood to gather for fires. Would you now have my mother and my sister blame me for a chill that our injured guest might suffer?" Snake asked with a smirk.

Just then, Cricket entered the tent and looked at the two of them as she carried a steaming bowl of porridge. "He has not drunk his tea," she said to Snake.

"He was busy. Besides, he said he does not like your tea."

Cricket was horrified and gasped. "He does not?"

Dark Moon interrupted frantically, "But he lies, Cricket. Do you not see the evil in his eyes when he speaks?"

Cricket became annoyed when she saw both of them grinning at her. Then, suddenly, Snake said, "I must go, for we will need more firewood tonight." He winked at Dark Moon as he turned to leave the tent.

Cricket and Dark Moon looked at each other.

"It was in jest," Dark Moon said.

"Eat your breakfast," she said crossly as she began to tidy up the area near the small stand where she set the porridge.

Dark Moon chuckled to himself as he watched Cricket gathering and straightening the area around his bed. "You must know that brothers can be evil tricksters if they are not watched," he said. "Look, I am drinking your tea."

She tried valiantly to suppress a smile, but she couldn't do it. Dark Moon loved the reaction she had to their play.

"You must understand that men always try to taunt and tease," Dark Moon said. "It is just the way of friends."

"And you are just as evil as my brother," Cricket said. "Do you think I will always let you torment me, with or without his help?"

He chuckled again. "I love your brother, and we are that way so we can learn to manage evil women who try to turn our lives upside down." He held out his hand to her. "Do you really believe that I do not like the food you bring me? I would eat rat turds if I saw that you brought them to me."

Cricket screamed, "You are not Dark Moon! You are just an image created by the evil spirit. What have you done to the other man, the one I gave my love to?"

"What? Are you telling me that you now lust after other men? What has become of the sweet girl who stole my heart? Are you an evil image of darkness that has come upon me, a poor injured traveler who wants only to be true and honest?"

Cricket rolled her eyes but went, smiling, into Dark Moon's arms.

Red Eagle and Calling Dove

R ED EAGLE WALKED SLOWLY through the village, acknowledging the calls of neighbors—waving, smiling, confident, and proud. He had become a hero during the great cold. The Salt Springs tribe survived the most bitter part of the Snow Moon, though the winter was harsh, and the Mahoning had frozen over completely.

And the loss of Dark Moon was gradually fading from the minds of the people as the travails of the winter had every day brought new crises and worries. His loss had brought the specter of death into their lives. But the presence of Red Eagle, assured and confident, was a constant reminder that through the cold, the stories of Red Eagle's efforts in bringing food for the Salt Springs and the stories of the bear he had slain after it killed and maimed Dark Moon, had conferred a mystic grace upon him that inspired all to look to him for advice and inspiration.

Toward the end of the fierce winter, Big Hand quietly stole into the forest one night and was never seen again.

Calling Dove remained troubled by Dark Moon's death. The rumors that he had been eaten by a bear were dreadful to hear and afflicted all her good memories of their youth together. Somehow, the great hunter, the cat who could haunt the forest and slay countless animals, including huge wood bison, was brought down by a bear, the likes of which he had slain many times over. She remembered his lean, thick, muscular body and shuddered at the thought of a bear slashing through it with his teeth and tearing his muscles asunder.

But as the great cold passed, life became less precarious for the tribe. Some of the Salt Springs people, especially the old ones, had died of the cold. And though the tribe did have enough food, they had to be careful that no food was wasted or spoiled. Some of the hunters, led by Wind, sometimes caught wolves, or large cats, or beavers, and these became the coats and covers for people against the cold and wind.

But then, after Big Hand died, Calling Dove grew distant and quiet. She had liked and respected the old chief since her childhood. He was the mainstay of the tribe, a man of wisdom, a man of gentle heart, a father to everyone, a settler of disputes, and an inspiration to all the men.

As the cold wore on, each day occupied her with the tasks of survival. She and her brothers and sister worked constantly to keep their lodge clean and warm. They cured animal skins, and gathered wood, and preserved meat, and cooked food constantly.

The ordinary chores that they did all through the year were always made harder by the cold. Outside the lodges, men would quickly be exhausted when they worked in the harsh cold air. Hunters could not search far away lest they be caught by the cold and freeze. They also had to be careful that the cold would not turn anyone's fingers blue and then black.

Everyone had to struggle just to live. One foolish turn, one rash moment, and a life could be gone. There was no forgiveness in the cold, and some of the Salt Springs thoughtless paid the price with their lives.

Toward the end of the winter, there was a brief warming. Everyone knew that the winter was not yet done, but the brief warming made it easy for people to come together to retrieve small animals and nuts—beavers, turkeys, and chestnuts—from the forest to augment the food supply that was growing thin.

But the sudden warmth also heartened all the Salt Springs that the worst of their ordeal was over. Suddenly, there was more noise in the camp. And children could be heard playing outside the lodges. Dogs would bark, and birds would chirp noisily, and wolves would howl at night. Everywhere there was movement and life.

Calling Dove and her sister brought ice from the river into the pots for melting. The job was onerous, and the weather was still not so warm that ordinary tasks became easy. One day, her sister nodded toward Calling Dove, a signal that someone was approaching from behind. As she turned, she saw Red Eagle.

"How are you?" he asked as he drew near her.

"I am fine. How are you? I have not seen you in many suns," she said.

"I was helping the hunters. We had to go into the small mountains to protect them from the Algonquins. We saw two Wenro who told us of the white ghosts and amazing stories of huge creatures that are a kind of giant dog and a bison. They told of men riding on the backs of those animals."

"Do you believe them?" Calling Dove asked.

"I tried to believe them. But I will leave those thoughts for another day. What are you doing now?" Red Eagle asked, changing the subject.

"My sister and I are gathering ice for water for her children and our old ones."

"I saw you putting stones into the fire," said Red Eagle. "That is hard work."

Calling Dove always expected that a day would come when she would choose between him and Dark Moon. But now there would be no choice. Dark Moon was gone, and she could not play the same game she had done in winters past, playing the two men against each other. Now, the chance was gone, and she had to decide—not between Red Eagle and Dark Moon, but between Red Eagle and another life.

In a way, she always knew that she would choose Red Eagle. And yet now, in a strange way, she was drawn to Dark Moon more. He was more complex and had secrets of his heart that he kept from everyone, especially her. Somehow it bothered her that a man could have dreams and hopes and thoughts that could make for him another life, unrealized by her. That bothered her, and yet it attracted him to her memory.

Calling Dove always knew what Dark Moon wanted, but she pretended not to know. She recalled those few oblique words of meaning that led her to know his wish. But she always tried to play and tease him. She couldn't face the kind of choice he would have made for her. She would have to love Dark Moon more than she would Red Eagle, to surrender more of herself to him, and would have to know him more.

Red Eagle would never give his soul to her, and would never ask for hers. With Red Eagle, it would be easy. She would surrender love, and for him that would be enough. He would offer her his proud looks, his chance for the future as chief, his love of adventure, his skill as a warrior. He would require less thinking than Dark Moon. He would never ask for all of her heart as Dark Moon would. She would not have to think about him. She would never have to try to lose herself to the depths of love that Dark Moon would want.

With Dark Moon, she would surrender her soul. With Red Eagle, she would never be asked. With Red Eagle, her life would require less commitment, less thought, fewer dreams.

Calling Dove always sensed that, with Dark Moon, there would come a day when she realized that he was her whole life, and she would be so totally his that losing him would be like losing life. That was what she feared—knowing that she would find herself so totally in love, so totally dependent on him for life's meaning that only the two of them could create.

Red Eagle wanted her body, not her soul. And that would be easy to give because it was enough. With Dark Moon, it would not be enough.

So, now, Calling Dove could give herself over to pleasure and to the comfort brought about by the envy and admiration of all the young women of the tribe. And she could cherish the thoughts of having a handsome and magnetic man as her husband because he would certainly be chief of the Salt Springs, and later, perhaps, the Great One of all the Erierhonon. All it would take would be for her to choose the life that Red Eagle was offering.

"Have you recovered from your ordeal in the forest?" Calling Dove asked.

"Yes, I am quite well," Red Eagle said.

"I have not seen you much this winter," she said.

He snorted. "Not many have gone out in this cold unless they had to."

She smiled. "Yes. The warmth of the lodge is very agreeable this time of year."

"Well, now that the bitter cold will begin to leave, the outside will be more welcoming. Perhaps we will see more of each other?"

"You could have come to see me," she said with a slight tease.

"Perhaps I should have," he said, almost to himself. "But you also could have visited me. My family has always liked you."

"You are right. We both might have tried to be more friendly."

"Shall we try now?"

"To be friendly?" she asked, smiling slightly.

"I am not talking about our families," Red Eagle responded.

She nodded. "I would like that."

He brightened. "I would, also. So, will I see you soon?" Red Eagle looked directly into her eyes as he advanced closer to her.

"Yes," Calling Dove said reassuringly, sending the message that he had hoped to hear from her.

As they parted, Red Eagle smiled to himself. Soon, that wonderful body would be his every night. He remembered the softness and the wondrous, smoothness of her skin. The glow of her face in the dark when they made love. His life promised glory in coming days.

He marveled at how simple it was. All he had to do was remove Dark Moon from the lives of the Salt Springs. And the Manitou did it so easily, saving him from sure death on the cliffside and sending the great, strange bear to kill Dark Moon.

Red Eagle, on one of the nights when he and Calling Dove were alone, told her about an incident that he and two warrior friends had with three strangers they encountered in the near upland forest.

"Did you know them?" Calling Dove asked.

"No," Red Eagle said.

"Where did they come from?"

"From the upper Mahoning—near the small mountains."

"And they were hunting?"

"Yes. In our hunting grounds. But they will not come this way again."

She was thoughtful for a few moments. "Did they return then, without food? But surely there is enough for all in these hills now that the cold is leaving?"

"They have now gone to the Manitou to hunt with him. These hills have always been the hunting grounds of the Erierhonon. If we let the Algonquins hunt there, then many others will surely come. And soon our children will be told that they are intruding on the Algonquin hunting grounds."

Calling Dove was quiet again. She didn't pursue the thought any further. She didn't want to know if Red Eagle and his friends had fought with them…or deliberately killed them. All her thoughts were centered on her marriage and her new status as the chief's wife.

They walked for a while as the sun set further. "The elders will meet tomorrow to choose a chief," she said finally.

Red Eagle snorted. "Did you think I did not know that?"

She shook her head. "I know it must be on your mind." She walked a few steps ahead, then turned to face him. "But you must know that you will be chosen?"

"One can never be certain of such things."

"But who else would they choose?"

"They might choose Wind."

"He has said that he does not wish to be chosen. He said Dark Moon was to be chief, and he would not do anything to mar that memory."

Red Eagle didn't answer her. After a long pause, he said, "I do not wish to talk of being chief. I have another question to ask."

"And what is that?" Calling Dove asked, smiling at him.

"You know what it is. Will you be my wife?"

"Do you truly wish to be my husband?" she asked.

"You have known that for many moons," Red Eagle said.

"But you did not ask me in those moons. Why?"

He was uncomfortable answering the question. "Because I wanted it to be as special as you are when I asked you."

"Now?"

"Now."

"So, you do think you will be chief."

He sighed. "Yes. I can think of no one else that they would choose."

She studied him for several seconds. "No one? If *he* were not dead?"

A spark of anger flashed through Red Eagle, because he resented even the thoughts of his old rival. "But Dark Moon is dead," he said emphatically. "If you will not be my wife, I will hereafter leave you alone."

Red Eagle turned and started walking back to the camp.

Calling Dove watched his back for a few seconds. She had to decide. There was no time left. Did she want to be the wife of the chief, and be first among equals among all the tribe's women? She now had to acknowledge what she always knew she would do—be the wife of the chief, whoever he might be. And now, Dark Moon was gone.

Suddenly, she ran after Red Eagle, calling his name as she approached.

"Red Eagle," she said breathlessly as she stood before him to block his path. "I should not have said what I did. It was a foolish thing to say. Forgive me...I would be honored to be your wife."

Red Eagle grabbed her and kissed her hard on the mouth. She was startled at first, not that he did it, but that she had to get over a momentary feeling of strangeness before she surrendered to his kiss.

Later that night, in the lodge of Calling Dove's family, her younger sister, Morning Song, quietly approached her as Calling Dove sat alone near the fire.

"Did he ask you?" her sister said.

"Yes," Calling Dove answered pensively and unsmiling.

"You do not seem happy. Did you consent?"

"Yes," she said softly.

Morning Song studied her for a few minutes. "Then, why do you not rejoice? You love him, do you not?"

Calling Dove had to finally say what she had never said before. "Yes, I love him."

The two women stared at one another for several seconds. Morning Song had doubts about Calling Dove and her future, but this was not the time to voice them. Perhaps there would never come a time. And as her sister studied her face, Calling Dove was grateful that she would never have to say such things again.

The Black Knives

CRICKET CAME TO DARK Moon's tent and stood before him as he looked up at her, curious about her presence at that time of evening.

"We must go outside to my mother's tent," she said.

"Is everything all right? Why are we to go now?" Dark Moon said.

"My mother wants to talk to you. Snake will be there also."

"Do you know why she wants me to be present?"

Cricket shook her head. "No. I know not why, but she wants us all to be there."

She helped him stand erect. He grabbed her outstretched hand and stood up, a move more easily done as each day passed.

"You are getting stronger," she said, smiling. "There was a time that you would have taken much effort to stand up, even with my help. Do you remember? And now you stand up easily."

He nodded assent.

"Come, Crooked Leg, hold onto me as we walk, and maybe it will not hurt as much to take the steps."

Cricket nestled against him under his left shoulder and put her right arm back around his waist. It took them several minutes to go the twenty-yard distance to the big tent.

When they entered, Snow Flower greeted them and pointed to a high seat where Dark Moon could sit easily. Snake sat beside him on a mat. Snow Flower was holding a small sack.

"What is this, Mother?" said Cricket. "I have never seen this bag before."

"No. I have kept it from you both because I was waiting."

"Waiting for what?" asked Snake.

"Waiting for a stranger to come among us … as my mother had foreseen," said Snow Flower softly.

"You mean Dark Moon?" said Cricket. Dark Moon said nothing and remained quiet, thinking that he was perhaps an unwelcome visitor to the gathering.

Snow Flower grew more serious before she spoke. "I did not know who the stranger would be, and I have often wondered if he would ever come," she said, nodding at Dark Moon. "But he was brought here by you and your brother. And when he lived, I knew that he had been sent to us by the Manitou. I knew then what I would do."

Suddenly, both Cricket and Snake were alarmed. "What will you do, Mother?" they asked in unison.

Snow Flower smiled and opened the bag. Then, she took out two small knives, identical in size, shape, and look with carved horn handles and black obsidian blades. She stepped toward both men and handed each of them one of the knives.

Both men examined the knives in their hands. "They were made by your father, not long before his ride to the Manitou," Snow Flower said. "He knew he would only have two children, so he made one for Snake, and one for the husband of Cricket's choosing."

Dark Moon was carefully examining the knife she had given him. He held it by the handle without touching the blade. He said, "I have seen other knives, but never have I seen one with such a blade, black as night."

"That man, who now has become your new spirit father, was a skilled maker of weapons, and he knew that these two knives were going to be special because they were his last," Snow Flower said.

"What is this black substance, Mother? I have never seen the likes of it," said Snake.

"Have care when you touch it. It is not large, but you will never see a knife as fine as this one." She handed Dark Moon an apple. "Use the knife to peel and cut this but have care."

"This stone, shining and beautiful…" muttered Dark Moon.

"It was found in the south, near the river Ohio," said Snow Flower. "But again, have care, for it will cut you even before you feel the pain."

Just then, Snake made a shrill cry as he held a bleeding finger, and Cricket jumped to bring a cloth his hand. "I merely touched it," Snake said in amazement, "and did not even try to cut with it." Snake smiled as he gathered the cloth around his finger. "I understand."

"How could he make such things?" asked Dark Moon.

"He had great skill, especially with small knives," said Snow Flower. "His own father, now your grandfather, was a hunter who ofttimes made long journeys into the forest. He told me that once he met some people from the south near the Ohio who were sick and starving…nearly to death. My husband said that he had never seen such creatures, men as tall as two of our women, taller than anyone of our tribe. But his father fed them and kept them warm for many suns."

She gestured with outstretched hands, showing ten fingers. She continued, "And your grandfather gave him the medicine that my mother and I had made. And they lived. My husband's father had saved and fed the lives of a man and his family, a man he did not know. In thanks, the family leader gave him two large, shining black stones as gifts, for it was all they had to give. These knives were made from those stones. And now they are yours, because you two have shown me that you both have the hearts of your godly ancestors. Therefore, my blessing is upon you with these gifts because you show kindness, love, and honor.

"Your father, over the years when he was not doing work for our family, would make knives. So, when you were born, Snake, he learned to hit one stone, especially flint, against other stones that made the finest of knives. But when he made these black knives, he saw that the pieces that were shattered were left with edges that would cut anything. So, in secret, he learned to make knives out of the black stones, and he saved the most perfect ones for the children and grandchildren he would never see. Since he had but one son, he made the other for the spouse that Cricket would have."

"But he is not yet a spouse," said Snake with a perverse grin. "What does a hunter need with such a knife? And Cricket's spouse may be unworthy of such a gift. Should I not have both knives and keep the one for the spouse that proves worthy of the gift?"

Dark Moon laughed. "Mother, perhaps you should give the black knife to your daughter in case she wishes to cut my throat someday."

Cricket exclaimed, "Quiet, both of you! Mother, do you hear these two fools show their disrespect? They should be sent to bed without food for their malice."

Snow Flower was grinning broadly. It was a pleasure to watch the two young men in her life chide each other and take pleasure in their play. Cricket also liked it, because none of them had ever seen such conduct between two men who cared very much about each other and played as they seemed to argue.

"You men must always be as you are now—brothers in our family," Snow Flower said. "Will you promise that to me? You three children have made the terrible misfortunes of my life become bearable. You are all my gifts from the Manitou. May you always be thus."

Snake and Cricket stood up to embrace their mother. Dark Moon stood behind them, uncertain of what he should do. When they stepped aside, he stood still, hesitating and looking. He wondered if he would seem the same as the other two in their mother's eyes.

Snow Flower sensed what he was thinking, so she opened her arms in greeting. He hesitated for a moment and tried to step forward, but in an instant, she realized that he could not move, so she stepped forward and hugged him. He stepped back, and his eyes ran with tears. For a few seconds, he couldn't speak, but finally he said, softly, "I have never had a mother to love...and I would watch other boys have the tenderness of their mothers' care, and I dreamed that one day, I could feel it. Now, I know that the Manitou has granted me that blessing."

Instantly, Cricket was in his arms, crying. Snake followed with a broad hug of the two of them. Snow Flower was speechless at the blessing that had come upon her. These three wonderful children had been given to her, almost unaware, as though she was always meant to have three children instead of two. And, as the Manitou wished, Cricket and Snake went out into the forest and did not find mushrooms or nuts but found another child for her.

She placed her hand on each of Dark Moon's shoulders and said, "My children sensed that there was a place in my heart for another child to love, so they went out into the forest for food, and they brought you home to me instead. So, sometimes, I will call you Mushroom because you were found hidden in the forest."

Snake and Cricket laughed when they heard their mother's words. They loved having another way to taunt the new family member when they played together.

Snow Flower had only one more cautionary note for the two boys: "Let these knives show a bond between you, that you are always special to each other. Remember that they can cut like no other knives. But since they are smaller than your flint knives, they should not be used roughly on bears or elk or deer. Your father, my husband, told me that such black stones, even though they can cut like no other, can be shattered easily. So, you must use them only for very fine work. Come now, Cricket. Let us have tea with these two evil ones."

Dark Moon Walks

IN THE DAYS AND weeks following Dark Moon's first step, he labored constantly to do more. He hated being awkward, so often falling and losing his balance. But Snake would always help him stand again. Sometimes, in frustration, Dark Moon would pound the earth with his fists after a fall. But each time, hearing the consoling words of his new brother, he would rise up, struggle to maintain his balance—and his temper—and continue.

At first, he always had help from Snake, but later he would insist on using his own strength to help himself up. So, Snake fashioned for him a thick cane that was sturdy and straight, and Dark Moon would use it to stand. As much as he respected his new brother, he was convinced that his recovery had to be personal and would only succeed through his own efforts.

One day, Cricket and Snow Flower walked out to the small knoll to watch Dark Moon struggle against his injuries. "How does he?" asked Cricket of her brother.

"He tries and succeeds ever more each day, but still he grows angry at himself when he falls," Snake said. "And he no longer allows my help, even though I know that he is tired."

"And yet he is much improved, is he not?" asked Snow Flower.

"Yes. But he sometimes forgets that he has made great progress, and then still tries to do too much," said Snake.

"I will talk to him this night before he sleeps," said Cricket. "Perhaps I can help him believe that he will hunt again."

"I know you will," said Snake. "Mother, you have seen other injuries, perhaps not as great as his. Do you think he will ever walk again?"

"I do," said Snow Flower. "And I know if we are patient and encouraging, he will have his wish."

Both her children nodded.

Snake said, "If anyone can get him through this journey, she can," and gestured toward his sister. He continued, "I will go now to encourage him that he has toiled enough for this day."

———◆◆◆◆———

Later that night, Dark Moon sat morosely in his tent waiting for Cricket to bring their ritual bowl of tea. When she entered, he stood to greet her.

"Do you know that only two moons ago you were unable to stand when I entered?" she asked.

Dark Moon was caught off guard by her words. "Have I acted so badly?"

"Yes, because it is not your true self."

He sighed and looked away from her. "I am ashamed." He shook his head. "I behave as a spoiled child. I wish you did not see me act so."

"But I do not know how you could be so unhappy after all the blessings we have been given," Cricket said.

"Do you not want the man who will be your spouse to be able to stand and walk beside you?" Dark Moon asked.

"Yes, because I know you wish it. But I wish I were enough to bring you peace, though I know I am unable to do it." And as she spoke, two silent tears left small trails of liquid across her face.

When Dark Moon saw it, he closed his eyes and took a deep breath.

Then, he shook his head. "I am sorry…so sorry. What a fool I am to pay no heed to your feelings!" He shook his head again and let it hang forward. After a few seconds, he asked, "Do you think I do not love you enough?"

Cricket shook her head but remained silent, not looking at him.

"I have never experienced feelings like this," he said. "I do not deserve you."

She looked back at him. "You must learn, or feel, that your happiness is my happiness, and your grief is my grief. I am not merely a shadow to your deeds anymore. I want to feel the hurt you feel—and the joy you feel. But if you do not wish to share with me, then—"

At that point, Dark Moon reached for her and rested his forehead against hers. "How could I forget that I am no longer alone? I am almost afraid to believe that you—and all this—are real. Suddenly, unlike all my past life, you have changed my dreams. And now I must learn to trust in happiness."

He paused for a few seconds, looking away from her. He took a deep breath and looked as though a new vision of life had occurred to him, before continuing, "Now…all my happiness is you."

Snow Flower and
the White Piece

TWO DAYS LATER, DARK Moon was again out in the small field near the two wigwams. For some reason, this day brought more pain than usual as he attempted to take more than a few steps at a time. He fell more often than usual, and the pain from his attempts to stride as he once remembered caused him to fall again and again.

Snow Flower approached her son and daughter, who were watching Dark Moon.

"He is in pain, but he will not let us help him," said Snake.

"But he still knows you have helped him and would do so again," said his mother.

"But now we wonder how long he can do this," said Snake.

"I do not want him to give up hope," said Cricket.

"Do you think he will give up this effort?" asked Snow Flower.

"I think he feels that he will die if he cannot walk," said her daughter. "And I do not think he wants to die."

"So, then, he will never stop," said Snow Flower. Cricket nodded in response.

They all watched silently for several more minutes as Dark Moon continued his labor. But suddenly, Snow Flower turned toward Snake.

"Go and bring my grandfather's white piece," she said softly.

"Bring it here?" asked Snake, puzzled.

"Yes," said Snow Flower.

Snake glanced at his sister who, herself, did not understand her mother's intentions. But he turned to do her bidding.

"Why are you doing this?" Cricket asked her mother.

"I am going to give it to Dark Moon," Snow Flower said, never taking her eyes off the figure who continually fell and slowly pulled himself erect with the aid of his heavy cane. Each time, he would grunt and wince and blow out his breath as the pain came against every movement that he made.

"What do you expect him to do with it?" asked Cricket.

"One time, when I was your age," says Snow Flower, "I asked my father what the great white piece was and where it came from. He did not know. All he said was that his grandfather's grandfather found it in the West near the greatest of all rivers. He said that the ancient one was in a forest and fell into a ravine and would surely have fallen to his death, except that he caught hold of this piece as he slid down the mountainside. It was sticking out of the hillside, and when he grabbed hold of it to stop his fall, it saved his life. Then, his friends pulled him up the hill and helped him dig the great white piece from the place where it was. It took them two suns to get it."

"But what is it?" asked Cricket. "Surely it is not wood, so it cannot be from a tree. Did he ever know?"

"No. No one has ever seen the likes of it. But one of the old women remembered that she heard shamans tell stories when she was a child that it was some kind of horn from a strange giant animal, very much larger than bison, that walked the land long before the oldest of our grandfathers lived. I remember once, long ago, I dreamed that the white piece was medicine lying in wait for a stranger, but I knew not in what way."

"Then perhaps it will heal Dark Moon if he can do something with it," Cricket said aloud to herself.

Snow Flower was quiet for several moments. Then, she said, "If he finds something to do with it, then he will not die, and you will have a husband."

Wind's Doubts

WIND SAT AT A distance from the campfire and was thoughtful. *How is it that Red Eagle is so relaxed when he tells his story?* he thought as he listened to the repeated tales of valor about how Dark Moon was killed, and how Red Eagle slew the golden bear in vengeance. Wind never liked the proud and arrogant warrior. He had known him to lie often as he exaggerated his exploits of battle. But his followers were always there to affirm his stories even when they sounded false and exaggerated.

But how credulous were these old ones? How foolish the young ones? They listened to Red Eagle as though he were the messenger of the Manitou. But what else could they think? If he were lying, what kind of lie could it be? Does anyone lie about such things? About the death of a friend? About a hero of the Salt Springs? Yet who was there to gainsay anything that was said? He and Dark Moon were alone in the forest, so his tale had to be accepted. No one else could say things contrary to Red Eagle if no one knew what had happened in the forest. Yet he brought Dark Moon's bow back and now brandishes the great bow as a totem of honor…and a confirmation of the story.

But if he was lying, what could have possibly happened? Could he have killed Dark Moon? Wind shook his head, trying to banish the thought. No. As much as he detested Red Eagle, he could not imagine him killing

Dark Moon. But if he did not kill him, and if Dark Moon were still dead, then what could have happened? Could someone else have killed him? But who? And why? What could Dark Moon have done to invite such calamity upon his life?

Book II

Seventeen Winters

Recalling Snow Flower

H<small>E WAS ALONE ON</small> the hillside, waiting in early morning for the deer to cross the small ravine. He held his bow beside him, quietly touching the string as his thoughts were on Snow Flower.

He missed her, and he knew Cricket and Snake missed her too. His daughters will never hear their grandmother's wisdom again, except though Cricket, who had also grown to be a wise and patient woman.

He thought he heard a noise. And he waited. Nothing. Slowly, he set the bow down beside him. It was too early. They might come for water when the sun was higher, just before the fog had completely burned off. He looked down at the bow. How many times had he used it to feed his family? How easy had it been to take revenge on the men who had driven Snow Flower's family from their land and killed their father? That was the last token in payment to the woman who had given him so much...the mother he never knew. She helped his life turn from sickness and anger to happiness and hope.

He remembered how desolate his life seemed so long ago. An old friend betrayed him, and that old friend took the bow that his foster father had shown him how to make and ran away.

No doubt it still had a place in the lodge of Red Eagle. No doubt it still gave good service. But as much as he felt the loss of the bow, he

131

could never think of it without recalling the betrayal that tainted all his memories of the Salt Springs.

Dark Moon, Cricket, and Calling Dove

DARK MOON RETURNED TO the lodge without his deer. Cricket approached him as he lay aside his bow and arrows, his ax, and his knife. He was preoccupied with his own thoughts and only sensed her when her arms encircled him from behind and locked around his waist. She rested her cheek against his back and held him silently.

"No deer," he muttered. "It was a waste of time."

"But you got something, did you not?"

He snorted. "Two turkeys," he said disgustedly.

"But is that not enough? We have never gone hungry, have we?"

"But if we have another winter like the great cold, we could all die."

"A great cold comes perhaps once in a lifetime," she said. "We have enough now. And there will be deer tomorrow."

He loosened her hands and pulled her around by her arms to face him. She came silently, looking up as she stood before him. He marveled at her. She was still beautiful and playful. He stared at her for several seconds.

"What are you thinking, Crooked Leg?" she said, smiling.

"I'm thinking...I did not ask the Manitou for you, for I did not know what I needed in my life. And yet, you came and found me, and as each day passes, my life is better."

She kissed him, then pulled away. "Is that true? Are you truly happy?"

"Do I not seem so?"

She was thoughtful for a moment before she answered. "Yes."

He frowned. "But you do not think I am?"

"Yes...But sometimes, when you have dreams, or when I watch you in quiet moments, I wonder if you long to return to the Salt Springs."

"Do you really think so?"

She hesitated again. "I worry that there is someone in the Salt Springs you want to see. Someone that you wish was not absent from your life."

Cricket turned away from Dark Moon when she spoke. He moved around to face her again. When he did, he could see tears in her eyes. "Who do I wish to see, Cricket?" he asked.

She looked at him but didn't answer. He studied her face. It showed the same disquiet whenever they talked about his past. "Calling Dove?" he asked.

"You still say her name in your dreams," Cricket said softly.

He shook his head. He grabbed her arms near the shoulders and held her in front of him so they were face-to-face. "But do my actions make you believe that I think of her?"

"Sometimes I think not, but then others...It was your home all your life, and you loved her in your youth."

"Cricket, before, when I thought of marrying her, I was still troubled." Dark Moon shook his head. "And love should not be troubling." He turned and walked a few paces from her and turned around. "Even then, I would often wonder if what I felt was really love. But when I was young and alone, I did dream of her in my bed. Now, I know that I would never have been happy with her."

"And you do not dream of seeing her again?"

"No," he said, shaking his head. "I have no home in the Salt Springs. My home is wherever you lay your head at night."

She closed her eyes and more tears flowed. "Then why do your eyes show that you still dream of the Salt Springs? Maybe the love you doubt is stronger than you think?"

"I doubted that love because I knew in my heart that there had to be something better." Dark Moon was quiet for a few seconds. "And then someone found me and brought me back to life, and I discovered what was missing in my love for Calling Dove."

Cricket took a deep breath, still not opening her eyes. "Then, what keeps troubling you?"

"I just wonder…did she marry Red Eagle? Did he become chief of the Salt Springs? Is he the Great One of the Erierhonon?"

"This is only curiosity, Moon. But it cannot be all that haunts the dreams in your quiet hours."

He seemed pensive for a few minutes, then said, "Why, when I was lonely for a woman to love me, did I find her so far from the valley of the Mahoning? And why out of all the lands you traversed, did you find yourself near a dead bear and discover me as I lay dying?" He was thoughtful for several seconds. "And why were the dreams of the old grandmother so prophetic that I would never be chief of the Salt Springs?"

Dark Moon turned back to Cricket and continued, "She told me that I would have three daughters, and she said that I would have a wife who was a stranger with pale streaks of light in her hair." He stopped longer this time. Cricket also remained silent, watching him. "And why," he finally said, "did he betray me? Had he always known he would do so? And why does the Manitou allow such things?"

"Red Eagle's malice is easy to know," Cricket said. "He wanted to be chief, and you stood in his way. And perhaps you were also in his way when he, too, wanted Calling Dove?"

He hesitated. "I know he wanted Calling Dove. He had slept with her the night of the yellow moon."

"Do you not see? Everything he ever wanted always brought the shadow of Dark Moon into his dreams."

Dark Moon didn't answer. Instead, he studied her legs, now bare, as she had taken off her outer dress and her moccasins. She was small and tan and lovely. But knowing her, she would feel intimidated by the tall and proud and beautiful Calling Dove. Dark Moon could see, in this small creature with light-streaked hair, intelligence and humility, but also sensitivity and wisdom. And even more, he cherished her playfulness, acquired wisdom, and gentle spirit. Yet she remained convinced that she could never take Calling Dove out of Dark Moon's dreams. He seemed to have no way to show her that the truth was the very opposite of what she suspected.

"How can I show you that you are wrong about Calling Dove? Every day I thank the Manitou for giving you to me. You see me touch your body. I look at your hair… I watch you walk and talk and work, and I see everything in the world that I could ever ask for. And yet now you still tell me that you think I dream of someone else?"

Cricket covered her face with her hands. He had never seen this in all their years together. He walked over to her and stood just a few inches away. In a few seconds, she raised her head to look into his eyes.

"Have you ever known me to lie to you?" Dark Moon whispered.

She shook her head. No, he had never lied to her… ever. And there he stood before her, asking to be believed, asking her to understand that he loved her.

"It is not you; it is I," she said. "I just think of all the other women out there, and your memories of Calling Dove—her beauty, her spirit."

"Many women have beauty and spirit," he said. "But none have the magic that makes my heart sing, except one. It is she who stands before me, who brought me back from the dead, who gave me three wonderful daughters. Who is also stubborn and resistant to all the truths that I am telling her."

She looked away, but then smiled, turning back to him. "You must be mistaken, but I will accept your words." She moved her body against his.

Dark Moon wound his arms around her. "You make me tired when you do this, as though I have dragged a bison home from a faraway hunt."

She laughed. "You are old now, and you will need the girls to help you."

"And will they all be like you, and drive their husbands mad because they imagine that he is dreaming strange dreams?"

"No. They are better than I."

"The Manitou has never made someone better than you," Dark Moon said, kissing her.

Snake's Late Arrival

"When will he come?" Dark Moon asked Cricket, as he paced back and forth in their lodge.

"He will be here soon, impatient one," Cricket said. "When you must travel as he does with so many children, it takes longer time."

Dark Moon began to work on some new arrows. Then he set them aside, unfinished. He walked out of their lodge and waited to hear any sounds. After a while, he returned inside. "Perhaps there has been some trouble on the way. Do you think I should go out after them?"

Cricket smiled. It did her heart good to hear her husband be so impatient about the arrival of her brother. The two men were great friends and, over the years, had become brothers in spirit as well as custom when one marries into a family.

"Perhaps one of the children is not well. Do you think it could be?" Dark Moon asked.

"Be still, Crooked Leg," she said, still smiling. She walked over to him and kissed him.

He put his arms around her. "Who do you call Crooked Leg, little one? Do you know that, in some tribes, men beat their wives for mocking them?"

Cricket struggled to get out of his grasp, giggling softly. He held her close and kissed her again. "So, you want to beat me, do you, Crooked Leg?" she said, taunting him.

"No, I tolerate your bad behavior out of respect for your mother," he said, still holding onto her. "But I have thought of a new way to tame you."

"What is that way?"

"I will throw cold water on you for your disrespect."

"And what am I to do for your disrespect? Throw cold water?"

"Oh, no. You must never throw water on the chief."

"Ha!" she said, laughing. "You are but the chief of one little family."

"The number does not matter. It is the wisdom and strength and greatness of the man."

"Let me go, oh wise Great One!" she said, pushing him away.

"You must pay tribute. What tribute do you offer?"

She looked at him for a few seconds. Then, she reached behind his head and brought it toward hers and gave him a passionate kiss. He began to be excited and kissed her harder the second time. She reveled in her ability to excite him as she always could.

"The children may come," she whispered, kissing him again.

He snorted softly. "Is it not evil for a woman to arouse her husband so and then warn him that his daughters lurk about?"

"You call me evil, crooked one?" she said huskily, kissing him again.

Just as they were both lost in their embrace, Snake from the River stood at the entrance to the lodge, surrounded by two girls and two boys. The children giggled to see their aunt and uncle acting like some of the young unmarried couples from a nearby tribe.

"What are you doing, Uncle Dark Moon," Snake bellowed, "to my helpless sister?"

He startled Cricket and her husband.

Dark Moon showed an embarrassed flush. "I was exacting tribute," he said as Cricket ran over to them to hug the children first, and then her brother.

Later that evening, the two men walked alone on the outskirts of their camp.

"Did you have enough food to eat, Snake?" Dark Moon asked.

"Yes. I have had plenty. And the children have also. I am not as good a cook as my sister, so they like eating here."

"You appear to do well enough," said Dark Moon.

Snake shook his head. "I know they miss their mother," he said, staring straight ahead.

"I am certain they do," said Dark Moon. "She was such a fine woman."

They walked for a while in silence before Dark Moon asked, "And you, my brother, do you often think of her?"

"More as each day passes," Snake said, his eyes glistening in tears. "The loneliness is so great sometimes that I almost go mad. Luckily, with two boys and two girls, I am busy enough that I fall asleep tired every night."

"Do you dream of her?" asked Dark Moon hesitantly.

"After she died, I did. But the dreams were so painful, that when I awoke and remembered them, my days were dreary. So, I have tried to forget the dreams. I wanted no more of them. And, strange as it is, the dreams have stopped. I do not often dream of her, and I am thankful. But not a day passes that she does not come into my thoughts, again and again."

They walked in silence for several minutes. Finally, Dark Moon spoke again. "You know, Snake, she is not gone altogether. I see her in each of your children, especially the girls. Do you not see her in them?"

He snorted. "Yes. But often I think that it is just my imagination wanting to see her." He paused a short while. Then he said, "Do you really see her in them?"

"Yes. Especially in the girls, as I said. Cricket does also."

Snake smiled in satisfaction as he turned to Dark Moon. "That is good to hear."

"Snake," said Dark Moon, "why do you tarry so long and far away? Your wife's family are leaving for the great north lake little by little. Why do you not return to us? My children would want yours to be with them. They would be brothers and sisters. And Cricket would teach your daughters what they must know about being women. And I would teach you how to shoot an arrow straight."

Snake was quiet for a few moments. "I have given it thought," he said. "Perhaps."

"But you must give it more thought! Do you not see me, surrounded by four women? I would thank the Manitou to have three men in my life. And I could teach your sons how to hunt…and to shoot straight, something their father must learn also."

"Perhaps," Snake said with a grin. "But I must prepare the boys for the boastfulness and pride in their uncle."

"If you return, I will lay aside my pride and arrogance," Dark Moon said. "I will only teach their father things he has not yet learned."

Snake laughed heartily. "It is so good to be with you again, my brother."

Snake's Family

I N THE DAYS THAT followed, the two families grew closer. Cricket worked tirelessly to feed everyone, and the five girls—her own and Snake's—bonded and became chattering, fun-loving, playful, and affectionate.

And the two boys enjoyed the way their uncle and their father got along. They had never seen Snake teased and taunted. And yet they were struck by the affection and respect between the two older men. There was humor suddenly in their lives, and the terrible pall of sorrow from the loss of their mother was dissipating.

They were amazed that, as they played their games with a leather ball that they would kick and throw, their swift and graceful father would chide his partner gently and dared to call him Crooked Leg. Even their Aunt Cricket would cheer and mock their uncle when he would hobble and gambol in his awkward, rolling gait that was funny just to watch. And though he heard the taunts and catcalls from the woman who emulated the jibes of their father, their uncle good-naturedly endured their jeering.

The youngest boy, Blue Hat, named after one of their games, asked Dark Moon as they rested in the shade and drank the cold water of a nearby spring, "How do you endure the mockery? Is it not insulting when they mock the way you run?"

Dark Moon put his arm around the boy and said, "None of them would ever wish any harm or evil to come to me. I know that, even when they tease me, their hearts are full of love."

The boy marveled at the tolerance of Dark Moon, and his open and forgiving spirit. Moon continued, "Do you know what a wonder it is for me to walk, much less run? I am thankful that I, who, many years ago, could not even take a single step, can now run, funny though it may be. And I owe it all to your aunt and your father and your wonderful grandmother. Without their help, I would never be able to run after a ball. They gave me back my life. And though now I am a turtle and they are rabbits, I am happy just to be able to move."

The boy marveled at the strange, non-belligerent behavior he saw between his family and that of Dark Moon and Cricket. Within his own family he had always known love and security, but he had never seen it between two different families. And he saw his father act, on the one hand, playful and mischievous with his sister and Dark Moon, and on the other hand, respectful and considerate.

He often talked of it with the other children, and they all noticed that something special had happened between all of them as the two families lived together. They all acted as though there was a secret undiscovered, something that they had never seen. When, in fact, they had never been part of a large and loving family before.

One day, the three adults were resting in the shade, talking about what they thought the winter would be like. Snake said he would have to go back north to see if anything was left of their camp—and if any of the young elk dogs were ready to travel.

"Travel where?" both Dark Moon and Cricket asked anxiously.

"Did you not implore me to move down to this plain with my children?" Snake snorted.

"But you usually do not listen to our wisdom," Dark Moon said, winking at his wife. "Usually, you find ways to cause yourself more trouble."

By then, Cricket was on her feet kissing her brother and throwing her arms around his neck.

"Perhaps I spoke too hastily," said Dark Moon. "You still have not learned to shoot an arrow straight."

"Hush, Crooked Leg," said Cricket, reprovingly. "Or he will find a reason not to return here."

Dark Moon chuckled. "Do not blind squirrels find acorns once in a while."

"We must gather what we need now to try to bring our food and stores back," said Snake. "We will need meat for the winter before we can relax our days. And I feel I must return to help my sister care for our growling old man with a crooked leg." Snake smirked and winked at his sister.

"Are you sure now?" said Dark Moon. "We will not tell our children if you suddenly begin foolish dreams and change your mind again and again."

In that moment, Snake nodded seriously. "Yes. They have found great happiness with your children, and it would be wrong to deny them such a good life."

"But what of their father? Does he have happiness here?" asked Cricket.

He thought for a moment. "These have been the best days of my life since losing Little Brook. I can be happy here…if I can go back to the north, once in a while, to breathe her spirit in the land where we had our children together."

Dark Moon stood up and put his hand out to Snake. "You have brought happiness to our lives. We will feel great joy to be with you and your children."

"But we must soon make the journey north before the cold comes. We must gather what we need and bring back the elk dogs before we can rest for the winter…." Then, he hesitated. "No, we cannot rest until we provide more meat for the cold that will come."

"But I will hunt for you," said Dark Moon.

"No," said Cricket. "We will build you a lodge in the time it takes you to go and return. Then, when you are here again—"

"But that is too much," Snake said. "I must do it myself. We should not be a burden to you."

"Do you want your brother to go mad, waiting for your return? He must have something to do," said Cricket.

"I would be honored," said Dark Moon, nodding to Snake. "For all you've done for me. or all the times you carried me from my wigwam just so I could take steps that any baby would take…and for your friendship. I will build you a lodge over there." He pointed to the leeward side of the small grove of trees that overlooked the whole plain.

"Well, then, after tomorrow we will leave," Snake said. "But then, when I return, if you build me a lodge, Two Bears and I will do a final hunt for the winter. He has long wanted me to take him to do a task that grown men can do. And since he is the eldest, I will go alone with him and talk at night of what it is to be a man. And then, in but a few suns, we will bring back food for the winter."

Cricket smiled. "My heart sings at this," she said, putting her arm around Dark Moon's waist.

Dark Moon Builds a Lodge

Dark Moon used the elk dogs to help him haul large trees from the forest to the small plateau where Snake's lodge was to be constructed. Once there, the largest logs were split, and their barks shorn to make a heavy covering that would protect the outer sides of the lodge from the north wind.

He had dug eight holes for the main posts that would keep the structure erect. Now, he and his three girls worked on the frame. They would tie the stays as Dark Moon would bend saplings down to where they could be joined. Little Dog and Mouse helped him bend the stays and hold them until they could be bound.

Each night, the girls would tell Cricket of the marvelous things they had accomplished by helping their father. Dark Moon was in his glory. He was building a finer lodge than the one they all had. His girls were helping him do something important, and they helped him do some things that he would not be able to do alone. And often at night, when the girls were asleep, he tormented Cricket with questions, like, "When do you think they will return?"

"No one knows, Dark Moon," she said. "Remember, not only does he have a large family to move, but he will also be bringing more elk dogs."

"Do you think the lodge will be large enough? Perhaps we should build another for his little elk dogs."

Cricket smiled. "The lodge we are building will be wonderful. And there will be more time to build one for the other elk dogs if we must. The winter will not arrive for several moons."

"Perhaps I should have gone to meet him to help," he said.

"Rest easy, Crooked Leg," Cricket said. "When Snake returns, he will have the finest lodge he has ever had. That will be a greater service than your help would be in the north. Besides, do you not want to hunt a few more times so that we are secure for the winter?" As Cricket spoke, she was undressing. "Are you sleepy?"

Dark Moon smiled. "Looking at you undressed has awakened me," he said.

"Then let us lie down," she said as she stood before him naked. She was still beautiful and desirable, and she knew it. And she knew that was all that ever mattered. She walked to their bed and lay down, smiling up at Dark Moon. In a few seconds, his clothes were gone, and he joined her.

Holding Cricket naked in his arms was always a surprise. He never lost the thrill he felt when he touched her. It was an experience like no other, the softness of her in his arms, the smoothness of her skin, the warmth of her breath against his face, the soft yielding lips, the way her body seemed to be a perfect fit against his. These feelings made him forget anything that troubled him. They always did, ever since that night so long ago when she first came to his tent. They made love slowly and talked more, but only of themselves. They still dreamed together, and her warm breath always gave him hope for a brighter future.

Cricket, the Mother

H<small>E WATCHED HER AS</small> she checked on the children as they slept. When she came to their private corner of the lodge, she climbed the two steps and brushed away the hanging skins that separated them from all the other sleepers and carefully set them back to assure their privacy.

She stared at him as he lay on the mat of skins that was set between two sideboards at the far end of their section. Slowly without changing her gaze, she quickly removed her skirt and then dropped her leather blouse beside her on the floor. She smirked slightly, knowing what the sight of her nakedness always did to him. Then, she walked over to him and knelt as he opened the deerskin to welcome her into his arms. He held her in his arms and kissed her.

"What are you thinking, O Dark Moon?" Cricket whispered.

"Nothing, evil one," Dark Moon said softly, "but suddenly I am no longer Crooked Leg."

"I have decided to speak to you with more respect now that you are old," she said as she laid on top of him, her face close enough to feel his breath.

"Who are you to call me old? I am but two winters before you."

"The two most important winters that make a difference," Cricket said and wiggled against his body and kissed him.

"You are a wonder, do you know it?" Dark Moon said as he stroked her back.

"As are you," she said.

"I am the most fortunate of all men," he said.

"Why are you so fortunate?" she asked. "Because we saved you from the golden bear?"

Dark Moon shook his head. "No, because I do not think that any man has known the happiness I have with you."

"Do you really think that, Crooked Leg?" Cricket asked. "What about the tall, beautiful girl who has had your heart in so many memories? The flower of the Erierhonon?"

"The yearning for her was not love. For then I knew little about love. But the first time I saw you, I knew that you were different. It was then that I began to learn of love."

Cricket smiled and kissed him.

Snake Returns

Dark Moon and Cricket and their three daughters were outside their lodge in the chill autumn air, talking softly about their day. The sun was setting, and the elk dogs grazed in the pasture behind the lodge. The fire kept the cold away and made them comfortable as they cooked their food.

Dark Moon and Cricket listened, as they often did, to the talk of their daughters. The girls were bright and funny and sometimes silly, but they were always playful and pleasant. Just then, one of the elk dogs huffed... then another.

Dark Moon turned toward them, then after a few seconds, he turned back to the girls and listened again to their stories. The girls continued with their banter and Cricket joined them. He sat contentedly listening to the four women who were the most important parts of his life. Again, he heard one of the elk dogs snort, so he turned toward the sound again. One elk dog had his head up, alert and seeming to hear something.

Slowly, Dark Moon stood up and walked to his lodge and got the great white bow and some arrows. He also grabbed his ax. He didn't want a hungry bear or cougar coming upon his family or the little elk dogs. Cricket noticed what he did and seemed to ignore him as she kept their daughters talking and preoccupied with their tales.

Dark Moon stood a few yards away from the woman, alert and still. One of the elk dogs looked up again toward the far end of the clearing, across the meadow that stretched up to the tree line almost at the end of eyesight. He listened carefully. He thought he heard a coyote bark in the distance. All the elk dogs were alert this time, looking at the clearing.

Then, Cricket was beside him as the girls still chatted among themselves. "What do you hear, Moon?"

He shook his head. "I do not know. Perhaps a coyote. The elk dogs have heard something for a long while. Take the girls into the lodge."

Just then, Little Dog was at their side. "What is it, Father? Something more than a coyote?"

She was the most like her mother, perhaps because she was the eldest.

"Did you hear a coyote bark?" said her father.

"Yes, but we often hear such calls in the evening, do we not?" she said.

"But look at the elk dogs," said Cricket. "They hear something also, perhaps more of a danger."

Suddenly, Dark Moon saw something move in the distance. "Go into the lodge now," he whispered. Everyone but Dark Moon went inside. He remained waiting and still, but hidden, as though he were hunting and expecting a quarry to move closer.

"Could it be an elk dog?" he whispered to himself as he saw distant movement.

Soon, another elk dog came, and then another, and soon there were many, as Dark Moon shouted to his family to come back out again.

A few seconds later, people emerged from the pack: Snake and his four children.

———◆▸▮◂◆———

Snake and his family rested for five days. They were amazed and grateful for the marvelous lodge Dark Moon and his family had made for them.

One night, Snake and Dark Moon stayed up late around a roaring fire. Cricket and all the children were sleeping. The cool night air was warmed by a crackling fire.

"When will you leave?" Dark Moon asked his friend.

"In a few suns," said Snake.

"Where will you go?"

"Where my brother, the great hunter, tells me."

Dark Moon paused for a few moments. He had never expected to be asked about where to hunt. His mind was transported back to those happy times when he and his old hunting companion, Wind, spent days together hunting for the Salt Springs. He had always been trying to forget the valley of the Mahoning. There were not many memories he cherished. Everything about the Salt Springs was darkened by the horrible memories of the slaughter of Elk Calf's tribe, and also the memory of Calling Dove's unfaithfulness on the yellow moon, and the final betrayal by Red Eagle.

But now, his was a good life. In fact, he felt that he was patterned with blessings that always followed his misfortunes. Though he lost his mother and father, he was rescued by Wise Apple, a man of honor who raised him as an only son and treated him with love and faithfulness. The old Grandmother also taught him many things. And he did have a few close friends. Perhaps there were happy memories. But then there was Calling Dove. The pain he felt in losing her to Red Eagle on the yellow moon lingered a long time, especially in the early days after he first found out.

Then, there came a bear, and that small girl and her brother who saved his life and brought new light into his world that suppressed all those dark memories.

"Moon?" said Snake.

"Yes," he muttered, awakened from his reverie. "There are western places you can go that are not too far south. And there are two great woods where you should find many deer. Remember that Two Bears has to help you bring the deer back home, so choose a small one."

"Are the woods near your homeland? Near the Salt Springs?"

"No," Moon said emphatically. "And be careful that you do not go too far to the east."

"Why?" Snake asked. "Is there no good hunting there?"

Dark Moon hesitated for a few seconds, then gave a deep sigh. "The hunting is good, but I wish you would not go there." He paused and took a deep breath, unsure if he should even tell his brother the story. He realized that it was time to do so.

"Many winters ago," Moon began, "I was in a hunting party with an old friend whose name was Wind. And we came upon the camp of another old friend, a Huron, who always offered us rest and food and whatever help we needed. They were never warlike, and their warriors were like those of the Salt Springs, fewer in number, but their job was only to keep the peace and to protect their small tribe from danger. Besides, their work was not hard because there were not many other camps in the region."

Dark Moon took a deep breath and snorted uncomfortably before continuing, "When Wind and I came to greet them and give them some of the carcasses we procured, we found them all dead. They were all killed; everyone in the tribe, even babies."

"And the young women? Were they taken?" asked Snake.

Dark Moon shook his head. "They were all killed. That was the strange part about it. Just madness." He hesitated again. "They cut them...almost like animals from the forest." Dark Moon grimaced. "You must never tell this tale to anyone, especially Cricket or the children."

He turned to face his brother.

Snake had a strange look on his face. He sensed that he had not yet heard all of the horror that occurred that night. "Is there more?" he asked.

"I will tell you, for it was the worst sight I have ever seen," Moon said. "The women were mutilated, and the men, even the babies, had their roots torn out and their heads cut open, and their brains taken." He hesitated again, looking up at his friend. "And they did something else. There was a hawk, a great brown one, whose wings were both broken, and it was unable to fly. They had clubbed it nearly to death. It lay there suffering when we came upon it."

"What did you do?" asked Snake.

"We killed it to end its suffering, and then we burned the camp...every one of the bodies. We knew it was an abomination in the eyes of the Manitou, so we returned their ashes to the dust so that the Manitou will not have to look upon such brutality again."

Snake shook his head. "I have never heard such a tale. I will believe it only because you tell me, and I know you always speak the truth."

"So, now you know why I told you not to go near the Salt Springs," said Dark Moon. "No one, except for Wind and a few of our young hunters, ever knew about Elk Calf's terrible story. All any of us could imagine was that a band of tribeless wanderers were overcome by madness and came upon Elk Calf's small tribe."

"Then, I will do whatever you say and stay away from the Salt Springs," said Snake. "Our journey will be barely a few suns. It will not take long for me to have some talks with Two Bears and give him the advice of a father now that he is a grown man. He has not yet met many comely young girls, but I know he will do so soon, perhaps in the nearby tribe we often trade with."

Gray Wolf

CALLING DOVE'S SON WAS now getting to be as great a warrior as his father. He was handsome, impetuous, proud, stubborn, and often cruel to anyone whom he vanquished in a fight or in sport. Gray Wolf was as swift a runner as his father, and he learned to fight with a knife and ax more lethally than his father could. He was the consummate warrior, gifted physically and socially, a natural leader that everyone in the Salt Springs knew would succeed his father someday as chief of the Salt Springs...and perhaps one day succeed his father as the Great One of the Erierhonon.

He was also the favorite of his mother, her only son. His sister was as graceful as her mother but did not have her height and spirit and strength. Instead, she was quiet and thoughtful and gentle and thought by some men of the Salt Springs to be as beautiful as her mother.

Both women idolized Gray Wolf. They spoiled and indulged him, often admiring him for the very traits Calling Dove abhorred in his father. His sister adored him as the big brother who every girl in the tribe wished was hers.

All the other girls brightened when Gray Wolf walked by. A word or smile from him was almost as thrilling as a word from the Great One, his father. Moreover, Gray Wolf was sexually available, while his father, though already married to the proud and beautiful Calling Dove, had to be more discreet in his pursuits of other women.

Gray Wolf would surely someday be chief. And any girl in the tribe would be admired and envied just to be considered one of the maidens he would possibly marry.

His sister was in a teasing mood. "Father will be angry with you," she said to Gray Wolf.

"He is always angry, except at you," Gray Wolf said.

"But you have not made arrows, or have not gone with the hunters to help them find meat."

"I am a warrior just as father was. I do not hunt. Hunting is for those who cannot be warriors because they either lack the courage or the skill."

"But there have been great hunters who have saved the lives of the Salt Springs people. Have there not?"

"But who remembers them? Who knows their names? Yet everyone remembers the names of the great chiefs who have fought battles that made the Erierhonon great."

"I remember one," she said.

"Who?"

"Dark Moon," his sister said. "I have heard the old ones say that when the great cold came, long before we were born, he could kill a bison with just one arrow. It was said that he was part cat, traveling through the forest without a sound. They talked of his bow. It is said that no one could shoot an arrow farther or truer."

"Bah!" said Gray Wolf. "I have heard that he was eaten by a bear, the very quarry he was pursuing. Is there any wonder that he is so remembered only in the fevered minds of the ancient ones? Who among the young ones—our age—remembers? Who was he, this Dark Moon?" He paused for a moment. "Remember these words, little sister. No one remembers hunters and food gatherers. They only remember those who bring glory to the Erierhonon in battle."

Snake and Two Bears Depart

THE NEXT DAY, IT rained, so the three adults sat under a deerskin awning and watched the rain while they drank tea that Cricket had brewed from summer chamomile flowers. All three felt peaceful and content as they watched their seven children talk animatedly under another awning several yards away.

"It pleases me so to watch them together," said Cricket. "They play and tease and laugh, but they are gentle and careful not to cause hurt." She paused for a moment and was thoughtful. "That is it. They show respect for each other."

The two men nodded in agreement. Then, suddenly, all the children began running through the rain over to the awning of the adults. "What is it?" Cricket asked as all seven arrived, breathless and wet.

"We have some questions we would like to ask you," said Two Bears, the eldest of the group.

The three adults looked at each other and smiled, knowing the conspiracy was well planned.

"All right," said Snake. "What do you wish?"

"Well, we have many questions for all of you...but we—"

"But we have more for Father," said Little Dog, the eldest of Dark Moon and Cricket's brood, interrupting her cousin.

"Sit here," said Snake, pointing to the ground in front of them. "We will answer what we can."

They all sat down cross-legged and smiling among themselves, content that their plans had so easily worked out. "Many of the questions are for Father," said Mouse, the middle child of Dark Moon and Cricket.

"Two Bears told us that Uncle Dark Moon killed a great bear by himself...with a knife only," said Blue Hat.

"He did," said Cricket.

"Will you tell us the story?" asked No Tail, the eldest daughter of Snake, addressing her uncle.

Dark Moon snorted. "Some of the story, I do not remember. When your father and your Aunt Cricket found me, I was nearly about to meet the Manitou."

"They saved you?" said No Tail.

"Yes. Without them, I would have died."

"Is that when you damaged your leg? And got the scars on your arms and your shoulders?" asked Two Bears.

Dark Moon chuckled and said, "You have heard your evil father and his evil sister call me such names, have you not?"

Cricket shoved his shoulder playfully.

"Was your leg straight in those days before the bear?" asked Blue Hat.

"Yes," said Dark Moon.

"The Erierhonon are often called the Cat People," said Snake, "and your uncle is part cat. Do you see that even with his crooked leg, he goes through the woods soundlessly as a cat."

Dark Moon shook his head. "I can no longer go into the woods as quietly as I once did," he said. "It is much harder to move as I did when I was young."

"But we have seen your bow. Why did you not kill the bear with an arrow?" asked Two Bears.

"Well, in those times, I did not have this bow. This one was given to me by your grandmother, Snow Flower. My bow, then, was a good one, but not as fine as this."

"But where did Grandmother get the bow?"

"It was not a bow, then," said Snake.

"It was a strange horn from a giant animal that the ancient ones always told us lived in this land," said Cricket.

"Then, your uncle carved the bow from the great horn and fashioned it into the one he has now," said Snake.

"Why did he not kill the bear with an arrow?" insisted Two Bears to his father.

"The bear came upon me when I was tired…and thinking of something else. I was not watchful as you must always be in the forest," said Dark Moon.

"And the bear attacked you from behind?" said Two Bears. "And you did not have your bow? Where was it?"

"I had set it down."

"Why?"

Dark Moon sighed, avoiding the gaze of his wife and his brother. "I was helping someone."

"What were you doing?" asked No Tail as all of their curiosity increased.

In fact, even the other two adults had never heard a detailed retelling of the story, so they, too, were curious.

"I helped a man climb from the side of a steep cliff. You see, he had fallen, and was caught on a narrow ledge of the hillside. And he could not move, lest he slip and fall to his death. So, I was able to throw him a cord and pull him up the hillside."

"Did he fall back when the bear came?" asked Blue Hat.

"No. He had reached the top, where he was safe."

"But then, why did he not help you?" asked Little Dog, who had never heard her father tell the story.

"I do not know," said Dark Moon.

They were all silent for several minutes, now wondering if the request to hear the story was a mistake. None of them had ever confronted evil, and their parents did not ever speak of it in their childhood. As children, they had never known liars or cheaters or killers, people who could betray friends in ways far more lethal than the mere informing of childhood confidences. But the story was unraveling in such a way that those images were coming into their innocent minds.

"Do you mean that he could have helped you but did not?" said Two Bears.

"Yes."

"And then you were attacked by the bear?" said Mouse.

"Yes."

"But what did he do?" she asked, incredulous. "Was he not your friend who you had just saved from death?"

"We were not the best of friends," Dark Moon admitted, "but we were not enemies—just childhood friends."

"He saw the bear attack you and did nothing?" asked Two Bears.

Dark Moon took a deep breath. "Yes."

"But the bear could have killed you," said Bee Teller.

"The bear would have killed me easily, but when he tore my leg, I was able to grab my knife. And when the bear turned his head, I struck him in the neck, and it entered his brain. I was favored by the Manitou. A greater gift of fortune was when your mother and your uncle came upon me from the deep forest."

"But what did they do? How?"

"As I said, I was in a dark sleep...near death. But they took me out from under the bear and brought me to their camp—this one here." Moon waved his hand. "To your grandmother, a wise and caring medicine woman."

"And how long did it take you to get well?" asked Blue Hat.

"More than one whole winter," said Cricket. "To take step after step, it took another winter."

"Your father, your uncle," said Dark Moon, gesturing toward Snake and Cricket for the children to see, "helped me out of my tent every day and picked me up whenever I fell down, and supported me when I was weak. Your mother, your aunt," he paused, gesturing toward Cricket, "washed and anointed my wounds every morning and night, changed my bandages, and gave me the medicines made by your dear grandmother. She also brought me food so that I would gain my strength."

"But whatever happened to your...to the other man?" said Two Bears.

"And what happened to your bow?" said Little Dog.

"The other man took it," said Cricket. "When we found your father, the bow was gone."

By now, all the children seemed perplexed and troubled. Such treachery had never been seen in their families. The betrayal, cowardice, and now the theft of the bow while someone was being killed by a bear—someone he did not help, after that very person had saved his life—seemed consummate evil.

"I would hate him so much, Uncle," said Blue Hat.

"Sometimes, as you get older and other things happen in life, you realize that hate seems to pass away like clouds on a windy day," Dark Moon said. He paused after several seconds and looked into the sky, as it seemed he was hearing something. "I have had too much grace in my life to keep hating for seventeen winters. Besides, I must teach your father to shoot an arrow straight. I do not have time to hate."

"Do you not get angry when Uncle says these things, Father?" Blue Hat asked Snake, enjoying the banter between the two men.

Snake chuckled. "He is right about my arrows, children," he said. "But I will never shoot arrows as he can. No one can do that."

"Is that true, Father?" Little dog asked. "Can you shoot an arrow straighter than anyone?"

"Your uncle overstates because he is my friend," answered Dark Moon.

"Mother?" Little Dog said. "Does Uncle Snake overstate?"

"No, children, I do not think anyone can shoot an arrow as does your father and uncle."

"Please show us, Uncle," they all said, as if in a chorus, but Dark Moon shook his head.

"Please," they insisted.

Snake stood up. "Come, Crooked Leg, show us."

They walked through the fine drizzle that came between the heavy rains down to a small flat field surrounded by trees.

"See that small tree in the distance, near the pine tree?" Snake said as he pointed to it. "I will try to shoot it."

"At that great distance?" said Blue Hat. "Should we not move closer?"

"No, I will try," said his father. Then, he drew his bow and fired. The arrow was true to the mark.

Dark Moon chuckled. "Perhaps I should no longer tease you for your shooting," he said.

Snake smiled. "At this distance, I would miss it as many times as hit it."

"No, you would not," said Dark Moon. "I am proud of you."

Snake's sons listened with satisfaction as their uncle praised their father.

"Go on, Moon," said Snake.

Dark Moon drew the great white bow and let the arrow fly. The audible hum of the bowstring was heard by all. As the arrow took flight, it truly made a different sound than that of Snake's bow, and in a few seconds, it thudded into the tree.

Snake smiled. "Now let us find another quarry...There! The bunch of grapes at the end of the clearing near the woods."

Some of the girls giggled when Snake pointed to the target. It was so far away that no one could reach it with an arrow, they thought.

"Watch me, children," said Snake. He drew his bow and let the arrow fly. The arrow whistled through the air and flew on a true course, but it landed many yards before it reached the grapes.

They were all amazed that the arrow had gone as far as it did and so nearly on the mark. "The distance was just too great, Father," said Two Bears.

"There are some who would say that the distance is not too great for one man," he said softly, nodding to Dark Moon. "Well then, Crooked Leg. You must reach the target for these children who do not believe that an arrow can go so far."

Dark Moon shook his head, reluctant to be forced to showcase his abilities.

"Go on, Moon. You know you can reach it. Show these children the gift that the Manitou has given you," said Snake.

Dark Moon picked up the bow and stared at the wild grapes, dangling far away at the beginning of the tree line. The children watched in rapt silence as he drew the bow back to what he knew would power the arrow to the target. Then he let it fly, with the same hum—only louder this time—as the arrow took flight. After a few brief seconds, they all saw the bunch of grapes seem to explode and throw berries everywhere around the arrow.

Cricket clasped her hands and smiled. "Well done, Crooked Leg," she whispered.

Father and Son Talk

S NAKE AND HIS SON had been jogging for two days, and they had not yet seen a deer, much less a bison.

"My uncle spoke the truth," said Two Bears. "This land has all manner of small creatures, but few bears. And we have never seen anything like a bison."

"Many of the larger animals prefer the forest," said Snake. "They often feel vulnerable when they are in these treeless meadows; most are not as swift footed as the smaller creatures."

"Did you hear the wolves last night, Father?"

"Yes, but they were distant. The pack is hunting for easy prey in these mild times."

They walked farther in silence, each of them wary of threats as they traveled across open fields and grasslands. The high prairie grass hid them, but sometimes, it also made them vulnerable to attack from a cougar or a bear hiding unseen in the tall grass.

Finally, Two Bears spoke, "Will we stay with Uncle and Aunt forever now?"

Snake looked at his son for a few seconds, studying his face, marveling at how much he had changed in the two years since his mother died. He was becoming a man.

"Father?" the boy said after a few moments.

Snake sighed. "It would be better for us if we were among people who cared for and trusted us, would it not? Dark Moon is as a brother to me. My sister is equally as wise and loving as your dear mother was. Their children love and cherish us, as we do them. I think, my boy, staying with them will enrich our lives far more than if we lived elsewhere and alone."

"But—" said the boy, who then shook his head and stopped speaking, seemingly ashamed of his thoughts.

"What do you ask, my son?" asked Snake softly, who began to be amazed at the new feelings that arose between them as they were suddenly just two men alone, talking of private things, much like he and his best friend Dark Moon had done so often.

"Well, Father, we will be such a small tribe, and I know we would be happy, but we would be..." he hesitated again.

"Tell me, Bears," said Snake softly, encouraging his son to say what was troubling him.

"But...do you not see? We will all be alone?"

Snake stopped talking for a few minutes, pondering the future his son would have, and wishing he had sensed, early on, what was troubling the boy. Two Bears was honest and sensitive and had lost his mother just at the time that she could have counseled and reassured him about young women and his feelings for them. And Snake, himself, was so overcome by his own grief of her passing that he never became aware of the new adult emotions that had come upon his son.

Yes, they would be a small tribe and happy together, content and never lonely. And all the children could grow up under the watchful eyes of Cricket and the two men who were the most important in their lives. After the death of his wife, his children's mother, the void in their lives was filled by Moon and Cricket and their playful, noisy, wonderful daughters, every bit as loving as his own. Yes, all of them were happy. All of them were fulfilled. All of them but one, the oldest of the children. Now, Two Bears was feeling different from the others. He alone had longings that were different...and unfulfilled. He alone would need more than they could ever give him.

"Where would I find someone like my mother or my aunt?" Two Bears asked. "For me? Where would I find a woman to sleep with me by night, who will give me children?"

Snake stopped talking for a few minutes, pondering the future his son would face. He realized that he had to help the boy fulfill his longings. "Bears, remember that there are tribes in the north that we will often visit and trade with. And I know that among them are many fine young women. There will be one among those many girls that will capture your heart."

Two Bears grimaced. "I wish it were so, Father," he said softly.

"Believe me, my son, if the Manitou wishes it, some fine young girl will warm your days as your mother warmed mine, and as your aunt warms the days of Uncle Dark Moon."

"Would that those days would come for me," Two Bears said softly.

Watchers

THE NEXT MORNING, SNAKE and Two Bears trod quietly through the meadow. They followed a young doe that was grazing a short distance from the tree line.

"She will be with the buck," said Snake to his son. "If we follow her, she may lead us to him."

They stalked her for more than an hour. Snake and Two Bears drew apart and carefully followed the doe, who had now been joined by another doe. Snake gestured to Two Bears, urging him silently to keep his eyes on the tree line to look for a buck who might join the two females.

As they stealthily followed the two does, Two Bears would occasionally make the sound of footfalls as he trailed. Snake would gesture for silence and point to the tree line. Two Bears concentrated on his task as a lookout. Then, suddenly, an eight-point buck entered the meadow, proud and self-assured. Both men saw the big deer at the same time. Two Bears' heart was beating faster as he drew an arrow from his quiver. Again, Snake commanded silence in a gesture that moved a hand across his lips.

Both men now had arrows ready. Snake cautioned his son to be patient. Both watched as the buck, emboldened by the peace and quiet of the meadow, made a further inroad into the field. Then he stopped, raised his head, looked around, and could not smell or hear the humans who were downwind and poised to strike him. His large brown eyes scanned the meadow carefully, only to assure himself that he was safe. He turned completely around, halting suddenly at a whisper of the grass caught by a soft breeze that overran the meadow.

The buck came nearer to the does, confident in his masculinity and enjoying the presence of the two does he had recently impregnated. Snake gestured for his son to be ready, both men resting their arrows against their bow shelves and holding for several seconds until the buck moved, giving them a better shot at their quarry. Finally, after several minutes, the deer lifted his head again, stopping to notice his does and checking once again for predators. Both men drew back farther on their arrows, increasing the tension on the bow for swift and deadly flight into the buck.

Two Bears, more impatient than his father, let his shaft fly first. Snake, upon hearing the hum of Two Bears's bow, let his arrow fly a split-second later. Two Bears's arrow hit the deer in the belly at the rear side of the animal, but Snake's arrow was the more deadly, catching the deer in the chest at the lower part of the neck.

The deer turned instantaneously upon feeling Two Bears's arrow strike his flanks. Then, as he was poised to run, the second arrow was so efficiently lethal that his steps were cut short. The deer took one more step, then fell dead. Two Bears screamed with joy as he saw the buck fall. Snake smiled and watched his son run toward the fallen creature, proud to be on the scene for the first great kill by his eldest son. His eyes surveyed the scene in pleasure as he slowly made his way toward the catch.

What neither man knew was that there were four other pairs of eyes witnessing the scene of a father bonding with his son in the ancient ritual. One pair belonged to a large, brown-colored hawk who watched from a tall tree at the edge of the tree line. The other pairs belonged to three men of the Salt Springs, who had strayed far from their band of other warriors.

———————

Snake and Two Bears bled the deer and made a rack to pull the animal back to their home.

"What say you, my son?" Snake asked. "I am certain that your uncle will be coming soon to help us with this deer. We should begin our return tomorrow."

Two Bears grinned. "If Uncle Dark Moon brings an elk dog, we may yet find a bison to add to this rack."

"I am not certain that he will bring one. But perhaps. All his life, he has hunted without one. Do you not think that we should return to our new home before the cold weather comes?"

Two Bears was silent for several seconds.

"We will do this again soon," said Snake. "In the spring, when the warm weather comes, I will help you find your bison."

"You would? In truth?"

"In truth. You are a fine hunter. Your bow is strong, and your arrows are true."

"As good as my uncle?" Two Bears asked.

Snake shrugged. "Someday, perhaps. But remember, Dark Moon is gifted by the Manitou as few other men are. But even if you are not his equal as a hunter, you may yet be great and respected by all who know you. And remember, you are already the better of your father."

Two Bears was surprised by Snake's words. "You believe it so, father?" he asked softly, smiling.

"Yes, my son. It is so. I am not so bad that my family would starve, but I am in the presence of two hunters whose skills are far greater than my own."

Two Bears put out his hand in thanks, and his father grasped it in acknowledgment.

"Let us cook one of the turkeys, and tomorrow we will turn toward home," said Snake.

Dark Moon Meets Wind

DARK MOON HAD OBSERVED the man from afar, coming upon him quietly and closing the distance between them. He moved stealthily and unseen. The sky was cloudy, and the day was gray and dull and promised rain.

The other man moved slowly, gathering branches and sticks to build a fire that would burn through most of the night. But he was preoccupied and worked silently, unaware of Dark Moon as he erected a small refuge that might protect him from wandering animals in the night.

As he had learned through countless hunts in his life, Dark Moon made his way slowly and steadily. When he was near enough, he studied the man whose back faced him. He loosened his ax that was bound to his side, then slowly drew his bow around his body and poised it so that, in an instant, he could drive an arrow in the man that would bring sure death. He drew the bow quietly, barely breathing, so the sound would not carry the twenty paces between him and the stranger.

"Hold! Do not move," Moon called, betraying his Salt Springs dialect he had learned so long ago. The startled man began to stand up, and Dark Moon shouted again, "I said hold, or you die! Stay down!"

The man understood Dark Moon. He spoke the dialect of the Erierhonon. But it was strange, attenuated in a way that he had never heard. There was something more, something in that voice. The man started to turn toward his stalker, but Dark Moon warned him again.

"Turn not, or you die."

The voice was different this time; it was deliberate and menacing, but softly spoken. *Who can this be?* Wind thought, as a chill traveled through his body. He felt the skin on his arms tingle. His legs also felt a chill that made him shudder.

"What do you want?" asked Wind. "All I have is some food and skins, and I mean no harm."

He started to turn toward his captor, but Dark Moon growled again, "Be still! Do not turn."

That was enough for Wind. He had heard that voice before. The memory of it lingered through all of seventeen winters.

"Moon?" he asked, this time bounding upward and facing his assailant. Dark Moon was startled.

"Moon? Can it be you?" Wind said again.

"I told you not to move," Dark Moon said as he instinctively lowered his bow.

Wind spoke again, looking puzzled. "Are you Dark Moon of the Salt Springs?"

"What are you called?" Dark Moon countered.

"I am Wind...of the Salt Springs of the Erierhonon. You speak our language."

Dark Moon took a deep breath, then slowly set down his bow. With his hand still resting against the ax tied to his waist, he took a few paces, moving around in a semicircle away from Wind. Both men studied each other, trying to understand what had just come between them.

Wind noticed the limp on the other man that he called Dark Moon. He also noticed the older face and the faint streaks of gray in his hair.

"Moon? Where have you been? Are you a spirit?"

Dark Moon snorted. "I am Crooked Leg now."

"But you are Dark Moon of the Erierhonon, the son of Wise Apple of the Salt Springs!" Wind exclaimed.

Dark Moon was about to respond, but he hesitated. He slid his hand away from the ax and encircled the man another few paces, his limp more noticeable this time. "You have not forgotten me, Wind?"

"I would never forget you, my friend," Wind said. He stopped as he listened to his own words. There had never been a moment in his life like this one. All those years he longed to talk to his old friend, as men often do in quiet times, waiting for an errant deer to come their way. When they learned from each other, when they talked of what they had seen and heard that added to their wisdom, they had become friends, had become men.

"You are different, Moon," Wind said softly.

"We are old men now, Wind," said Dark Moon, "nearly forty winters."

"But where have you been?" Wind whispered, shaking his head as though believing he was talking to a ghost. "But if you are a spirit, then you should not have grown old."

"I am not a spirit, Wind," said Dark Moon.

"But Red Eagle said—"

"Said I was dead, did he not?"

"By a great bear with golden skin. He said he slew the bear who had eaten of your flesh."

Dark Moon's expression changed, and Wind notice the scowl on his friend's face.

"The bear was dead, but not by Red Eagle," said Dark Moon.

Wind looked up at the sky, closed his eyes, and shook his head. "Lies," he whispered to himself. "I sensed that he was lying, only I had no way to gainsay it."

"He was always a liar, was he not? How many times did you warn me about his conceit and lies as he boasted of his powers as a warrior? Does a man who lies all his life tell the truth about such things as a friend dying?"

"But where did you go? Why did you not return to the Salt Springs?"

"I was near death from the bear, but I was rescued by a man and his sister from a faraway tribe. They took me to their camp in the north, and their mother made the medicine that helped me walk again, even though I must limp."

"But why did you stay there?" Wind asked. "You might have returned to be the Great One of the Erierhonon."

"The one who rescued me was a man whose heart is as great as any I have ever known. Every day for two winters, he helped me learn to walk, and when I would fall—either with lack of courage or with despair—he would bring me up again. He never wavered. And, always, the next morning he would be at my tent to help me face the pain and to bolster my lack of courage. I only walk today because of him. In that winter, I came to love his sister, who is now my wife and the mother of my children."

Wind listened intently, and when Dark Moon stopped talking, he shook his head. Then, he said, "And was the life you had with the young man and his sister good enough to persuade you to forget your home in the Salt Springs?"

"Yes," Dark Moon said. "My happiness was such that I never wanted to be anywhere without their family."

Wind was shaking his head as Dark Moon spoke. "Do you know what you have done, Moon? You have doomed the Salt Springs. If you would have returned, everything today would be different. Do you know what has happened? Red Eagle is now chief of the Salt Springs and…" He hesitated. "He is also the Great One of the Erierhonon."

Dark Moon sighed deeply. "Has he been a good chief?"

"No," Wind growled in disgust. "He is mad with power. He struts and sings sweet words and bathes himself in the sighs of women and foolish men who enjoy power as servants of the chief. No one hunts anymore. We have had three starvation winters since he has been chief. The feeble old ones were told to leave the lodges so that there would be food and warmth for the young. Most of them died. The few who lived, like the mother of my wife, who lives in my lodge now, were made to feel ashamed for taking food from the young and the healthy. Only because I am a hunter was I able to keep her in my lodge."

Dark Moon stared at him for several seconds. "And you blame me for this?" He advanced three or four steps closer to Wind, not trying to hide his ungainly steps. "Did not the fools of the Salt Springs, even the supposedly wise ones who should have known better, vote for Red Eagle? Did they not dream visions that could never happen?"

"No one but you could have changed their minds," Wind said.

"Did you not try? You are also a man of respect. You and I both saved them from starvation in many winters," said Dark Moon, still resenting the accusatory words of Wind.

Wind huffed. "I did my best. I spoke out often and am now lucky that my wife and children still live, for I am considered a traitor by some of Red Eagle's men. Without my hunting skills and the food that I provide, I would have lost my wife and children, and also my own life. But I was not Dark Moon."

"Then you did what you had to do," said Dark Moon. "I did the same. And the happiness I knew more than atoned for my feelings of loss of the Salt Springs or the pain my injuries brought."

"And Calling Dove? Did you not wish to see her again?"

"She slept with someone else on the yellow moon. Did you not tell me that? As time passed, I began to understand that she is one who would run both with the stag and with the wolves, then rejoice with the victor."

"Did you stay away because of her?" Wind asked.

Dark Moon shook his head.

"So, why are you here, stalking me, and aiming your arrows at my heart as though we were both strangers?" Wind asked. "Could you not return even after the bad winters?"

Dark Moon huffed and smiled cynically. "Because I have the love of a woman who graced my life with happiness, and who gave me three daughters and her mother, whom I loved, and her brother, who I now consider my brother. They nursed me back to health. I am happier now than I have ever been."

"Moon, the Salt Springs tribe is lost. It is as if we are taken over by a strange sickness by which we will all perish. Very few see it, or even wish to hear it."

"But who is responsible for those who are willfully foolish, who believe the words of men who are known to be strutting liars?" Dark Moon said. "Are you the only one who sees what is happening to them? Are they not cowards who hold their ears whenever you tell them the truth?"

"There are those who want leaders who croon to them," said Wind, "who, when the dark winter comes, blame others for the starvation, and revile the old and the infirm merely because they want a bite to eat. Red Eagle is a man who daily lives for the adulation of well-fed fools who swear that his lies are the truth of the Manitou."

Dark Moon stared at him in disbelief. "Has it come to that? Where are those who would support you?"

Wind shrugged. "I have just a few close friends. But there are many more who hate me because they know that I think Red Eagle's words are false. Many are also cowards and only care that they will not starve in the winter. And some, like hungry dogs when offered a piece of meat, want to believe the words that Red Eagle says, even if they know in their hearts that he speaks tall stories.

"No one hunts or works, except for my small band of hunters, and a few generous women who care for the sick and the aged. The rest have forgotten how to hunt or raise crops. They dream fantastic dreams that have made them weak as women. They wait for the day when a war leader like Red Eagle will lead them to paradise. But, in truth, they only lie to themselves in dreaming that, in a war, none of them would perish."

Wind stopped and stared at the ground as though listening to the echo of his own words. Then, he looked up at Dark Moon to say, "And the ones who loved you lost heart when they were told that the great hunter had been killed by a strange bear."

"Did no one suspect that it was a lie?" asked Dark Moon softly.

Wind did not look at him for several seconds. Then, he turned around toward him. "Whether it was a lie or not, you were still gone. The loss of heart was greater than the doubts about Red Eagle's lies." He hesitated again. "You see, Moon, you were someone they believed in. And if the Manitou could allow a strange bear to kill the man who had fed us through so many dark winters, a man of courage and respect, who would begin to question the words of Red Eagle who feigned sorrow at the loss of a friend?"

"And you, Wind," said Dark Moon, "were you afraid?"

Wind looked directly at him. "I was afraid for my family. I had lost my best friend, so there was no way to gainsay what Red Eagle told us. And remember...I told you that you should not have gone hunting with him. There were bad omens in my mind about him." Wind hesitated a few seconds. "But even I could not imagine that he would stand by and see you eaten by a bear and do nothing."

Dark Moon hung his head in silence for several seconds. Wind just watched him. Suddenly, the man who had come upon him as a cat, who could have easily killed him, whose voice was harsh and bitter, was now forlorn.

They were quiet for several more seconds, then Wind said, almost in a whisper, "Why have you come here, Moon? What are you looking for?"

"I am looking for the man who saved my life, the brother of my wife," Dark Moon said. "He is hunting with his son, and I intend to help them return the creatures they killed during their hunt." Dark Moon pondered and continued, "Wind, you have never hunted here before this far from the Salt Springs?"

"I am sick of what has happened to the Salt Springs," Wind said. "And I have heard stories of coming winters that will bring more death and starvation. I am looking for a better hunting field for the Cats."

Dark Moon responded, "Wind, the Cats you are trying to help are mere playthings for Red Eagle. He does not deserve you or your men—or your families. If the Salt Springs are doomed—and I believe what you say—then gather your families and come to live with me. All my family will bond with yours, and our wives will be friends as you and I are."

Snake and Two Bears

THAT EVENING, THE CAMPFIRE warmed the area as Snake and Two Bears cooked their turkey. The pleasant odor of meat cooked over an open flame wafted into their nostrils as they drank tea and talked, awaiting the final cooking of the bird.

"We should do this more often, Father, just you and I," said Two Bears. Snake smiled. "We will, often, I promise."

He wished regretfully that he would have gone out with his eldest son more often, but also, remembered how his own loneliness had disabled him as he mourned for his lost wife. The boy, who sometimes had been remote and contrary, seemed to glow in satisfaction and appreciation at their latest adventure where he and his father hunted alone in the woods as equals. It was the final bonding of two grown men, long in coming after the loss of the woman they both loved. Snake was satisfied and content as his son sprinkled salt on the turkey, now glistening as it cooked.

Suddenly, a sound in the air penetrated his consciousness. In another second after Snake heard the sound, he heard Two Bears gasp and yell. An arrow had cut through his thigh, and he fell forward into the fire, rolling through it to the open ground. Two Bears tried to stand up but fell to his knees as the arrow lodged itself deeper into his leg.

Snake was suddenly struck in the right shoulder as he screamed for his son to run for cover. He was then kicked and fell face forward, trying to brace his fall to keep the arrow from coming farther and deeper downward into his lungs. He screamed at his attackers.

Both father and son were on their knees, looking up at their attackers who stood before them. Two Bears was kicked in the back.

"Where are you from?" a young man said, coming forward. He was tall and lean. His eyes were cold, and his face was grim, and his mouth tight.

"Where are you from?" he asked again.

Both men were dumbfounded by the suddenness of the attack, and both could feel the blood oozing from the wounds. Snake's mind cleared enough to speak, "We are a small tribe from the north on the other side of this forest, beyond the hills."

"And what are you doing here?" said the tall man.

"My son and I are hunting before we go back home," he said. "Why have you attacked us?"

Once again, he was kicked as he spoke. "Do you not know that these are the hunting grounds of the Erierhonon?" asked the leader.

The pain in Two Bears's leg was growing worse. "We did nothing to you!" he screamed. "Why have you done this to us?" He clutched his leg that was now soaked with blood.

"What tribe are you from? Are you Iroquois?"

"No," said Snake. "I told you, we are but a small tribe of two families. We are of the Dakota and the Mandan, far to the north and to the West."

"Why are you here?" asked the leader.

"I told you," said Snake. "My son and I wanted to do one more hunt before the cold came. We have only taken one deer."

"But that deer you took comes from the land of the cat people, the Erierhonon. This forest is ours."

"How can you own a forest?" cried Two Bears.

"Surely, one deer will not bring starvation upon the tribe as great as the

Erierhonon," said Snake. "The Salt Springs are a great distance from this forest, and we chose not to come to your lands."

"Did you not take two turkeys? Were they not from our forest?"

"But turkeys are as the stars in the sky," rasped Snake. "They cannot be counted…and we merely took it to feed ourselves."

"A kill from our forest is a theft from the Erierhonon," the leader said.

"But here, there is an abundance of animals to hunt, more than any of us would ever need. Our families want none of your land. We were just traveling through this forest to hunt as men always do."

The leader advanced upon Snake, his face lowered to look into Snake's eyes. He looked merciless and cold. "You have been here before," he snarled.

"We have not," cried Two Bears, fearing that the leader would harm his father more.

The leader turned back suddenly toward Two Bears to advance a few steps forward.

"Wait," called Snake, as the leader turned back to him. Snake could see the murderous confidence as the man walked between him and his son. The thought of destruction was no longer an issue. If ever there were a time when he was unsure of what they would do to him and his son, there was no doubt now.

They all moved with swagger and assurance, with the confidence of people no longer troubled or doubtful about the rightness of their actions. But to make matters worse, Snake could see that these young men had become easy killers and were comfortable with their intent…confident that what they do would be satisfying, even pleasurable, and would allow them many hours of posturing around their campfires, as they honed their story into personal legend.

The leader stared at the blood oozing from Snake's wound. He knew that the arrow had done so much damage that he was dying. Suddenly, the leader struck him with a blunt club that crushed Snake's shoulder and landed in the crook of his neck, crushing the bone near his jaw.

"Father!" cried Two Bears as his father moaned softly, then struggled to get back to his knees.

Some of the other men were fascinated by the display, but one of the others was staring uneasily at something he had never been brought up to imagine, much less witness. He felt the pangs of guilt at being part of a ritual assassination, haunted by the thoughts of telling his own father of this monstrous act.

"I entreat you," said Snake, "he is merely a boy. Let him return, away from this forest. Do what you will with me."

The young leader smiled and turned again, as though to advance on Two Bears. Then, suddenly, he whirled around and struck Snake again. This time, he crushed his jaw and sent him sprawled over backwards with the arrow lodging ever deeper into his chest.

When Two Bears saw his father's face crushed and distorted, blood gushing from his mouth and nose, he screamed and lunged fitfully toward Snake, his arms outstretched in the almost childlike gesture of a babe wanting his father to embrace him.

Snake was conscious enough to see his son, as the boy stumbled toward him. One of the men slashed Two Bears's arm with a huge ax and severed the limb at the elbow, blood gushing from the open wound. Snake screamed in horror as he saw the lethal blow struck against Two Bears. He knew in an instant that the vision he had of his own sure death would also be that of his son. Both men screamed as a realization of each other's deaths set upon them in their last conscious moments of life.

In another second, two final blows were struck, each splitting the heads of both Snake and Two Bears, killing them in an instant. Then, the others advanced on the bodies and hacked them with their knives and axes in a frenzy of blood.

The leader stared silently at the two bloodied corpses. Some of the others began stripping the bodies in satisfaction for what they had done. For several minutes, there seemed to be complete silence of the forest. One of the men held up a small, black obsidian knife.

The leader took it and smiled thankfully. "This is my prize in victory," he said as he put the knife into a pocket near his chest.

Above them, they heard a hawk crying into the night, circling overhead and raining down upon them an eerie cascade that made some of them shiver uneasily.

"A hawk, at night?" one of them said to his nearest companion. "Have you ever heard such cries at night?"

The Search

DARK MOON WAS QUIET for a few minutes. Finally, he spoke as though a revelation had occurred to him. "Wind, why are you here?"

Wind looked at him curiously. "Did I not say that the Salt Springs will need more hunting if they would not starve in the coming winter? My group of young hunters will help me if we can find a forest that has not been overly hunted."

"This region where we now sit is not the best one," said Dark Moon. "There are forests farther south and West that are better. We will see them soon. I think my brother has gone there to hunt in the one I recommended."

"Can you tell me how to find it before I must return to the Salt Springs?" Wind asked. "Are those regions far away?"

"Perhaps three suns. But I can show you, if you will come with me. There you will meet Snake from the River and his son."

"Snake from the River?" said Wind.

"We call him 'Snake' now that he is growing older. You will like him, I assure you. He has heard me talk of you for many winters. I know you will become friends."

"You would take me there?" Wind said. "That far?"

"Yes. It would bring me great joy to hunt with you again, as we did when we were young and sometimes foolish."

"But can you walk well enough to hunt now? At that distance?"

"I have learned to hunt even with a crooked leg," Dark Moon said. "In fact, when Snake and my wife want to tease me or make fun of me, that is what my name is—Crooked Leg."

"It would indeed be a pleasure to hunt with you again," said Wind. Then, he hesitated. "But time is growing short, and I must return to my young hunters of the Salt Springs. I am certain that it will take too many suns for us to get there now."

Dark Moon shook his head. "We will be there in fewer than two suns," he said. Wind grimaced doubtfully. Dark Moon hesitated, but then spoke, "There is something you must see before we lay our heads down this night."

"Where?" Wind asked. "Do you wish to travel in the dark?"

"Yes, because I must show you something."

Wind huffed, not wanting to show how much he was skeptical of Dark Moon's enthusiasm.

Dark Moon understood. "It is not a great distance, and you will be glad for the journey," he said.

"You are certain?" Wind said.

"I ask you to trust me."

"Well, then, let us go. There is still much we have to speak of, like how you were injured and why Red Eagle has told his lies to the Salt Springs."

—⚬✦⚬—

Old memories seemed to haunt them as they ran through the last part of their journey, a treeless quarter mile that gradually sloped upward. When they reached the top of the hill, they both stopped to catch their breaths.

"Do you remember when we could do this all day long?" Dark Moon said.

Wind nodded in agreement. "Old age creeps up on us, does it not?"

Dark Moon shrugged. "I run slowly and steadily...much slower than I did when we hunted together."

"Then, let us continue," said Wind.

Dark Moon shook his head. "We are there," he said.

Wind looked around from side to side, puzzled. "Here?" he asked skeptically.

"Be patient, and you will see...over there."

Dark Moon pointed to a small grove of trees. And this time, Wind heard something, so he quickly drew his bow, ready for danger. But Dark Moon gestured for him to put down his bow as he turned to sound out a whistle. Suddenly, they heard a loud shuddering sound in response.

"What is that?" said Wind anxiously.

"Come, I will show you."

When they were clear of the thicket, Dark Moon stopped and whistled again. Suddenly, a large horse emerged, running up to Dark Moon, who fed him an apple.

Wind was amazed, yet not frightened because of Dark Moon's calmness and trust in the creature.

Dark Moon turned toward his friend. "We will not have to run tomorrow. He can hold us both," he said.

"Do you sit on him?" asked Wind, amazed as he had never been. "What is it called?"

"They are called elk dogs. The man you will soon meet has many of them. They can carry us on their backs, as you will see. And they have great strength and endurance."

"But where do they come from?" asked Wind. "I have never heard of such creatures."

"They come from some tribes across the mountains of the morning." Dark Moon shrugged. "It is said that strange white ghosts who appear to be men came in great canoes and brought these beasts with them. They eat grass much like a bison does. The newly born ones are quite small and gentle."

"Are these great ones dangerous?" said Wind.

"No. They are slow to anger and would rather run than fight. But almost no animals are as swift or have their endurance."

"So, you have others of these?" asked Wind.

Dark Moon shrugged. "We have a small group, and we will have more because some of our females will have offspring soon."

Wind was dumbfounded. Of all the things he learned in the last two days, this one was the second most astounding. "You have made me believe that I am dreaming—first, seeing you alive, and now seeing this huge creature. I hope that I will not soon waken and learn that my fantastical dream has vanished. Will this beast really carry us tomorrow?"

"Yes," Dark Moon said. "You will see what it can do."

———

The rest of the evening, Dark Moon and Wind exchanged stories about their lives—their marriages, their children, and how they now lived after their parting seventeen winters past.

Dark Moon addressed his friend, "Tell me of your wife and children."

"Two girls and a boy."

"And your wife?"

"Shadow Cat. You might remember. She is two winters younger than I."

Dark Moon snorted. "As is mine, exactly. What is she like?"

"Like none of the ones we desired when we were young. She is a quiet one. And she never slept under a blanket on the yellow moon."

"But she became yours?"

"Yes," Wind sighed, looking away from Dark Moon. "But she is different. She is darker than most of our women, but when I see her naked, she stirs my blood. And that is all she desires. She never became one of those who taunt and tease and enjoy foolish talk."

"She sounds like my own, easy to desire and wiser than the others," Moon said. "Was she the kind that you knew in an instant that there was no one better?"

Wind snorted. "Perhaps we married spirit sisters. Or perhaps we are enough alike that we had to wait to find two girls who were also waiting for us. They must meet someday, Moon."

Dark Moon sighed. "I cannot go back to the Salt Springs, Wind. Too much of my life is lost from there. What about you? Will you live among those who would want Red Eagle to be a great warrior chief who will lead you all to glory?"

"Many depend on me, especially the old and the feeble ones, for food in the winter. If I leave, no one will teach the young men to hunt. And until they learn by themselves, the Salt Springs will starve."

Dark Moon shook his head. "They should not depend only upon you and a few of your men." He looked away from his friend. They were quiet for several minutes.

"Where did you find your wife?" asked Wind.

"She found me. I would have died if she and her brother had not found me and carried me home to their mother, who brought me back to life."

"But why were you so near death?"

"A yellow bear."

"A yellow bear? Then, Red Eagle was not lying…at least about that."

"Many strange animals have come from far away in the north, because in that region, the great cold had killed so many of the other, smaller creatures they would eat," Moon explained.

"But why did you not kill the bear with your own bow?" Wind asked. "You had done it many times before."

"I had no bow in my hands," said Dark Moon, who stared at his skeptical friend. He had never lied to Wind, but his friend knew that Dark Moon had not told him the full reason for his disappearance.

Then, finally, through the night, he told Wind the outline of the story of Red Eagle's treachery.

Wind was disgusted by Dark Moon's story of Red Eagle's betrayal. The tale seemed even worse now because their world, which had once showed such promise for them both, was now darkened by stories of regret and missed opportunities. Their dreams of peaceful contentment and prosperity were gone.

"Why do people have such evil within them, Moon?" Wind said. "We asked nothing more than the enjoyment of our friendship and the peace of having a woman to love and to bear us healthy children. What makes people seek out evil and favor it, even though it causes pain and misery? Why does it have to be?"

"I wish I knew, Wind," Dark Moon said. "Some men wish misfortunes on others when they have no cause. We could have all been friends, and our children could have grown together in friendship, and perhaps some could have chosen love. Why did it have to be thus?"

The next morning, they set out on a southwestern course that Dark Moon often hunted in the years following his recovery from his wounds. At first, Wind seemed skeptical about two grown men riding a single animal, but soon he became accustomed to the easy, steady rhythm of the horse's gait, and he began to enjoy the comfort and ease provided by the creature. They rode all day, stopping only a few times to share water and pemmican, and to let the horse rest.

"We should be near the first forest I would wish for you," said Dark Moon. "The hunting will be good, and there will be a river we can follow to an even better place."

That evening, they rested and talked more of the glory days of their youth, of who is now living and who has gone to the Manitou. Dark Moon sat cross-legged and stared out into the night sky above the tree line of a distant field, addressing his companion without looking at him.

"Wind, do you remember that night when we were all weary and sought refuge from the cold? And found Elk Calf's whole camp slaughtered, as though they were herd of elk or deer?"

"I will not forget that as long as I live," said Wind, curious about Dark Moon's question.

"I often think of that lately, and I know not why." Moon stopped for a moment and turned toward his friend to change their somber mood. "I will skin an apple for you. Do you remember, when we returned from our hunts, that the older women of the tribe would have their daughters roast chestnuts for us?" Dark Moon rose and reached for the sack that lay near them. "And how the chestnuts would burst sometimes, and the women would be frightened as they considered it an omen from the Manitou that we would never choose one of their daughters to wed?"

Wind chuckled as Dark Moon spoke, looking away from his friend to the distant willow trees that clung to the water's edge. When he looked back, he could see Dark Moon trimming the skin from the apple with a small black knife.

"These kinds of apples, though the elk dogs like them, have sometimes bitter skins, and they taste better without it," Moon said.

As Dark Moon worked the blade on the apple, Wind took sudden notice of the knife. He looked in astonishment as he watched Dark Moon skinning the apple. Dark Moon suddenly realized that Wind was staring with a strange look on his face. "What is it?"

"Dark Moon? Where did you get that knife?"

Dark Moon looked curiously at his friend before answering. "It was a gift from Cricket's mother. Why do you ask?"

"I have seen that knife before," Wind said.

"No. You did not, for there were only two such knives that were made by the father of my wife before he died. The only other one was given to my brother, Snake, who you will see tomorrow or early the next."

"Let me see it, Moon," said Snake.

"Here," said Dark Moon, as he extended the handle of the knife toward his friend. "Be careful, Wind, for it is sharper than every other knife you have ever seen. It may cut you before you even see the blood from its wound."

Wind shook his head when he examined the knife as he brought it closer to the firelight and studied it. "Moon, I have seen this knife before."

"But my friend, there are only two," Dark Moon said patiently. "There may be another one with the black blades, but my wife's father made them as he was dying, long before Cricket and I had ever met. Look again. Surely you are mistaken."

Wind shook his head as he examined the knife again, turning it slowly by the firelight. "It is this one," he said, turning toward Dark Moon.

"But I tell you..." Dark Moon said. Then he stopped, troubled by the manner of Wind's certain look. "Where did you see that knife?"

"I saw it only few suns ago...in the Salt Springs."

"But you could not have. Snake would never part with his knife. Cricket's mother gave one to Snake and one to me, long ago. Who was it that had such a knife?"

Wind suddenly closed his eyes and let his head bow forward. He stayed that way silently for several seconds, then took a deep breath with his eyes still closed.

"Wind?" said Dark Moon, now becoming frightened by the behavior of his friend. "Wind, what are you thinking? You know you cannot be right."

Wind hesitated, then said, "Are you certain that there were only two such knives?"

"I am certain. But why are you so troubled? It is merely a harmless mistake."

Wind gazed at Dark Moon and shook his head very slowly. "Moon? Do you know who has possession of that knife and began wearing it around his neck but a few suns ago?"

Dark Moon still didn't understand. He shook his head in wonder.

Wind spoke again, "He is the son of Chief Red Eagle of the Erierhonon. And he displays the knife as a token of battle victory for all the Cat people to see."

Dark Moon bounded upward clumsily, almost falling as he stood erect. "Red Eagle? Does he have a son?"

"Yes, only one, and a daughter…and some smaller children of his dead brother. The boy is called Gray Wolf, and he is much like his father and has taken to wearing the knife as a token of conquest that will foster his dream of succeeding his father as the Great One."

Dark Moon had a strange expression, seeming not to believe the thoughts that were occurring to him as they talked. "How much like his father is he? Does he crave attention and talk always of his great worth?"

"Did not his father proclaim the same boasts about his adventures and victories that no one but a few of his men had ever seen or heard? His son is as boastful and false as his father, but perhaps even more cruel."

"Wind, do you think it could have been Red Eagle who led the slaughter of Elk Calf's tribe?" asked Dark Moon, suddenly acknowledging ideas he had always tried to suppress.

"Was it not Red Eagle who watched a defenseless friend being killed by a bear and did nothing to save him?" Wind replied. "Who then returned with your bow to the Salt Springs and told lies to all the people of how he slew the creature that killed his friend, proclaiming a fantasy that made him seem noble and innocent?"

Dark Moon didn't answer. He shivered slightly, and Wind took notice.

"You have not had food, but I have pemmican in my pack," Wind said. "Let us eat."

They were awake for several hours in the moonlight, stacking more wood on the fire to last them through the night. Dark Moon, in response to Wind's persistent questions, told him the entire story of rescuing Red Eagle from the cliff, and when he was safe at the top ground, stood by and watched the bear attack.

"My old bow, the one I used when you and I hunted together, lay there on the ground before his eyes," Dark Moon said.

"And he did nothing? As the bear tore your limbs?"

"He picked it up and walked away, leaving the bear to devour me. This knife," Dark Moon said as he drew the long flint blade from a leather scabbard to show his friend, "was what killed the golden bear. It was to be the last moment of both our lives. But shortly after the bear died, my wife and her brother found me and saved my life. They took the knife from the neck of the bear and returned it to me the day I took my first steps alone after two winters."

"And now," Wind said sardonically, "Red Eagle parades your bow as a thing of honor, something that reminds every one of his bravery for killing the bear that destroyed you. He makes no reference of your saving his life from the cliffside."

"And also, you say that his son wears a black knife that was made by my wife's father," said Dark Moon. He paused for a few second, then said softly, "Wind, do you suppose…"

Wind stared at him silently. "I hope not, my friend. I hope I am a fool and am making a senseless mistake."

Dark Moon was quiet as they rode the elk dog toward the one place that he knew would have the best hunting, the south forest that he had described to Snake. Wind was thoughtful and quiet as they rode. Both knew that there was little chance that the thoughts that tormented their imaginations could not be true. Still, both ardently hoped that they were wrong. Could there be a chance that Wind was wrong about the black knife? Could there be a chance that Snake would voluntarily part with such a revered treasure … and yet be unharmed?

The day passed slowly as they made their way toward the forest where Dark Moon hoped to meet his brother. He was quiet and sensed something wrong, perhaps a strange smell in the air. And in the quiet, he could sometimes hear a hawk cry, the same eerie sound that always tormented him. The anguished cry that always cascaded over hills and forests as he traveled, and always foretold havoc.

He looked over at Wind, and his friend said, "Are you hearing something, Moon?"

Dark Moon's head dropped forward, and he huffed. "Did you not hear something, Wind?"

Wind shook his head, remembering other terrible times when his friend heard the cries of a hawk that no one else could hear.

Dark Moon closed his eyes. He could hear water running, and he could also smell the moisture carried on the wind. He sensed discord in all the sounds around him, especially the damnable cries of the Ghost Hawk that no one else could hear. He knew he had to collect himself. He had to find a way to suppress the madness that haunted all his thoughts. He had to conquer fear more than anything else. Could Snake be safe? Could he and Two Bears be hunting and bonding, unaware of what danger they might be in?

When they rested, Moon sat quietly on a log and pondered what could happen soon. Perhaps he would find Snake and his son as safe as they were when he last saw them. And Snake would laugh at Dark Moon's fretful worries. "You always worry too much," Snake would say.

But what if he were not the jovial and spirited man who teased him and taunted him constantly? The man who smiled often, someone so truthful and just, a man as fine as anyone in the Ohio. What if he were badly injured and in need of help?

Dark Moon sat staring at the forest. He knew he would have to con-front reality—that Snake was either safe and awaiting his arrival or had traded the black knife for good reason, perhaps safety for him and his son. But what if the knife was stolen from him and he did not even realize it? Or what if he were also unable to stop the person who now has the knife? But that could only mean...

Dark Moon abruptly stood up. If there were killers lurking in this for-est, he would have to find them, to stop them from any damage they could do, from any violence they might inflict. What if they were not merely passing hunters, preparing themselves against the great cold?

Moon looked at Wind. Here was a man who he had known all his life. What if Red Eagle's son's men were marauders and killers that he had seen recently, not realizing that they had stolen and killed for the black knife? And yet here he was in a region he did not know and faithfully adhering to Dark Moon's guidance, standing by him, even if danger was awaiting them.

Dark Moon cursed himself for allowing strange phantasms to blind him from what he must do. He gathered his bow and nodded to Wind.

——◆◆◆——

Wind was worried about his friend's preconceived notion. "What are you thinking, Moon?"

Dark Moon shook his head. "I am wondering if my brother and his son are still alive and imagining what my life would be like if they were dead." He took a deep breath. "And what I would say to my wife if I had to tell her that her brother was gone."

Wind had never seen such behavior in Dark Moon, never in all the years they learned to camp and hunt in the forest. But he still tried to console his friend. "Perhaps I was mistaken, Moon. I should not…"

Dark Moon was shaking his head as Wind spoke. "I have known you so many winters, and I have never known you to be wrong about something like the black knife, something so important." He paused again for several minutes, looking away from his friend. "But what would I say to his sister if your understanding is true? And what would my life be like if he is no longer in it?"

"Let us see what the Manitou has wrought for us, Moon. Perhaps we are hasty in imagining his loss. You said he was a man of skill and honor. Perhaps they stole the black knife, and he didn't realize it. Perhaps he and his son are waiting for us now… and I will have a new friend."

"But what if you are wrong, Wind?" Moon asked. "I know you. And if you have a thought, it is always colored by truth. So, what if he is lost to us?"

Wind looked away for a few seconds. "I know not, Moon. All I know is that when I lost you to a golden bear, I found a way to survive. I had to, as you must, because there are too many hearts that depend upon you. My friend, you must be the totem for those whose lives you cherish. Someday, when you meet the Manitou, he will tell you the reason for your terrible loss. And if we find your brother living this day, then you will know that the Manitou has chosen yet another path for your life."

Wind paused again. "Think of it. Would you have ever imagined that you would be attacked by a yellow bear after you saved the life of a comrade? And would you ever have imagined his evil and cowardice as he left you to be eaten by the bear? Would you have ever dreamed, when we were young and carefree, that your life would be saved by two women and a man who were strangers to the Ohio, and came upon your body that was so damaged?"

Dark Moon just looked back at him and sighed, then nodded his head. He answered softly, "Wind, would that the Manitou had blessed me with wisdom, as he has done for you." He shook his head. "I am fortunate indeed, to have you as a friend, and I hope to thrive by your counsel the rest of my life."

"Then, let us go, Moon. We must confront a story that will stay with us forever."

Discovery

HE ELK DOG CARRIED them steadily for the rest of the day. Finally, Dark Moon reigned in the horse as they approached a small river that led to a much larger lake. Dark Moon knew it well. There was an opening along the creek where camping was easy because of its safety and nearby firewood. They decided to rest there.

The two men walked slowly into the small clearing. Suddenly, Dark Moon took a deep breath as he closed his eyes to shut away a closer look at the mangled bodies of Snake and Two Bears. He fell to his knees as he braced both hands against the ground to keep himself from falling face first.

Wind continued walking toward the bodies, looking at their mangled limbs and shattered heads. He stopped and shook his head. He had seen it before, so many years ago—the slaughtered remains of good people, cut apart by cruel and depraved men that were worse than animals because they were conscious of what they were doing and not driven by animal hunger.

Suddenly, Dark Moon was beside him. "This was not done by animals, was it Wind?" Wind shook his head, and Dark Moon continued, "We have seen this before, have we not?" Again, Wind nodded. "A fine young boy about to be a man, and one of the best men I have ever known who was not yet a grandfather."

"Where did he keep the black knife, Moon?" asked Wind.

Dark Moon hesitated for a moment, then said, "In a small pocket near his chest."

Wind walked toward Snake's dislocated body and looked through all the garments that partially covered the torso. He felt and examined every other part of the dismembered corpse. Then, he looked around the ground near the body. He walked back to Dark Moon, who was standing awe-stricken, seeming unable to move toward the bodies. "If he had the black knife, it is now gone," said Wind.

"By your words, it is in the Salt Springs," Dark Moon answered as Wind nodded in assent.

—————◆◆◆◆◆—————

The rest of that day, Dark Moon and Wind labored over their terrible task, gathering every particle or possession that could be used as keepsakes for the family, and placing the bodies onto wooden pyres, supported about two feet above the ground.

Sometimes, they would have to stop because Dark Moon would be overcome by the scene before him. He forced himself to act without thinking, and not imagining that he was gathering the body parts of two men he loved. But sometimes the thought of what they were doing was too much to bear for both men. They both knew that these images before them had to be stricken as much as possible from their minds as they lived the coming years without Snake and Two Bears.

So, they set flat stones into shape as curved platters that became receptacles for the ashes that would be left from the burnt bodies. Finally, after a short prayer to the Manitou, they set the kindling ablaze. "These ashes will be buried in our camp," said Dark Moon. "Their final rest will always be among us."

Then, he quietly bowed his head as tears dropped to the ground in front of him. Wind put his hand on Dark Moon's shoulder and stood quietly beside him as the fires blazed.

They watched the fires as night came, talking many hours about the task that was before them. When the fire was gone, they grabbed the ashes of each man and placed them into leather sacks. Then, they slept a few hours until they heard birds making morning calls at daybreak.

The two men rode the elk dog east to the point where they first met in the forest. They both knew that each would return to their home camps but would surely meet soon again. Dark Moon and Wind, as they dismounted from the horse, faced each other for a goodbye.

Dark Moon spoke first. "You must come to live with us before the cold comes, Wind. You know you can no longer stay in the Salt Springs."

"I know," said Wind. "But what will you do now?"

Dark Moon shrugged. "I do not know how to tell my wife. I know not if she will be able to withstand the loss."

"When will we meet again?" asked Wind.

Dark Moon didn't answer for several seconds. Then, he said, "I will be at the Salt Springs on the next Moon of Falling Leaves."

"But then, what will we do?" asked Wind.

"Prepare for a journey. Take all that is necessary, that you can carry to travel in safety. The rest we can provide upon your arrival at my home." Dark Moon shook his head. "I know one thing for certain. Whatever else we do, I will avenge my brother and his son."

"Moon, you must be careful," Wind said. "Both Red Eagle and his son live only to fight. It is all they do. How will you be able to—"

"If one of them is dead, then the other will be weaker," said Dark Moon.

"But Moon, I must help you. We can meet before—"

Dark Moon interrupted him, "I cannot fight his way, but neither can he fight my way. I will use my mother's bow to avenge Snake. Once I kill

Gray Wolf, the other will be lost...and then I will kill Red Eagle to avenge Elk Calf."

"But how will you do that? Your leg is not what it once was. If he brings the fight to you, you cannot fight him with a knife or an ax."

Dark Moon pointed to his bow. "I wonder if my new mother, Snow Flower, would have ever imagined that I would use it to avenge the murder of her son."

"I wish I were as trusting as you," said Wind. "Those men kill for pleasure. You do not. On their side is a lifetime of killing without remorse."

Dark Moon nodded his head, confident that he suddenly knew what he could do to avenge his brother. "Remember, Wind, the Moon of Falling Leaves. I will be on an elk dog, and they will not know what I am. They will think me a ghost."

"I wish I could be as hopeful as you," said Wind.

"The next full moon, Wind."

Wind nodded reluctantly. "Take care, my friend. I have lost you once. That is enough."

"Make plans for when we leave the Salt Springs, Wind, who you will bring with you other than your own family. And remember that no one must know our story beforehand, or you will all be in danger."

Wind nodded. He was frightened for Dark Moon and frightened for his own family, and for keeping his chosen friends safe.

Dark Moon understood Wind's fear for the safety of his family and friends.

"The Manitou will favor us for bringing justice to the Salt Springs," Moon said. "They have brought disgrace upon a once great tribe and have hidden their evil by lies and killing. The Grandmother once told me that the Erierhonon will be gone from the Ohio. Now, it will be so."

Two days after they parted, Dark Moon rode northwest toward his small tribe, and Wind traveled on foot to the Salt Springs. Both had heavy hearts in parting and for fearing the future.

Dark Moon agonized over how he could tell his family—and especially Snake's children—that their father and brother were now gone. He knew that he could never describe the horror of what happened to the two men. And what could he tell Cricket about the loss? Would she even believe that it was true? And how could she abide the loss of her brother, the only companion in her life as she grew up, other than her mother and father?

The Moon of Falling Leaves

I T TOOK WIND THREE days to return to the Mahoning Valley. He had no interest in hunting on his way, but instead thought always about what was ahead for the Salt Springs. He made good time, but he often thought about what he would say to Shadow Cat. Everything was different now. And he had to tell her what was to become of them. But first, he had to convince her that Dark Moon was still alive and that he would return by the Moon of Falling Leaves.

How would he tell his closest friends among the hunters that he was leaving? Would he have to convince them to come with him? And if they would come with him with their own families, could they prepare to come with him in the few short days before Dark Moon arrived? Would that commotion not be noted by Gray Wolf and his father? And what if Red Eagle tried to stop them?

Both Red Eagle and his son were vicious enough to try. But would it come to that? Would his few friends and their families of the Salt Springs rise up against Red Eagle and his son, and dare to leave? Would they let Wind and his family leave peacefully if only he alone wanted to leave?

This was a dramatic turn in his life, and first, he had to convince Shadow Cat that leaving would be the best choice. He was tired. He thought of Dark Moon's elk dog. How easily those beasts made the fatigue of life and travel so much lighter.

Finally, he came to the Salt Springs, and he entered wearily into his lodge. Shadow Cat ran to him and kissed him, as well as his two daughters and his son, each making a welcoming embrace of their father.

———❖———

That night, Wind slept after he had bonded with his family, and awoke at dawn the next day. Shadow Cat felt him move beside her and stood up with him.

"Something is within you, my Wind," she said. "Do you have something to tell me?"

He shook his head. "Later. Let me think more of it, and we will talk tonight after the children are asleep."

"Is there trouble in our future?" Shadow Cat asked.

"It is because I lack love and affection," he said smiling.

She pushed against his chest, setting him off balance a couple of steps. "Who do you say does not show you affection?"

He shook his head, looking away from her. "My wife. She did not feed me or bathe me after my return from a long journey."

Shadow Cat screamed as her hands went for his throat. "I have spoiled you all our lives, and our daughters also. And our son believes that you are a friend of the Manitou."

Wind grabbed her and pulled her face up to his. "They are right about the Manitou. I am one of his favorites. And you must all show me more respect."

She kissed him fully. "Is that enough respect?"

"Certainly not. My status requires much more."

"And how much more do you require, exalted one?"

"I will explain all your new duties this evening…after the children are asleep, but today we must talk of other things."

Shadow Cat stared him for a few seconds before saying, "This will not be you and I playing together, will it?"

"No," Wind said. "But it involves us and our children. And I must know what you think. But since I am weak from hunger, perhaps I will be unable to tell you all of my story."

This time, she was puzzled, because Wind's attempted humor was also an attempt to distract her. She stepped away from him. "Will you tell me before we tell our children?"

"Yes, of course," Wind said. "But first, I must have nourishment, or I may fall down." He grabbed Shadow Cat's arm and pulled her toward him and kissed her.

When they caught their breaths, she said, "Come, I have something on the fire outside. It has been there all the night and is now ready for the mighty hunter, who has much to tell his wife."

Later in the day, when all the wood for the fire had been split and stacked, and when the food was cleaned and chopped and cut, Wind and Shadow Cat relaxed as they watched their children play a tag game with a leather ball.

"There have been stories about the camp," Shadow Cat said. "Gray Wolf and his tales of wonder."

"What stories?"

She sighed, acknowledging that the story was fostered by braggarts, and grimaced as she spoke, "There were stories about one of our hunting parties being attacked by a strange tribe who were scouting in the great forest." She grimaced, showing her doubts. "Men from the northwest who would seize our lands and come to the Salt Springs to steal its abundance."

Wind turned toward his wife. "From the northwest? Never have intruders come so near to our Valley from the West, especially through the dangers and distance of the great swamp."

She shrugged, uncomfortable with the story she was telling against her husband's doubts. "It is just what is being told around the campfires," she said.

He turned toward her. "Was anyone injured? Or killed?"

"No. All were safe, even though it was a great battle against many more men than our few."

"Not one serious injury?" Wind asked. "In a fight against so many more men?"

Shadow Cat huffed, "Well, since Gray Wolf is such a great warrior, it takes far fewer men to defeat their enemies." She smirked.

Wind snorted. "So say the wives and mothers of those men," he said. "Does anyone really believe that they fought a battle against a tribe that greatly outnumbered them, and no one was killed, or even injured? My men and I, when we go on a hunt for turkey and beavers, are grateful when we return home with mere scratches and cuts."

Shadow Cat was thoughtful for a few minutes as she put some broth and bread out for her husband. Finally, she said, "Do you think they are lying?"

Wind smiled affectionately and held his arms open for her to come into his embrace. "Part of your goodness is that you believe people easily, because your heart thinks only the best of people."

She kissed him. "But why must they always tell such false stories?" she asked, sitting next to Wind and massaging his back as he slowly drank the soup and ate some bread pieces.

Wind brought her hand to his lips affectionately. "You know Gray Wolf. He is his father's and mother's son, arrogant and proud beyond example. Can you not believe that he would tell stories that seem to make him valiant and strong in the face of danger, more courageous than ordinary men?"

She jostled his shoulder. "You are right. I have never liked him. And I am glad that our daughters have not caught his eye."

"I just know this," said Wind. "These braggarts never tire of telling all the world how brave they were in battle. Yet, who is ever here to gainsay their story? Well, I have met someone who has shown me that their story is a lie. That instead of bravery, they are murderers and cowards who only attack a peaceful hunter and his son and cut them to pieces as one would cut a slain deer."

Shadow Cat looked at him, stunned. "Is that so? Are they truly killers of innocent people? Who told you of this?"

"Dark Moon," Wind said sardonically, knowing how she would react.

"You jest about such a thing by invoking the name of a dead person?" she asked impatiently. "A friend of yours...just to tell your story? How can you speak thus?"

Shadow Cat frowned and shook her head, and rose to turn away from Wind and leave. He grabbed her wrist to stop her. "Let me go," she said, slapping his hand away.

"Please, Cat, sit here beside me, and I will tell you my story," Wind said. "Please."

She looked at him, dumbfounded, as though she hardly knew him. "I ask you again, how you can dishonor the dead by speaking as you did?"

He pulled her toward him, and helped her kneel down in front of him. Then, he snorted, shaking his head and looking away from her for a moment. When he turned back, he said, "What if I told you that it was not a lie, or even a jest?"

She made a face. "You have never done this to me. Why are you spoiling such..." She shook her head, trying to banish everything he was saying. Then, she tried to stand up, but Wind held her arm.

"Please," he said. "I must tell you something that you may not believe, though it is all true."

Shadow Cat was shaking her head as though pleading with him to say no more.

"Cat," he said, "I know what you are thinking. "But I have never lied to you, and this is not a lie."

"But," she said, shaking her head, "I just cannot do this."

"A strange man came upon me in the forest," Wind continued. "I knew not who he was, perhaps a raider or a scout for marauders. But we had the same speech patterns, and he called me Wind after we had barely spoken a few words."

Wind hunched his shoulders and shook his head. "It was indeed Dark Moon of the Erierhonon."

"But he is dead. Did you not tell me that so many times in our lives? How could he be alive?"

Wind gazed at her for several seconds, silently. "Who told us that Dark Moon was dead? Was it not the man whose words are baited traps for anyone they can ensnare?"

Shadow Cat held her hand to her forehead as though trying to hold Wind's words from being heard. "But how does a spirit come to you and speak? Why, at that time and that place?"

"He was returning home through the forest," said Wind. "He was as shocked to see me as I was to see him."

"But where did he come from?"

"He lives in the north, not far from the great north lake. He has a wife and three daughters. And when he walks, he walks with a limp. The limp he has because of the damage that the great bear did to him when he was attacked. And he and I traveled together to the West and found his brother, the brother of his wife, slaughtered like a turkey or a beaver…as was his son."

Wind stopped for a minute to ask, "Do you believe me?"

Shadow Cat shrugged but had become fascinated by the strange tale

Wind was unfolding. "Continue," she said softly.

He nodded and began, "You have seen that beautiful black knife that Gray Wolf wears so proudly? Well, it was stolen from the neck of the man who is the brother of Dark Moon's wife. You see, the entire story that Red Eagle told about coming upon the body of Dark Moon that was half eaten by a bear was a lie. He watched Dark Moon being attacked by the bear and did nothing, even though Dark Moon's bow and arrows lay at his feet. When he was certain that the bear would kill Dark Moon, he took the bow and quiver and ran away to return to the Salt Springs as a hero, a man of honor who killed the golden bear who was devouring Dark Moon. He was a hero of his own false imaginings.

"And now, Gray Wolf, who is as much a murderer as his father, has killed Dark Moon's brother and the brother's son. Dark Moon was saved by a girl and that same brother, who lived in a small camp. Their mother was a healer who kept Dark Moon from death. Though now he walks with a limp and is sometimes called Crooked Leg by his family in jest, he is married to the girl who rescued him from beneath the dead bear. The brother of the girl who helped carry Dark Moon to their camp was but a few suns ago murdered by the son of Red Eagle."

She looked at him. "Is this story really true? Dark Moon still lives?"

Wind snorted and smiled slightly. "Have you ever known me to lie to you?"

"But what will happen now?" she asked.

Wind didn't answer her for a few seconds. "That will be your—"

"What are you saying?" Shadow Cat interrupted. "Do you expect me to decide what we will do?"

"You must help me make a decision. Whatever I decide will not be if you do not agree with it."

She frowned. "You are thinking of something that will change our lives?" He nodded, so she continued, "What is it you wish?"

209

Wind took a deep breath. "I would leave the Salt Springs forever. I would take you and our children to the north, where we would live in the camp of Dark Moon and his family."

"But what of my brothers and their families? You would have me leave them and never see them again?"

"They could come with us if they wished, but we must never tell anyone until it is time," he said.

"But if they will not come? What will we do?"

"If they will not come, it will be their choice. But I think that the evil that is among us must be banished from our lives."

"What does that mean? How would we—"

"Red Eagle and his son are evil. Gray Wolf and his men killed the brother of Dark Moon, not even a moon ago. You have seen the small black knife that Gray Wolf wears as a token of honor? Well, it was stolen from a defenseless and trusting man, who was the brother of Dark Moon's wife. Gray Wolf killed both the man and his young son."

"How do you know this?" Shadow Cat asked. "Are you taking the word of a friend of your youth who never returned to the Salt Springs in…how long?"

"Seventeen winters," Wind sighed.

"How can you trust him if he did not ever come back to you? You have often told me that he was the friend of your life."

"He was badly injured and was unable to return. Even today he walks like a man who endured great pain just to learn to walk again."

"But do you think that you can trust his word that Gray Wolf killed these men? You have not seen it, yet you are believing the story from a man you have not seen in seventeen winters?"

Wind snorted, staring at her silently. "You still do not believe me," he said grimly. "You think I am lying."

"I believe what you are saying, but you are asking our whole family to be uprooted and go live with someone who has not spoken to you in seventeen winters. Who is his wife? Who are his children? What if the words he says about welcoming us are false? Or what if, even if he is truthful, his family does not agree? You expect us to go among them and become another family? Among people who know us not?"

Wind was thoughtful for a moment. Usually, Shadow Cat would be exactly right. And all her reactions would be normal and prudent. But she did not see the slaughter of Elk Calf's tribe, the women and children who were dismembered and mutilated as though they were animals. Neither did she see the cruelty that Gray Wolf inflicted when he killed Snake and his son, people whom he had never seen before and by happenstance were found on a hunting trip that would bind them together as two adults, father and son.

Though he loved Shadow Cat with all his heart, he knew she could never imagine the savagery that Red Eagle and Gray Wolf were capable of. Truly, for most people, their deeds were hard to imagine, like the slaughter and dismemberment of small babies.

Wind walked toward her and took her in his arms. "Your heart is as tender as any I have ever known," he said softly. "And the words you say show kindness and wisdom. But now I ask you to set aside your doubts and trust me. I have seen the deeds of both father and son, one who is now chief and the other who will be so chosen in the future. I ask you to consider that Red Eagle and his son are not merely boastful fools but are men capable of the worst kinds of deeds. Our tribe seems to tolerate their vainglory because they have been convinced that without Red Eagle's protection, peace would never come to the Salt Springs, that without them, raiders and marauders would destroy this valley."

He stopped for a moment and stepped away from her. Then, he shook his head, as if trying to banish her doubts. "But I have witnessed the evil that they have done just a few suns ago, and also many winters ago when

Dark Moon and I were very young men. We both saw it. But it is just now, after seventeen winters, that we have been awakened to the truth. The truth that we both found difficult to imagine—that Red Eagle could have lied to everyone about the great bear killing Dark Moon. We have always accepted his boastful pride because this valley was such a wonderful place to raise our children. But I am telling you now that the Salt Springs of old will be gone forever in but a few more winters."

Shadow Cat didn't respond. Instead, she walked up to him and hugged him. Then, she said, "Why did you not tell me of these feelings you have?"

"Because I have difficulty thinking of those things when I am with you and our children," Wind said. "The joy of being with you has always overcome the evil of those men. But now, when I know that my lost friend, Dark Moon, lives, I think I can imagine all of us together in happiness without the evil killers that have made this valley a place of fear and sometimes starvation."

She stepped back from him and smiled playfully, smirking. "What is his wife like? Is she another tall and beautiful one like Calling Dove? Or is she small and plain like me?"

"I don't know if she is as evil and disrespectful as you," Wind said. "You know that though you are small and slender, you are still quite beautiful."

Shadow Cat came forward and kissed him. "As long as you think I am, then I am satisfied."

Wind seemed a bit more serious in his response. "Truly, Dark Moon said that his wife is also small and beautiful. Do you think you have a spirit sister somewhere in the north?"

She smiled back at him.

Wind said, "My little one, we must be careful. We must tell no one yet about Dark Moon's return on the Falling Leaf Moon."

She was surprised. "Will he really return?"

"We will know in a few suns," he said. "Meanwhile, we must quietly prepare for our departure and tell no one except those few who we can trust who may want to leave with us. I will do the same with those hunters I would want to come with us...if they wished."

"But what will we do when Dark Moon returns? Would not everyone know that we are leaving then?"

Wind was thoughtful for a few seconds before replying, "Dark Moon considers the brother of his wife as his own brother. He told me much about what that man did to help Dark Moon survive the bear attack, for he was unable to walk, and his new brother, called Snake from the River, helped him learn to survive." He paused and was thoughtful. "I know Dark Moon comes for vengeance, and for that we must prepare."

Dark Moon Comes
Upon a Boy

THE WOODS SEEMED ESPECIALLY quiet as Dark Moon pushed through the thickets. He had been trailing the river, but at a distance from its banks. As usual, all his senses were alert to any strange occurrence in the forest—an uncommon sound, the call of a distressed animal, or a vague silence that could hint at lurking danger.

He walked carefully, but steadily, and came upon a small clearing. Then suddenly, he stopped. At the far end was a young man poised to strike something in front of him. Dark Moon crept silently forward around the edge of the clearing that was bordered by the tree line. He moved slowly, careful to not make a sound that would give his presence away.

The young man had killed a rabbit and was binding it into a leather sack over his shoulder. He had entered the woods from the east and made his way through the thicket. Dark Moon snorted in disgust as he cursed himself for the unwieldy leg that might betray his presence or cause him to make noise that would alert the boy that he was being followed.

Soon, he came upon the boy from behind. The young man had stopped to rest, sitting cross-legged as he drank some water. Dark Moon snorted softly in satisfaction. All he had to do now was to come silently from behind and subdue him.

Slowly, he circled behind the boy who was sitting quietly, lost in thought. Dark Moon, trying to be as furtive as he was in days gone by, but knowing that he really was not, used patience to make up for his loss of cat stealth.

As he advanced at the back of the young man, Dark Moon breathed heavily once, then held his breath. After one more step, he reached out with his left hand, encircling the boy's head and pulling him backward toward his chest. In the other hand, he held a knife to the side of the boy's neck.

"One move, and you are dead," Dark Moon said softly.

The boy, sensing that he could have easily been killed, did not struggle because he knew that there was some reason that his assailant let him live. Dark Moon quickly bound his arms with leather straps. Then, he roughly turned the boy around to face him.

"What do you want?" asked the boy. "Why have you done this?"

Dark Moon could tell from his speech and accent that he was not one of the Erierhonon. He sensed that he was from one of the tribes across the endless mountains, perhaps an Iroquois. But their languages were similar enough so that each understood the other.

The boy was afraid of the scowling, murderous look on the face of the older man. He noticed that his small knife blade was made of shiny and deadly looking black substance, the likes of which he had never seen. Again, he spoke, "What do you want from me? I have nothing. I am only passing through this land."

"Where are you going?" asked Dark Moon.

"It is a long journey," he said, "to where the waters have food and flowers."

Dark Moon held his knife before the boy, threatening him with the slight move toward his chest. He growled, "Do you think me a fool that you could tell me such nonsense and be believed?"

This time, the boy was frightened. "But it is not fool's talk! The lake is far in the West. We go there to make our home."

"Where are you from?"

"Across the great mountains."

"And why came you here?"

"Our tribe has been destroyed...almost all. In a dream, our father learned that the Black Wolf people had to leave their homeland and go on a great journey, far to the land where the sun sets. There, we will find the lake of flowers and food, and we would be safe."

Dark Moon studied the boy. There was nothing false about him. His words seemed true, and his actions showed both fear and honesty. "Where is the rest of your tribe?" Moon asked, lowering his knife.

"We were once a small tribe, but then we scattered after the war. Some died of a strange sickness. Others remained out of fear of going into lands where stories are told of great monster bears and huge cats."

"Why are you alone? Why did you not stay with some of the others?"

The boy looked away, and again Dark Moon's anger arose.

"Answer me," Moon growled.

"I cannot tell you," the boy said weakly. Again, Dark Moon's knife was poised at his neck. The boy shook his head slightly.

Dark Moon was troubled by this boy. He seemed as innocent and sincere as his own nephews, and his eyes were as honest as those of his own daughters. *What is he not telling me?* Dark Moon thought.

Finally, the boy shrugged. "I know you will kill me," he said. He stopped and raised his face to look into Dark Moon's eyes. "Will you do something after I am gone?"

Dark Moon shook his head in amazement. "Why would I do anything for you?"

The boy sighed. "Not for me, for someone else."

"Who else?"

"Someone who means you no harm, who has never done anything to you or to anyone."

Now, Dark Moon hesitated, then snorted, "Am I to believe you? A stranger from the tribe of killers?"

"Killers? No! Someone who is…She is a child, as innocent as a baby deer in the forest."

"A child? You travel with a child?"

The boy nodded, then made the curious gesture of moving his head slightly sideways from left to right. "She is hidden…out there." He nodded to the left. "I left her to rest so I could hunt for food. We have not eaten in two suns."

Dark Moon lowered his knife again.

"I know you want to kill me," said the boy, "but she has done nothing to you. She has barely twelve winters."

His words shocked Dark Moon. For a few more seconds, he studied the boy, wondering what there was in his own eyes that made the boy believe that he was a killer.

"What have you done that you expect me to kill you?"

The boy seemed puzzled. "But why else are you so angry? What do you think I have done?"

Suddenly, Dark Moon walked behind the boy and cut his bands with his knife. "Nothing," he said softly, then hesitated. "I have just lost two men of my family who were murdered by men more evil than any other creatures under the sun."

"Where are you from?" the boy asked, looking up at Dark Moon. "I come from the east, in the direction of another great lake."

Dark Moon gestured with his arm. "I do not know these parts," he said. "But I have long hunted the forests of the Erierhonon to the south."

"Is that why you came upon me as you did?" the boy asked. "And did not face me in friendship?"

"I have learned not to trust strangers in these woods," said Dark Moon somberly. "The loss of my brother and his son has turned me into a wounded animal. It is easy to hate when you have seen the senseless killing of those you love."

"Do you know who the killers were?"

"I know some, but they seem like ghosts. I have seen their work before...when I was little more than your age. They are people who enjoy killing and destroying. But this time, just a few suns ago, I came to know just who they are. And I mistrusted you, thinking you might be one of them." Dark Moon held up his other knife, the black obsidian one. "There is another just like it, stolen from my brother who was killed. And now, today, the killer wears it as a token of conquest among the Salt Springs people who know not that he is a man of dishonor and shame."

"And you thought that I could be a killer?" asked the boy.

Dark Moon took another deep breath, then shook his head. "No."

The boy was thoughtful for a few minutes. Then, he said, shaking his head, "I must leave. My sister awaits me, and I know she is already frightened by my late arrival."

By then, Dark Moon was completely relieved of all his suspicions and mistrusts of the boy. "I will come with you. I can get you to your sister before it is dark."

The boy looked at him with skeptical eyes. "Are you...mocking me?"

Dark Moon realized what the boy could be thinking, so he said, "I do not jest. Come. I will show you what I mean."

The girl gasped when she saw Dark Moon standing beside her brother.

"Hello, Star," said the boy softly. She never took her eyes from Dark

Moon as she advanced slowly toward her brother.

"Walker, why have you tarried so long? I feared harm had come to you," she said, hugging him.

After a few seconds, she moved away and looked at Dark Moon, her eyes questioning and fearful. The boy turned to Dark Moon and said, "I do not know your name."

"I am Dark Moon, once of the Erierhonon."

Star looked back at her brother for guidance, troubled by the appearance of Dark Moon, and sensed something to fear about him.

"He is a friend, Star," said Stone Walker.

Even Dark Moon was surprised at the boy's acknowledgement. The girl stared at him for several seconds. "Why are you in these woods?" she said to Dark Moon.

"Why are you here?" answered Dark Moon, with a slight bemused smile on his face.

Star looked at her brother. "But we are on a journey," she said, expecting him to support her curiosity.

"As is he," said Walker.

"I was returning to my home," said Dark Moon.

"You have not yet told me what you seek," said Walker. Just as he spoke, the horse made a loud shuddering sound that startled the girl. She shrieked softly, clutching Walker.

"It is the elk dog," said Dark Moon, not showing any surprise at the loud sound.

The girl frowned. "What is an elk dog?" she said, turning toward her brother. "Is it one of those monsters?"

Walker looked toward Dark Moon for a few seconds, and the older man nodded and gestured at them to follow. In a few minutes, they broke into a small clearing, and the girl saw the horse.

"What are these creatures? Where do they come from?" Star asked in amazement. The horse stamped a leg upon seeing her and nodded its head as it shuddered loudly. The girl screamed and ran toward her brother.

Both men laughed softly as Dark Moon walked to his horse and fed him an apple. Then, he turned toward the girl and said, "Come touch him. He will not hurt you."

Star hesitated but was overcome with curiosity. Dark Moon was smiling in response to her questioning and doubtful looks. "Touch him here," he said, showing her how to stroke the horse's neck.

Dark Moon handed her an apple and motioned for her to offer it to the horse. She held it before the horse as he ate it from the palm of her hand.

"Are they always as gentle as this?" she asked, looking directly at Dark Moon.

"They are seldom angered," Moon said.

"But where do they come from? I have never seen or heard of such creatures."

"My spouse and her family have them, and they raise them."

"But where did they find them?" said the girl.

"I do not know. It was from a tribe of white faces who came across the endless waters long ago—from the time of her grandfather."

They camped that night in the small, secluded clearing where the boy and his sister had stopped. It was cool and clear, and the moonlight shone on the whole clearing and lit the faces of all of them as they talked by a fire.

Both young people, especially the girl, seemed suddenly to be bright and talkative. They asked questions of Dark Moon, and he, in turn, asked questions of them. Dark Moon liked the two young ones because they were unguarded and friendly, and yet seemed harmless and innocent.

They were just children, much like his own and Snake's that he had left behind. And they found themselves enthralled by the easy talk occurring between them.

When they had talked through the early night, and through two fires replenished by wood they had gathered before the darkness came upon them, Dark Moon grew quiet.

He turned away from them, seeming to be grappling with an idea he had turned over many times in his mind as he grew closer to the young people. "Where are you going now?" he said suddenly.

"As I said," Stone Walker replied, "we go to the land where the Manitou has made food grow in the lake."

"But must you hurry?" the older man asked. "To a place so far away?"

The boy looked at his sister. She also had a questioning look on her face. "Why do you ask this?" said Walker.

"I am returning home now," Moon said. "You can both come with me and stay at my lodge. Soon there will be a great cold, and you will not be able to finish your journey, and you might starve or freeze in this land that you do not know. We have food in plenty, and you can stay with my family through the winter."

They were both silent for several seconds. Then, Walker said, "You would offer us food and shelter?"

"Yes. You would be part of my long house."

"How many are in your family?" the girl asked.

"I have three daughters, and my wife's brother now has one boy and two girls in his lodge. They have all lived about as many winters as you."

"Does your brother have a wife?"

"No. She died some winters past."

"Why do you treat us thus? Never on our journey has anyone given us what you offer," said the girl.

Dark Moon smiled slightly. "Because you put me in mind of our own young ones, mine and my brother's." He hesitated a few seconds. "And because I was once helped by strangers who knew me not and who brought me back to life when I was near death. I have owed such kindness to others long since."

Walker and Star's Secret

ON THE LAST NIGHT before they arrived at Dark Moon's camp, all three rested quietly before sleep, and Dark Moon spoke softly to the young pair. They stared curiously as he seemed to struggle with his words.

"There is something I must tell you…and that I must ask you," Moon said.

Star and Walker seemed puzzled by his hesitant behavior.

"This terrible killing of my brother and his son will bring great sorrow to my family," he said. "I know not just how…or when…I can tell them. My wife will be especially sorrowed because she has lost her mother and father, and now I must tell her that she has lost her brother and his son. So, I am asking you to not do or say anything that will reveal this terrible story. I alone must choose the right time to tell them."

He was thoughtful for a few seconds before continuing, "It would be the greatest thanks you can ever offer me. And if you wish to stay among us forever and live your lives as part of our family, you are welcome. But if you ever tell this news to anyone before I do, then I will consider it an act of betrayal and will never forgive you. Do you understand what I am saying? You can do right, or you can do wrong. You can be a comfort to our whole family, or you can hurt them and me by betraying the trust that

I have now placed in you."

Stone Walker and Little Star looked at each other and stepped toward Dark Moon. The girl put her arms around Dark Moon, and her tears fell on his shoulder as he held her in his arms. She looked up at him to say, "We have hardly ever known a mother or a father, but you have shown us more favor and love than we have ever had. You speak to us as a father would, and you offer us a life that we would never have."

Dark Moon held the girl in his arms and spoke to them both. "If you remain with us, you may call me father, but only if you obey my words and honor my wife." He was thoughtful for a few more minutes, then said, "You may ask her someday if it would cause offense to call her mother."

Walker advanced toward the two, with the girl still within Dark Moon's arms.

"The Manitou brought you to us," Walker said. "You are a blessing to our lives."

—◆∘••∘◆—

Cricket was amazed at the sudden appearance of the two young strangers. She had always known that Dark Moon was a man of many mysteries, but she never expected him to bring home live creatures from his hunts.

But within a few days, she had become the mother of two new children to care for along with those of her own and her brother's. They all called the new ones Dark Moon's rabbits.

Star and Walker, in turn, had never been treated as part of a family, having been orphaned and on the run since they were mere children. The two learned a new kind of behavior, based upon respect and affection, and another kind of behavior they had never witnessed—one of playful humor.

The girl had never before beheld young women treated with a special kind of respect. Dark Moon's daughters were warm and kind and welcoming. The boys were not mean or brutal, but instead were affection-ate and gentle, but also funny and mischievous. And each would show her and Walker new skills, foods, animals, and beliefs. Walker and his sister realized that there was something very new about these people. Not only did they have the strange new creatures called elk dogs, but they had a way about them. A kind of lifestyle that was new to the boy and his sister. They also had leisure, and that was something that Star and Walker could barely understand.

Calling Dove's Emptiness

WHEN RED EAGLE BECAME chief, Calling Dove enjoyed the new elite status it brought to her and her family. When he became the Great One of the Erierhonon, their stature increased even more.

But it was not as satisfying as she expected. The deference shown to her and her husband was exactly what she had always wanted, but somehow it was not enough. Unfulfilled satisfaction seemed to haunt her waking moments. And the actual realization of its presence brought the beginning of the silence. It started slowly, in small instances, then grew into longer voids.

Both she and Red Eagle began to notice it, but neither one would try to bridge the silence. She would often ask herself, "Why is this life not more gratifying? Why am I unhappy?" So, the silence became part of their very existence, as though it was in the air they breathed. It was their life.

When Gray Wolf was born, Calling Dove had expectations of great happiness again. But strangely, though she dutifully cared for the baby and accepted the adulation of all the tribes of the Erierhonon for giving birth to a strong, healthy child, even that attention was disappointing. It was something pale and incomplete. And yet, it was something she could not change, because she knew that there was nothing more within her to give. She loved the boy, and in the emptiness that grew between her and her husband, Gray Wolf was all she had to live for.

One of the worst turns was the loss of her other male child that died in infancy. The other surviving child was a girl who was smaller and less beautiful than her mother and who did not have the same flirtatious and aggressive personality. The two women were never able to establish a special bond between them like the one Calling Dove had with her son. Since she and Red Eagle so seldom made love in recent years, the chances of her becoming pregnant again at her age were beyond hope. She also knew in her secret heart that there were many younger women among the Cats that willingly provided her husband with any relief he sought.

And so, as Calling Dove lived for Gray Wolf, he grew tall and handsome, a more perfect replica of his father. She could see in him the same traits that captivated her in her youth when she looked Red Eagle...yet those things gradually began to repel her.

In quiet times, when Red Eagle was out visiting other tribes of the Cat Nation, and when her now grown son was with him, she was haunted by new thoughts she could not banish from her mind. Even though she loved Gray Wolf as any proud mother would, she saw so much of his father in him—the smug arrogance, the casual self-assurance, the presumption of greatness, and worst of all, the coldness and tendency toward brutality.

Gray Wolf had his choice of many young girls of the Salt Springs, even of all the Erierhonon. Whatever contests he entered, he won. But in victory, he was never gracious; instead, he was contemptuous of vanquished comrades.

The traits she perceived in her son were nothing but the honed, more perfect likenesses of his father. And the lying that rolled so easily off the tongue of Red Eagle was perfected into an art by her son. Yet, despite the fading love that she could feel for them both, she still gloried in the envy of the other women, who saw her entice the one and give birth to the other.

Moreover, no one would remind Calling Dove that the beauty of her youth was fading, that her skin had become less elastic, and the tighter skin seemed to pull the lush softness from around her eyes and her cheeks. She was still a great beauty, but she also knew that she was losing herself to time.

"Are you hungry?" she said to Red Eagle, who had relaxed in a soft bed that made him seem drowsy at its touch.

"No, I have eaten," Red Eagle replied. "We stopped at a small group near the Mahoning, where the little falls exist. They fed us."

"Who did you eat with?" she asked.

"Talking Sun."

"Was his daughter there with him?"

"Yes…as was his wife."

"The girl is quite beautiful now, is she not?"

"I suppose she is," he said absently. "But Gray Wolf seemed not to notice her."

"But his father did notice," she said.

"I did not pay her much attention," Red Eagle said, casually ignoring her meaning.

She knew he was lying, and it angered her. Her son had told her of his day spent among the Falling Waters, and that meant his father would have had time alone with the girl. So, she tested him one more time.

"Do you want me to wait in your bed tonight?"

"No. It is not necessary. Perhaps tomorrow. The journey was wearisome, and it would be best if I rested."

Calling Dove turned away and began hanging Red Eagle's boots and jackets near the fire so they could dry.

Dreary Life

THE NEXT DAY, RED Eagle was quiet and moody.

Finally, Calling Dove said, "What troubles you? Are you not well?"

"I am well," he said. "You know a great cold is coming, as it was in our youth?"

"Some of the women have talked of it," Calling Dove said. "Do you think it will be as bad as the year..." But she caught herself, almost mentioning the one name that haunted her husband all his life, the one name that had wedged itself between them all the days of their marriage.

He still bristled at the rumor, often whispered in the shadows, that Calling Dove would have married Dark Moon, that Red Eagle was really the second choice for her bed. And even though she had tried strenuously to convince him that it was not so, the truth was that she didn't know if it was true.

But Calling Dove learned early on that in Red Eagle, there was no substance. He was brilliantly physical and dynamic. But beneath the external pomp, there was nothing. *What would have it been like,* she allowed herself to wonder, *to discover that Dark Moon's thoughts were only of me? That the man who came as a child stranger to the Salt Springs could today have a lodge that was redolent of love?*

But today, those thoughts were always in vain. He was gone. And she would never know what might have been.

Red Eagle was not a stupid man, though he was not insightful. But when he saw the distant expression on her face as she forced herself not to say the name of Dark Moon, he knew she had thought of him. And his anger began to surface.

"The year that Dark Moon died?" he asked, sneering.

She didn't answer.

"The year that Dark Moon died?" he asked again, more loudly.

"I was thinking of the cold," Calling Dove said, lying as he knew she was doing.

Suddenly, Red Eagle advanced on her, raising his hand to strike her, but he held back. She stood still, facing him, not cringing but not defiant. Instead, she was simply resigned to him and to the colorless, empty life that another beating would adorn.

"Only of the cold," she said, lying again.

The Ghost Hawk at Night

URING THE NIGHT, THE sounds of the forest seemed muted. It was cool and clear outside, but inside, the lodge was smoky and warm. Calling Dove's rest was troubled, but that was not unusual; she often heard things in the night. Sometimes, the sounds tormented her so that she would awaken sweating, her heart beating heavily.

There! It was above the lodge. Perhaps a squirrel. But at night? She fell back to sleep, then awakened again. She got up, left her husband's side, and quietly walked through the lodge to the entry. Everyone was asleep.

Outside, the whole camp was still. Tomorrow, it would rain. The trees rustled softly in the wind. Where are the squirrels? She looked around the lodge and saw nothing. No squirrels or mice...no animals. In the still night, there was no sign of life or movement. Even so, she felt almost as if she were dreaming.

Yet, there was something. Suddenly, she was startled by a strange movement in the darkness, a creature sitting atop the lodge.

There it stayed, watching her, but making neither sound nor movement. It was large, perhaps an owl? No, this seemed larger. When she called to it, it didn't move. Again, she called and it remained still. Then, she was frightened. What kind of large bird comes and rests on a lodge at night and makes not a sound?

She made a throwing motion with her arm. But it didn't move. She reached out and grabbed a stone to hurl at the creature. "Why do you come to me?" she called, holding the stone in her hand.

Then, impulsively, she threw the stone, hoping to frighten it away, yet it stayed. "Why do you come to me? What evil do you bring?" she called.

There was no answer, no movement—only now, she could see two yellow eyes peering at her from the darkness.

She returned uneasily to the lodge. Again, no one stirred. She lay down on her mat and tried to sleep but couldn't. Then, she heard a noise and the flapping of wings, and finally the fading call of a hawk. She lay her head down in silence.

Gentle Rain and Calling Dove

GENTLE RAIN CAME QUIETLY to the entrance of the lodge. She softly called the name of Calling Dove, and the door opened from the inside.

"Why did you not just come in?" Calling Dove asked the younger woman.

Gentle Rain shrugged. "I did not want to bother you, if you were busy."

"You are never a bother to me. Come, have some tea." Calling Dove gestured to the stool covered in deerskin. The girl quietly sat on the stool and waited wordlessly for Calling Dove to turn toward her with the hot tea.

Calling Dove could see that the girl was troubled. "You have not been here to see me for many suns," she said, handing the girl her bowl.

"I should have come. I wanted to—"

"But then, why did you not?"

"Because it seems that all I do is tell you my troubles," Gentle Rain said. "I know you must tire of hearing me complain."

Calling Dove was closer to this girl than she was to her own daughter. She never considered why it was so, but it was evident, as her own daughter was growing ever more remote from her as she grew older.

"I never tire of talking to you, ever since you were a small child," Calling Dove said. "You were always my favorite among the children of the Salt Springs. You know that."

Gentle Rain looked away, lowering her eyes to her hands folded in her lap. "I have always been honored by the attention you gave me," she said.

"So, what is your trouble? Is it my son?"

Gentle Rain didn't look up, didn't answer.

"What has he done?"

Gentle Rain was quiet, avoiding Calling Dove's eyes. The older woman stared at the girl. She was beautiful, but it was a quiet beauty that seemed to reflect her nature. It was only when someone knew her, knew the sweetness of her thoughts, that her beauty seemed to suddenly burst forth. Only then did one look at her eyes, her nose, her mouth, and realize how lovely her face was, with her skin the color of the afternoon sun.

Yet now, there were tears rolling down the flawless cheeks, unleashed by the closing of her eyelids.

"Did he strike you?" Calling Dove asked, more insistently.

"He has not done so in a while," Rain answered.

"But he has lied to you?"

Morning Rain took a deep breath, then nodded.

"Tell me," Calling Dove said.

The girl grimaced. "He does it so often, it is hard to tell you. This time, I was told that he slept with Rabbit Wing on the yellow moon. Then, when I asked him, he said he did not, and he grew angry and walked away." She hesitated for a few minutes, looking away from Calling Dove. "But several girls have told me that he did, that they saw them naked under a blanket."

Calling Dove nodded. "I have heard as much," she said, almost in a whisper. She studied the girl. She was exquisite, the only woman in the tribe who was her match in beauty. No wonder Gray Wolf gravitated toward her. There was no one in the Erierhonon who would seem a more suitable match for him.

"But," the girl said finally, "he lies to me, even when there is no need to do so. I do not question him or judge him. Yet he lies to me…over nothing."

Calling Dove's heart sank. The one truth she always hated to admit was what this girl expressed about her son. When she realized that he was an inveterate liar, she excused it by fantasizing that it was a normal part of young male behavior. And in her quiet moments, she would strive to banish the unwanted knowledge that he was just like his father.

But now this poor young woman, in all her innocence, was admitting to Calling Dove what she always forced herself to suppress. Her son was a liar, someone whose falseness was so ingrained that he was often unable to distinguish truth from falsity. Reality was only what he imagined, whatever suited his purpose. He was incapable of guilt…and yet she had brought him into the world.

But what would she do now? What does one do when she admits to herself the truth, that her husband, and now her son, are incapable of true love? If it ever existed, it vanished in the miserable years she spent being his proud wife and bearing Gray Wolf. This after she had brought forth another male child who did not survive even a week after birth. But being male and a survivor, Gray Wolf made his father the envy of every man in the Cat nation.

"He is just like his father," Calling Dove said finally to the girl.

Gentle Rain looked at Calling Dove, startled, amazed at what the older woman had just said. "Is the Great One truly like that?" she asked, grimacing at the very thought of what she was saying.

"His lies are as numerous as the stars in the heavens," said Calling Dove.

"Does he strike you?" the girl whispered.

"Does his son strike you?" Calling Dove asked in return.

The girl nodded.

"But why?" Gentle Rain said. "My father, my uncles, my brothers... They do not strike their wives, and they do not lie."

Calling Dove sighed and shook her head. "But there are some men who lie as easily as they talk. Their eyes can look into yours, and you would never know that they were lying."

"How can you stay with him?" the girl asked.

"Where can I go? I do not know medicine; I cannot weave; I am not a storyteller. Where would I sleep if I left this lodge? And when I am too old to gather wood, who will do it for me? Who will bring me food in the winter? These men? I sometimes feel that the great spirit is angry with us."

The girl was crying uncontrolled now. And Calling Dove, as much as she despaired of finding happiness for herself, pitied this sweet girl who, despite her innocence, would probably be destined for the same miseries that she, herself, endures.

Calling Dove went to the girl and held her in her arms. Suddenly, she held her away at arm's length. "Tell me something," Calling Dove whispered, still holding the girl to face her.

"Yes, what is it?" the girl asked, her face contorted into a frightened frown, dreading what Calling Dove would say.

"When you walk alone, do you ever hear..." But Calling Dove stopped, wondering if she should ask the girl about something that the girl might never have known or understood.

"I hear the cry of a hawk," the girl said softly.

Calling Dove closed her eyes and let her hands fall to her sides, away from the girl's shoulders.

"Do you hear it too?" asked Gentle Rain.

"It is called the Ghost Hawk, and I can hear it when no one else around me can."

"It is the same with me. None of my friends can hear what I hear. And I think sometimes that I am going mad. What does this mean? Why does it happen to us?"

Calling Dove shook her head, looking back at the girl. "I do not know," she said softly. Then, she turned and walked away a few paces, trying to imagine how all these strange visions could be coming to them together. She closed her eyes again, and her skin grew cold. She turned around to look at the anguished girl whose face still seemed to have questions for what Calling Dove knew and what she did not.

"Rain," said Calling Dove softly, "did you bleed this month?"

"No," the girl said, looking down away from Calling Dove's eyes.

"When was it due?" Calling Dove said.

"It is past due," the girl answered.

"Were you with a man in recent time?"

The girl hesitated.

"Who, Rain?"

"The only man I have ever been with is your son," Rain said.

Calling Dove wrapped her own arms around her head, forcing it downward as she fell to her knees, emitting a strange wail as she began to cry. The startled girl came to her, imploring her not to show such horror.

"He said I was to be his wife," Rain said as she touched the other woman's shoulder, and she shrugged. "I believed him."

Calling Dove reached for her and held her in her arms, still wailing softly and swaying back and forth.

"What is it? Do you not want me to be the mother of your grandchild?" said Gentle Rain.

Calling Dove didn't answer at first, then she said, "No, child, that is not my sorrow. I have loved you since the moment you were born. But—"

"But?"

"But do you not see? You and I are the only women in the Salt Springs who are haunted by the Ghost Hawk. None of the other women of the tribe can hear it but you and I. And what does that mean for us? Now you have a child within you, and still, we hear the hawk calling? There is something in these stories that binds us together. I am afraid there is anger that the Manitou has for us."

Cricket Learns of Snake

ONE LATE AFTERNOON, EVERYONE seemed to be subdued and quiet. Cricket wondered what Dark Moon was doing since he so seldom came to their lodge lately. She had not seen him the whole day and realized that he was deliberately staying away from her. She went outside to find him. He was alone in the small hut binding leather thongs for his journey. Dark Moon looked up as she entered.

"You come home with two strangers and never touch me, and never smile, hardly ever speak. And now I find you leaving our marriage bed to sleep in this…" She waved her arms around at the piles of wood.

He answered softly, "First of all, those children have never known the love of a family as all of our family has. Even I, who never had a mother until Snow Flower, was more fortunate than they. And even if your heart is against them…"

"I have never said one word against them," Cricket said. "Do you feel that much bitterness about me to imagine that? Did you not see me treat them with the warmth and love that I do our own children?"

"It was you who called them strangers," said Dark Moon. "And you must also know that if they were to continue their journey and not remain here safely under our care, they will surely die this winter—from cold, starvation, or from wandering marauders who kill for sport. They are as innocent and trusting as our own children…and equally as vulnerable."

She was quiet for a few seconds. What he said about the two new children was true, that he acted with his heart by bringing them to their home. But now there still seemed a kind of shadow that hid her vision of him. There had to be something else.

"I must go," she said quietly as she turned to leave the small shed.

"I will never leave you," Dark Moon said to her back.

Cricket leaned against a beam for support. "Please do not torture me so. If you must have her, then go to her and leave us alone."

He didn't answer. Neither of them moved, seeming not to know what to say or do. Suddenly, Cricket turned to leave.

Dark Moon said, "Snake will not come home, Cricket."

She turned to face him. "What did you say?" she whispered.

"Our brother is dead, little one."

Cricket stared, holding her hands to her ears, wishing she had never heard his words. Finally, she said, "What?"

"He and Two Bears were killed by renegades."

She screamed, waving her arms as if to banish him from her sight. He stood closely in front of her. "Leave me!" she screamed hysterically. "Go to your tall woman and leave me and your children. I care not. Is your scorn so great that you wish only to hurt me by saying such things?"

"It is the truth, though it hurts my heart tell you."

As she was crying, Dark Moon reached for her and she tried to push him away, struggling against him until she couldn't do it anymore. He held her tight to his chest until she grew still in his arms. Then, she spoke softly again, not raising her head to look at him.

"He is dead? Is it true?"

Dark Moon nodded. "I saw it myself. Wind and I came upon them as we rode the elk dog into their camp. I saw what they did to him and his son."

"But who? Who would kill someone so worthy? And why? What had he done to them?"

"Nothing. He was killed by men from the Salt Springs." Moon stopped for a moment, then shook his head. "I wish I knew why. Wind told me that he had seen my black knife before, worn by someone from his tribe. I told him that he could not have seen it, for Snake and I were the only ones who had such knives."

He stopped to take a deep breath before going on, "But when we searched your brother's body, his black knife was gone. The killers had taken it." He stopped again for several seconds. "Wind had seen it just a few suns earlier. The black knife was around the neck of Gray Wolf, the son of Red Eagle, the man who abandoned me, and who is now the chief of the Salt Springs. Wind has a wife and three children in the Salt Springs. He had to return to save them. If the men who killed Snake would sense that he knew of their treachery, Wind's family would surely be killed."

Cricket stared at him, then shook her head. "How am I to believe this fantasy that you are telling me? You have lied to me before."

"I have never lied to you," Dark Moon said. "And I would never say such words about Snake even if I hated you."

"You tell me so easily that you never think of Calling Dove, who I know you long for even after all these winters. You call her name in your sleep, and after all the lies you have told me."

"I have never lied to you," he whispered again.

"You go away, and you return with two children that you found in the forest. Then, you tell me that the brother I love is dead and that I will never see him again. You wander outside our lodge at night, you ask me to treat two strangers as though they were our own children, and you ask me to trust you when I know you long for Calling Dove because she forever torments your sleep."

"Do you really want to hear what I have seen?" Dark Moon said angrily. "He was destroyed! Wind and I burned the bodies ourselves." He gestured with his arm, pointing to the outside. "The ashes of your brother and his son are concealed in the wooden box in our lodge by our own bed. He was killed by the son of Red Eagle of the Salt Springs. And when we cleaned their camp after we had burned the bodies, we agreed to meet again at the Salt Springs on the next Moon of Falling Leaves."

"To do what? Will you not see the tall one?"

Dark Moon hung his head in frustration. In all the years he had known her, he had never seen this in her. *Did she always think of me as a liar?* he thought. *As someone who has made a fool of her and her love? Someone who thinks I love someone else, even as I sleep beside her in our bed?*

"I have brought the ashes of Snake and Two Bears to be buried here where he has given and received so much love, where your wonderful mother, who became the mother I never had, lies buried," Moon said. "Do you remember the many times I would fall, and each time he would pick me up and make me stand and try again? Do you think I could ever forget that? Have you always held this mistrust in your heart for me?"

"Then, why are you so intent upon leaving us?" Cricket asked.

"I must go back to get that black knife that was taken from your brother. I go also to accuse Red Eagle and his son for the evil that they imposed on Elk Calf's and Snake's families. Is that not valid reason? I told you that I would return. But it is something that I must do if I never do anything else again. I go not for the 'tall one,' but I go for vengeance. I will see their blood drip into the soil of the Salt Springs. And then, I will return. Because I know that your mother, Snow Flower, and Snake and Two Bears would rest among us."

Cricket started to walk away, then turned back to him. "You do not know what my mother would wish. But when you return with the tall one, I will go away and leave the girls so you may have them with you."

The Argument

IT TOOK HIM ALMOST a week to get ready for his trip to the Salt Springs, but finally, he was prepared. He had chosen two of the best and most sturdy elk dogs and made sure they were prepared for the journey.

He was in the small storage-room lodge where he spent most of his time during the day, and where he now passed all his nights. Whenever he and Cricket were together, they tried to seem civil to each other for the children's sake, but all the children knew that they were estranged. The girls, especially, were aware that something was wrong. They immediately sensed the self-imposed distance between them.

More importantly, now they knew that their parents did not even share the same marriage bed, that sacred place where Cricket and Dark Moon always kept them as children. Whenever they were sick or frightened, they could share the warmth of the two bodies of their parents, which always made them whole and safe.

They would often secretly discuss how disjoint the atmosphere of their camp had become. Parents who were known by everyone as loving and almost magically close, now only talked in terse and formal exchanges. None of them knew why, and Walker and Little Star dared not violate the dictate of Dark Moon by betraying his confidence to the others. And, in a way, it was also a shock to them because each had only a few ephemeral memories of their own family. There had been such turmoil before its disintegration that their family's life was only a dim memory. But after they had been absorbed into the lives of Dark Moon and Cricket, they finally knew what family love could be.

So, the atmosphere around the camp was strange but tolerable enough that everyone could do the work they had been assigned. And the courteous but reserved behavior of Cricket and Dark Moon was tolerable. Besides, the coming cold preparations occupied them. Everyone was busy. But Walker and Little Star were still troubled by what they saw as the disintegration of an obviously devoted family, the likes of which they had never known.

One day, Cricket approached her husband from behind as he stared at the evening sun, now falling below the horizon. "When will you leave, Moon?"

He shrugged.

"Will it be tomorrow?" Cricket asked.

"You have seen my preparations," he said. "Why are you asking me this?" His response was not friendly, nor was he smiling. He couldn't help thinking about how their partings used to be, and how heavy his heart always was to leave her. But this, above all other partings, would be different. In this one, he might never return, might never survive, and he was leaving sorrow and enmity behind him.

She shook her head, and tears filled her eyes. Each day since his return, their private exchanges had become more bitter and resentful. And suddenly, he did not want to reconcile anymore. He no longer cared if he said something that would hurt her. Now, for the first time since he had ever known her, his words were rough and angry.

"What is it you want?" he said coldly.

She closed her eyes and took a deep breath. She was not used to their talking that way. But she went on. "Blue Hat wishes to go with you," she said softly.

Moon snorted and shook his head to himself. "He is just a boy," he said roughly to her.

"But he is barely two winters younger than his brother, who is now gone."

"What could I say to him? He has lost a father and a brother by the work of savages. Should I tell him that he should not seek revenge on the killers? What if I am killed first? Would he not surely be destroyed? And would not Snake's two daughters ache forever for their loss?"

Cricket shook her head. "I don't want either of you to go on this journey. And yet, how could I lie to him that he should do nothing in revenge? He has lost a father and a brother."

"But you have said it to me! You call me a liar. You do not believe...do not listen to anything I tell you. Did you not say it these many times as I tried to tell you what was in my heart? You believed nothing of what I said. Liar! How easily the word fell off your tongue. And now you want to send a young boy who is unskilled as a fighter with me to his possible death, which would be certain if I am killed first."

Cricket held her hands to her ears as tears flowed down her face.

Moon was silent for a few moments, then he spoke again in an even harsher way than he had ever imagined he could. "You can save your tears, for I am sick of them. They mean nothing to me. Tell the boy I will take him if he wishes. He could ride the other elk dog."

Finally, Cricket said, "I just want you to protect him. He has lost so much."

"But you are talking to a liar, are you not? If he is killed, you know I will return here and tell lavish tales of how I valiantly tried to protect him. But in your heart, you will know I will be speaking falsely. That is my way, is it not?"

He paused for a few minutes but made no attempt to draw closer to her or to speak more calmly and with less anger.

"I will leave tomorrow," Moon said. "Tell him that he should pack for the journey. At dawn, I will feed and prepare the elk dogs. Then, we will depart."

She took a deep breath. "Dark Moon, you know that I wish you a safe journey and return. I—"

"No worry, Cricket. If I return, I will lie to you about my exploits. And I will keep the boy as safe as I can and tell you a fable of all the punishment I put on the Salt Springs chief. Who knows? Perhaps I can show Blue Hat how to lie also, so we can both pose as heroes in victory."

When Cricket heard him speak to her as he had never done in his life, she fell to her knees, her head bowed and silent.

He just stared at her. "You have done this before, and I have lifted you up. But not this time. I have only one duty that I must accomplish. I will bring back your brother Snake's black knife, and then you and I will be done with each other."

Talk of War

A few days later, Red Eagle came back to the Salt Springs earlier than expected. The Iroquois were coming into the great forest and hunting and trapping on the windward side of the endless mountains. It bothered him that the Iroquois were there, and some Onondaga and Oneida, hunting in the territory of the Erierhonon who had lived along the Mahoning and Chenango rivers forever. And though there was never a shortage of deer and bears and beavers, it was still troubling to share their abundance with strangers.

Could they be coming even as far as the valley of the Mahoning, even as far as the Salt Springs? There were many times when such hunting parties were destroyed by the Cats for having strayed too far into the Salt Springs.

All tribes knew that the land of the Salt Springs was that of the Cats. Only they were welcome there. No one else.

———◈⋆◈———

He walked into his lodge without saying a word and began undressing, and laying aside his bag and knife and ax.

"Are you hungry?" asked Calling Dove.

He shook his head.

"Are you well?" she continued.

"No one had good hunting this day."

"Only that? But you are not a hunter, and you seem troubled beyond your care for hunting."

"It is the Iroquois," Red Eagle said bitterly. "They have begun hunting and trapping on this side of the endless mountains."

"Are there many? Who told you this?"

"Some Wenro traders. They often sell to the Iroquois."

"But how many did they see?" she asked.

"Only a few. But when they encounter our abundance in these woods, they will come back often."

"And what will you do then?"

"Then, we will make war upon the Iroquois."

"War? Against so many? They are many times the number of Erierhonon."

"We have vanquished many times our number in other battles."

"But perhaps we can treat with them," Calling Dove suggested. "Perhaps trade. They may want to have more of the beaver and deer in the Mahoning Valley?"

"The land is ours," Red Eagle said emphatically. "They may come and trade with us, but they will not do their hunting in our forests."

"And how would you stop them?" she asked.

"Kill them. Let it be known that anyone who encroaches on the lands of the Salt Springs will die for their efforts."

"Will you sleep now?" she said, changing the subject.

"Yes," he said, lowering himself to the bed, where blankets were arrayed.

"Would you like me to sleep with you?" Calling Dove asked.

He shook his head. "I am tired," he said.

In a few minutes, Calling Dove felt relief as she heard Red Eagle's soft snoring. She did not want to sleep with him. Making love was a labor for her as much as it was merely relief for him. She didn't enjoy it. It had become a dreary duty that she performed less and less often as time passed.

The worst of it was that, when they were first married, the exultation she expected never lasted. All the girls of the tribe talked about it, about what it would be like. That yellow moon, when she slept with Red Eagle, there was at least the excitement of doing something mysterious and thrilling for the first time. But it was unfulfilling still, and she could not understand why. Somehow, the shadow of Dark Moon hovered over all her musings.

It also troubled her that she was disappointed because the excitement and passion that she expected somehow never came. Could it be her fault? But how and why? Could it be his?

Red Eagle was handsome and gifted, the dream of every girl her age. His body was lean and graceful. But it troubled her to realize that their love-making never achieved the promise that, for all his physical gifts, Red Eagle could not deliver. Perhaps he did not know how to be a good lover. Perhaps he felt that his body alone was gift enough, or that there could be anything more than what he had to offer. Or perhaps it was that she, despite her own physical gifts, lacked something that did not stir Red Eagle to feel that he was favored more than any other man in the Salt Springs, to have a wife that made even the Manitou jealous.

Whatever it was, as their passion waned over the years, their lovemaking diminished from expectation to unfulfillment to merely relief.

Wind was the tribe's best hunter. And Calling Dove could see that "something," that look that Shadow Cat and Wind shared in their marriage. Many of her own married friends would sometimes still talk of making love in amazed and joyous tones. Though Wind was neither as tall or imposing as Red Eagle, he and his wife seemed to have joy beyond anything that she and Red Eagle ever dreamed.

How could such things happen?

The Children Learn of
Snake and Two Bears

T HE DAY AFTER DARK Moon left, Cricket assembled all the children in her lodge. Everyone but Star and Walker was unaware of the loss of Snake and Two Bears. They both sat quietly on the edge of the group and listened as Cricket told them the terrible news that she had relayed the night before to Blue Hat when he left with Dark Moon.

In all their young lives, none of the children had ever experienced the loss of a dear loved one. Cricket tearfully and gently conveyed the idea that though the loss of their loved ones was hurtful, the departed ones were now at the camp of the Manitou, where they would be content and loved.

After two days of weeping and mourning, and with the quiet, consoling words of Cricket to give them comfort, the children began to sense the beginning of relief and consolation. Even Cricket herself felt some comfort as she convinced the children that their uncle and cousin were happy with their beloved grandmother, Snow Flower, in the garden of the Manitou.

As the days passed, the children's lives seemed slowly to return to normal. And all of them, including Star and Walker, could feel comfort from the closeness that they all shared with each other.

That closeness also affected Cricket. She thought long and hard about her life and how barren it had become, and she realized that not only had she lost her brother and mother, but also she had forced the loss of Dark Moon.

Red Eagle Hurts Calling Dove

R ED EAGLE WAS DRINKING tea as he sat in his lodge. It had been a restless night. He would sleep a short while, then awaken. And if he did fall back to sleep, he always awoke a short time later.

Calling Dove came in from outside. She carried breakfast of deer meat and bread.

"How do you feel now?" she asked, unsmiling.

Red Eagle didn't answer. He just looked at her as she carried a tray with the food.

"Do you need more tea?" she asked as she set the tray in front of him.

He still didn't answer and didn't turn to face her. She stayed by him for a few seconds, then turned away. He took a bite of food, then, without a word, threw the tray, and all the food, across the room.

Calling Dove screamed, "Have you gone mad? I was awake early to prepare this. You ungrateful man! What is your trouble?"

"You trouble me," he growled. "You cook the same food every morning. I am sick of it."

"I cook what we have," Calling Dove replied. "What the hunters return, what every member of the tribe has."

"But I am the chief," he said. "Should I not have something more to eat than any child or old woman?"

"But you know that has always been the way among the Cats. The chief eats as the others eat, the way our children and all the people do."

"Our children should have more than other orphans and old enfeebled ones. They did nothing to deserve to eat as the rest of us, as grown men do."

"Would you starve our children?" she asked. "How could you say such a thing?"

"They are not my children. Only you call them that. Most are the children of my dead brother."

"You promised him that you would raise them as your own, yet now you treat them as though they were strangers wandering in from the forest."

"The chief should never have to feed his own children the same as those abandoned children without mothers or fathers," Red Eagle said.

"I knew one who was found wandering through the forest and was brought to the Salt Springs," Calling Dove said. "He never had a mother, yet he grew up among us, becoming a great hunter, beloved of many...and the Salt Springs never had hunger as long as he and Wind provided for us."

Red Eagle snorted. "And you still dream of that hunter, do you not? How many nights do you lie awake dreaming that it was Dark Moon sleeping beside you instead of me?"

"You know nothing of what I dream...nothing of what is in my heart."

"I know that you tried to raise all these children to hate me."

"The children learn to hate you on their own," Calling Dove said. "You treat them as though they were beggars who constantly seek food and affection from you. And you make it seem that they are a burden that you cannot wait to dismiss from our lodge, that they do not belong here."

"It is you who have turned them against me," Eagle said. "You always make it seem that I am the source of all their grief."

"There was nothing to turn. They saw you please the children of those women you have lain with more than themselves. Gray Wolf was not treated so because he is your only true son, and now he has become what you are—a dog prowling after its aunts and mothers."

"Be quiet, woman," he said. "I am sick of hearing you."

"You listen to the foolish talk of the women you sleep with. But not words from me or your own children."

"I have told you, they are not my own children!" Red Eagle shouted. "My only children are Gray Wolf and our daughter. You could give me no others."

"You barely know their names as it is, and you are not ashamed when you call them by names of the other women's children, those you sleep with, to your shame," Calling Dove said.

He stood up and stared at her. "Silence!" he said angrily.

"I will not be silent in my own lodge!" she yelled.

"You will be silent whenever I tell you, wherever I tell you."

"Is the Great One now the lord of all the sky? Are you equal to the Manitou? No, I forget myself," she said with a smirk. "You think you are the Manitou."

He hesitated only a few seconds, then lashed out at her, hitting her fully in the face and causing blood to flow from her split lip. She fell down in front of him but didn't make a sound for several seconds.

Then, she said, "You may now boast how you, the Great One, have beaten a woman, and point to my face as a symbol of your magnificence. The great woman beater."

This time, he kicked her in the side, and she was really hurt. She cried softly as the pain became almost unbearable. He spat on her and walked out of the lodge.

Dark Moon Returns

THE TWO MEN RODE until Dark Moon waved for them to stop.

"Are we there, Uncle?" asked Blue Hat wearily. He was still enfeebled from the terrible news of the loss of his father and brother.

"Yes, my boy," Moon said. "But this is where you must stay. Look there. Do you see the smoke from their fires? Do you see the lodges?" Blue Hat nodded. "You must keep watch from that boulder…" Dark Moon pointed to a place where the boy could hide yet see all the sites in the camp. "I will go to that ridge on my elk dog where I could be seen easily from the camp."

"You want them to see you, Uncle?"

"Yes. Because they will think I am a ghost, and that will enable me to avenge your father."

"But what if they come to attack you? I do not think I can bear the loss of another loved one."

Dark Moon sighed. "Have courage, my boy. Your father and brother are watching us, and they will witness our victory. But this battle cannot be fought in the usual way, by you and me against their multitude. I must keep the battle only between them and me—the chief and his son. If I win, then the truth will help us to victory, because both father and son will be revealed as liars and cowards. I am hoping that the people of the

Salt Springs, once they realize that they have been deceived for seventeen winters, will realize that those men are not worth fighting for."

"Do you think they will realize that?" asked Blue Hat.

"It is my hope," said Dark Moon. "Besides, there is one man among them who will tell them the truth. He is the other best friend of my life, called Wind."

—————————◆◆◆◆◆—————————

Wind was inside their lodge, sorting his arrows and repairing others that could be salvaged. It was a quiet and peaceful day. Shadow Cat was being helped by their two daughters preparing for the evening meal. His son, a boy of twelve winters, was outside playing in a ballgame with his friends. The late afternoon was clear and warm.

Suddenly, there seemed to be commotion outside. He could hear people running past his lodge. Shadow Cat looked up from her work with the same questioning look that Wind had. He walked to the entry and drew back the skins. He saw what seemed to be the whole tribe running but not rioting yet seeming for purpose. There was no violence, just hurried motion.

"There is a creature on the long hill," one man said.

Both Wind and Shadow Cat proceeded to run with the crowd toward the strange sight. When they got to the bottom of the long hill, all the tribe seemed to be collected at its base, looking upward at the creature.

"What is that?" someone in the crowd asked him.

Wind looked up at the strange sight. It was Dark Moon, astride one of his horses, still and quiet as he peered into the valley.

Wind turned to his wife and whispered, "It is Dark Moon."

Shadow Cat was trying to guess what the crowd was seeing. They knew that it was a man dressed as they often did for their own ceremonies. But he was silent and motionless as he stared at the throng before him.

Soon, Red Eagle's son came forward through the crowd. Calling Dove was walking behind him with a proud look, almost defying anyone to ask about her cut lip and swollen face.

When Red Eagle turned back to her, he said in a low, menacing voice, "I told you to stay in the lodge. Have you no shame to show yourself this way?"

"I just wanted to see the strange vision that all these people were seeing," she said defiantly. "I do not care if they ask me how I came to have it. Do you not want them all to see what the Great One does to his wife?"

"Silence, demon!" Red Eagle raised his hand as if to strike her, but then he realized that those standing nearby were now watching them.

Suddenly, someone shouted, "Look! It gestures!"

No one but Wind and Shadow Cat knew who the creature was, and they said nothing. Someone else shouted, "He gestures! It is the sign of the coward."

"What is that creature he sits on?" someone in the crowd yelled.

Everyone knew that the question was meant for Red Eagle.

"Father," whispered Gray Wolf, "have you ever seen such a creature?"

"Once I heard someone from another tribe near the mountains tell of a creature that a man can ride like the wind," said Red Eagle. "But I believed it was his fancy—a dream. I have never seen such."

The crowd seemed to become louder and more insistent. "What is that creature?" became the murmur throughout the group. "What will we do, my chief?"

Again, the vision made the gesture of the coward. Gray Wolf had never had that experience. He grew up in an era when his father was respected without question as the Great One of the Erierhonon. But his legend came before any doubts about his worth or authority. Now, many of them looked to him for protection, or at least to ease their minds about what this invader could be. And, if he was a threat, what would Red Eagle do?

"Father," said Gray Wolf, after hearing the murmurings of the crowd, "let me attack this man. He may sit on that strange creature, but he cannot withstand one of my blows unless he is a spirit."

The crowd was getting more fearful after each gesture that the vision made. The man on the creature kept gesturing the sign of a coward. Suddenly, an unseen woman yelled to Red Eagle, "What does he want from us? Who is the coward that he signals? Is it someone from this tribe? My chief, what does he seek? Who is he?"

Suddenly, Wind walked forward and stood at the base of the hill a few yards away from the gathering of all the Salt Springs people. He was slightly elevated so that he could be seen by everyone. Then, he shouted out, "You who are not children should know him! I will remind you because you knew him well. He is Dark Moon of the Erierhonon, one of us from the Salt Springs."

"Do not speak nonsense," cried one woman. "If it is Dark Moon, it is only his ghost!"

"Yes, nonsense! Dark Moon is long dead!" another shouted.

But upon hearing Wind, who was held in great esteem by almost everyone in the Salt Springs, the group was suddenly confused.

"Are you telling us that Dark Moon still lives?" asked one man who was elderly and a friend of Wind.

Wind gazed over the crowd. The entire Salt Springs tribe was suddenly aroused and disoriented. Over his shoulder, far up the hill, the creature stood mounted on the horse but was still unmoving except for the occasional gesture of cowardice.

"All of you my age knew him well!" Wind shouted. "He is Dark Moon of the Salt Springs."

"You speak nonsense!" shouted one of Red Eagle's supporters. "Dark Moon is dead."

"From whom did we hear that Dark Moon was dead, that he was killed by a great bear? Yet, there he is. Dark Moon of the Salt Springs." Wind gestured with his thumb over his shoulder.

"How do you know that the creature is not a spirit vision?" said another one of Red Eagle's comrades.

"Ask your chief," said Wind, gesturing toward Red Eagle. "He knows that Dark Moon lives."

"I know not of Dark Moon!" Red Eagle shouted to the crowd.

"But you have said that he was eaten by a golden bear, did you not?" asked Wind. "And that you burned the remains of Dark Moon after you slew the bear with his own bow, the one you have in your lodge today? Did you not tell us that lie?"

When Gray Wolf heard the murmurings of the crowd in response to Wind's appeal, he grew angry, especially toward a man he disliked because of his easy acceptance by all the Salt Springs as a heroic figure, and a great friend of the legendary Dark Moon. He grabbed an ax and started walking toward Wind, but as he advanced, he was unaware that the creature on the horse had an arrow poised for release. No one was worried about the threat of an arrow from so far away. The distance was too great.

Wind, as Gray Wolf advanced toward him, was unarmed. He reached instinctively toward his sash, but he realized that his ax was gone.

Calling Dove, knowing that Wind was always a fierce fighter from her memories of long ago when he and Dark Moon were hunters, screamed, "No, Gray Wolf! Do not do that! My son, no!"

Gray Wolf hesitated before taking another step toward his victim, and stopped and turned toward his mother. Just then, an arrow from the sky suddenly sounded to everyone nearby as it pierced the neck of Gray Wolf. When he was struck, he turned in disbelief toward his mother and father. He never in his life had been thwarted in doing anything at all.

But the arrow had brought instant death to him as he looked at his father and asked, "How?"

Red Eagle ran to his son and grabbed him as he fell to earth. "No!" he screamed. "My son! No! No!"

Calling Dove ran to their sides as the crowd was aghast and fearful at what had just happened, the terrible death that had just taken place.

"Why?" she screamed at Red Eagle. "Why did this happen? What have you done?" She was merely voicing the question that all the members of the tribe were now thinking.

Red Eagle's world had suddenly fallen apart. The life he was living as the Great One, honored by all the Erierhonon, was suddenly gone. He let Gray Wolf's lifeless body rest on the ground and stood up to face Calling Dove.

As he did, Wind spoke out so everyone could hear, "You know, Red Eagle, that there is only one man who can shoot an arrow from that distance. That is Dark Moon sitting on an elk dog at the top of the hill." Then, he turned toward the crowd. "I tell you all. Dark Moon still lives, and that is his arrow of vengeance upon Gray Wolf, who killed Dark Moon's brother and his son without mercy—a man and his young son, a mere boy of sixteen winters. The black knife that you have all seen him wear around his neck was stolen from Dark Moon's brother, who was the brother of his wife. When Dark Moon married, his wife's mother presented Dark Moon and that brother with two identical knives—this one that Gray Wolf stole, and the one that Dark Moon still has around his neck. Today, Dark Moon has come for that black knife."

Calling Dove was almost crazed when she heard Wind's story. She turned toward Red Eagle and said, "How could you lie to us all…to me, especially? You told us that you slew the bear and burned Dark Moon's ashes."

"In fact," Wind shouted, "he left Dark Moon, who had just rescued him from sure death as he clung to the cliffside and would have fallen because there was no way he could have ever found a way to climb! When

Dark Moon was exhausted from saving Red Eagle, he knelt down from his efforts of pulling the rope. It was then that the great bear attacked him, moments after Dark Moon had rescued Red Eagle by pulling him to safety at the top of the hill. He had Dark Moon's bow and arrow right at his fingertips and yet did nothing to stop the bear as he attacked his rescuer. He stood by as the bear destroyed Dark Moon, then he turned and ran away. A coward."

There were gasps and loud murmurs from the crowd. When Calling Dove realized the truth, she screamed at Red Eagle, "Then the sign of the coward is true! You are the coward. You have lied to gain all of our trust."

"Dark Moon killed the great bear," said Wind, "but today, he must walk with a limp. He was saved by a girl, who later became his wife, and her brother, the man that this wretch, Gray Wolf, killed. Their mother was a healer of great wisdom, and they saved Dark Moon's life. It took more than two winters before he was able to walk but a few steps." Wind stopped for a few moments as he scanned the crowd that was listening to the lurid story. Then, he continued, "But there is something else. Red Eagle himself is also a killer without mercy. It was he who slaughtered Elk Calf's small tribe that some of us remember in friendship. Men, women, children, even animals were slaughtered as though they were a group of geese or turkeys. I was there to see the devastation, and so was Dark Moon."

By then, everyone was so horrified by Wind's story that the death of Gray Wolf seemed justified. Calling Dove was so stricken that she stood beside her son's body and screamed at Red Eagle, "Coward! Coward! You have lived on the lies you told us all. You are the Great One only through lies. Now, our only son lies dead at your feet, because you allowed him to grow as a liar and a killer in your own image."

By then, the chant arose from the gathered crowd, and they screamed, "Liars! Killers! Shame!"

Red Eagle was unable to deal with the revelations coming out about what he did. It had unraveled his life so much that everyone could see what a wretch he truly was. All the years he basked in glory and fame were now revealed to be shame born of cowardice and murder.

When he heard Calling Dove call him a liar and a coward once again, in front of all of the Salt Springs, he took his ax from his cincture and struck her in the neck. She cursed him in that moment before she fell dead near her son.

Red Eagle, with the blood of his ax covering his hands, turned toward the crowd. "I am the chief, the Great One. I will kill anyone who says that I am not. I have always been a warrior, and you have known my leadership. You are safe in your lodges at night only because of me. And if you listen to these weaklings, you will someday find our tribe overrun by marauders who wish to steal the Salt Springs from us. And he," Eagle said, pointing to Wind with the bloody ax still in his hand, "is the one you must blame for bringing all this misery and misfortune."

Red Eagle paused for a few more seconds, then started toward Wind, who had no weapon with him. Before he came within ten yards of Wind, Red Eagle was struck by another one of Dark Moon's arrows. The large shaft came into his chest from one side and protruded through the other side. He took one more step...and fell dead.

The moment Red Eagle fell, a huge brown hawk flew over the scene of the Salt Springs tribe assembled and let out fierce cries as it flew, over and over again, each time emitting one loud shriek after another.

This time, Wind also heard the hawk, just as everyone else did, and he looked up at Dark Moon and pointed to the hawk overhead. Each time as it drew near, the people of the Salt Springs gazed fearfully at the creature as it passed. Wind nodded to Dark Moon and waved his arm, calling him to join them.

Shadow Cat ran to Wind and hugged him with tears streaming from her eyes.

"Let us go, my love," she said. "This place will never be home for us again. Not ever."

The Journey

FORTY-NINE PEOPLE TRUDGED wearily through the forest as they headed north toward Dark Moon's camp. The two horses carried loads of home goods, tools, and garden implements for the families. Dark Moon and Wind had spent lifetimes on foot, but almost everyone else, especially the women and children, were not used to distant travel, especially on long treks through the woodland forest.

"It will take us several more days to reach our camp," said Dark Moon to Wind. "The two old ones and the lame child, especially, and all these children are exhausted each night when we rest."

"I have forgotten how long the journey was for people who do not often travel from their homes, as you and I did," said Dark Moon.

"But is it not painful for you?" asked Wind.

Dark Moon shrugged. "I have been walking the forest all my life, so even though I am sore sometimes when we rest, I usually feel better in the morning."

Wind looked at his wife as she helped her mother through the thick part of the forest. "I think she will be a good friend to your Cricket."

"I very much wish it so. My wife took her brother's death with such pain that our marriage has been greatly strained."

"How so? Surely, she does not blame you for the massacre done by savage killers? Will she not be happy to know the story we have just witnessed?"

Dark Moon huffed. "I am not sure. I know she will be pleased that two killers are dead, but..." He hesitated to say it. "But she thinks that I have love for Calling Dove. When she and her brother found me and brought me back to health with her mother's medicine, I would call out names in my sleep. I would call your name and my father's. But I also called out such names as Calling Dove and Red Eagle because I kept dreaming of the bear and Red Eagle, wondering how he could have done what he did. And in my dreams, I knew he would be chief, and that he would have Calling Dove. So, now, Cricket is convinced that I still long for Calling Dove, even though, since the moment I ever saw her, I knew my heart belonged to Cricket. She is a blessing and the joy of my life. I thank the Manitou every night that I did not end up with Calling Dove. But now I believe she is done with me. So, I must stay away from her."

"But you cannot!" said Wind. "This is madness. If you love her, you must not let her go."

Dark Moon shook his head. "I do not know, Wind. She has withdrawn. She does not care if she ever sees me again."

"But what will she say when we return?"

"Blue Hat, who you see helping that elder man over there, is the son of Snake. She will rejoice when she sees him. I know she will welcome all of you because she knows of our long friendship and the kind of man you are. But I cannot enter our camp." Dark Moon reached into a sack and took out the black knife. "Would you give this to her? I know this would be more meaningful than anything else. And tell her that I kept my promise."

Wind shook his head in exasperation. "Dark Moon—"

"Please, Wind. I ask you this with my heart. I cannot go back. I will travel to a place farther north that I have sometimes hunted in the last seventeen winters. I will still be nearer to all of you than I was, and you and I will still hunt from time to time."

"When will you go?" sighed Wind.

"I will help the old ones because they will not be able to keep up with all of you. And when they are nearby the camp, I will guide them forward...then I will depart."

"Moon, this is wrong. Come back with me. You know we all want you with us, just as you and I have been together since we were children. Even if she is unwilling, we need you. You took the yoke from our shoulders without a war. You killed the two men that did not deserve to live. You have ridden the Ohio of a curse."

"Wind, I cannot stand living in the same camp where she is a stranger to me. I cannot watch her outside coming and going, yet acting like she has never seen me before."

"But surely, in any marriage, there are disputes. Always, when there is love between the partners, there is a way to solve differences."

"The differences are resolved because of love between the two," said Dark Moon. "But when that love is gone, differences become unmendable." Dark Moon paused for a few seconds. "Do you think there was love between Red Eagle and Calling Dove?"

Wind shook his head. "It is hard to believe that love ever existed between them. They spoke to each other with such malice. When a man kills his wife as though she were a small creature from the forest, there could not have been love."

"But how does happiness turn to hate? I always felt that Cricket was the greatest gift of the Manitou to me, though I was undeserving. And yet, we are now strangers. There must be some way that happiness can be replaced by hatred." He paused. "No, Wind, I have to go."

"Moon, I have known you all your life," Wind said. "Do you really think that what you had with Cricket was just like what Calling Dove and Red Eagle had? You always knew the Red Eagle was a man without honor.

In your heart, despite the fire in your loins, you knew that Calling Dove was not the kind of woman that a man could give his heart to. She was never like your Cricket or my Shadow Cat. She lived from her outside, because there was an emptiness within her, something that a good man deserves that she was unable to give."

"You are right, Wind," Dark Moon said. "But if I cannot be with Cricket, then I cannot see her every day, going on with her life and never needing or thinking of me. I have to go. You know I will be near enough to come to your aid whenever it is needed. You have but to send for me."

Cricket was outside, waiting for the rocks to be heated by the fire enough to cause the water in the pot to boil. The children all seem to be occupied with their daily duties, some gathering water, some harvesting vegetables from the garden, while the two boys tended to the horses, especially the newly born ones to keep them from predators.

She thought she heard something, a faint noise from the forest, not something like daily animal sounds. After a short while, the sounds grew more intense and more like the sounds of humans. Finally, she could see movement in the distance. Men, women, and children were walking toward her camp.

Wind emerged from the group, leading them toward her compound. When Wind saw Cricket, he held up his hand to stop the group. "Stay here," he said to them. "I must tell her that we mean no harm."

He walked alone up the long, slight grade to the campground. Cricket sensed immediately that he meant no harm, so she waited.

"I am Wind, of the Erierhonon," he said. "These people and I are from the Salt Springs, and we wish to join you in your peaceful camp. I am a lifelong friend of Dark Moon."

She closed her eyes as her heart sank. Surely, Dark Moon was dead, or he would have been leading this group. She fell to her knees without responding to Wind. He immediately advanced to help her up. Her eyes were full of tears as he helped her stand.

"Is he dead?" she said softly.

In that instant, Wind knew that she was still Dark Moon's gift from the Manitou.

"No," said Wind. "He lives in good health."

"Then where is he?" Cricket asked, wiping the tears from her eyes. "Did he stay with Calling Dove?"

"No, he is with us, but he is with other families in our group. There are ones who need help walking, so he remained with them. They are perhaps one sun behind us."

"So, he is not injured?" she asked. "He is coming forth?"

Wind nodded.

"With her?" she continued.

"He is not with her. Calling Dove no longer walks this earth."

"She is dead?" Cricket whispered.

"Yes. Red Eagle killed her."

She frowned. "Did anyone see it?"

Wind sighed. "Everyone saw it. It was before the eyes of the whole tribe. But I do not want to talk about it now. There are many people at the bottom of this hill behind me that are weary and hungry. We have no place to go. Dark Moon has asked us to settle here among you and your family. He said that you would accept us. Will you do so?"

"There are old or sick ones among you?" she asked.

"Yes. My wife's mother, another old woman, and a lame child," he said.

She drew her breath. "Bring the old women and the crippled child first. You are all welcome. We will talk later. My children will prepare food for all of you. We have lodges enough to feed and shelter you, and we will build more lodges for families to live together."

By night, the travelers had been fed and parceled out to sleeping quarters, and it seemed that everyone was comfortable and safe indoors. Cricket, when the children were resting and all was quiet, walked outside her lodge to breathe some fresh air. When she did, she could see Shadow Cat. Cricket gestured for her to approach. Shadow Cat nodded and came forward.

"Is everyone provided for?" Cricket asked.

"Yes," said Shadow Cat. "We thank you for your kindness. Are you certain that you are willing to let us live among you?"

Cricket nodded assent. "Your husband and Dark Moon have been friends since their childhood...more like brothers than just friends."

"I learned the story of your brother and his son, and it is fitting that their murder was avenged," Shadow Cat said. "They turned on each other."

"Calling Dove and her husband?" said Cricket.

"Yes. He killed her before the eyes of all of us—the whole Salt Springs tribe."

"But why do it thus, before the eyes of everyone?"

"Dark Moon stayed away at the top of a hill," Shadow Cat said. "When my husband told the people that Dark Moon lived, Calling Dove went mad and called Red Eagle a liar and a coward. He struck her with his own ax; one blow and she was dead. Then, when he turned to strike my husband, who had called out his lies to the crowd, Dark Moon killed him with an arrow, as he had killed their son, Gray Wolf, earlier. When the tribe heard of their treachery, Red Eagle was certain that he had lost their favor. All he could do was to strike out at his wife and my spouse, who was unarmed with a weapon. He was a coward until his end."

"And Dark Moon killed him as he was about to attack your husband?" said Cricket.

Shadow Cat nodded. "My husband had addressed all the people and told them of the treachery of father and son, so it was natural that he would attack a man who did not have any weapons of war on him."

"That was when Dark Moon struck him?"

"Yes."

The two women were silent for a few minutes, just standing, looking at each other. Finally, Cricket spoke, "When will the others arrive?"

Shadow Cat grimaced. "I think by night tomorrow."

Cricket sensed her hesitation to answer. "What are you thinking?" she asked.

Shadow Cat shook her head, unwilling to answer.

"What is it?" Cricket repeated.

"Dark Moon will not be among them," she said.

"How do you know? Is there something wrong with him?"

"He told Wind that he would not return. He would only bring the other families and their old ones to this place, but he would not enter."

"But where would he go?" Cricket asked.

"I know not," Shadow Cat answered. "When Wind tried to convince him to stay..." She stopped speaking. She shook her head, unwilling to proceed.

"Wind tried to make him stay?"

"Yes," she whispered softly.

Cricket waited for her to continue, but Shadow Cat shook her head again and stopped. "Did he say why?" Cricket asked.

Shadow Cat simply looked at her. "You must know why," she said.

It suddenly dawned upon Cricket just what Wind and Shadow Cat were hesitating to say.

"Please tell me," Cricket said softly, her eyes filled with tears. Shadow Cat huffed softly. "Please," Cricket whispered.

"He told Wind, who had tried to dissuade him, that he could not live in a place where he would see you daily and never be able to touch you or even speak to you," Shadow Cat said. "He said that he could never make you believe that he loved you and never cared if he ever saw Calling Dove again."

Cricket held her head in her hands, moaning softly and crying. Shadow Cat embraced her and held her in her arms as she sobbed against her shoulder. "My dear," she said, "what can we do to help you?"

Without looking up at her, Cricket said, "All my life, I have tried to live according to my mother's teaching. To be kind…and just…and faithful. But at the most important time to do just that, I rejected the one person I have loved more than life itself. I would never believe that he would love me more than someone as beautiful and striking as Calling Dove." She hesitated for a few seconds. "When he told me that he did love me when he returned with my brother's ashes, I acted as though he was false, a liar, unlike anything I had ever known about him. And now I know that the worst act I have ever done in my life was to spurn the love that he pledged to me so often. When the time came to trust and believe in him, I failed. I will be cursed by the Manitou for not trusting in love, from him to me and from my own heart to his."

Cricket began sobbing again.

Shadow Cat held her in an embrace as she cried against her shoulder. "This cannot be," she said. "There is too much love between you for you to be apart. Come with me."

She lifted Cricket and guided her toward the lodge where Wind was resting. She called to him, and he came outside quickly, astonished to see the crumpled, helpless figure in Shadow Cat's arms.

"What is happening?" said Wind.

"We cannot let Dark Moon go away," said Shadow Cat to her husband. "They love each other too dearly to be apart. We must take her to him."

Wind looked at Cricket and held the black knife before her. "He made me promise to give you this."

271

The next evening, the rest of the party arrived at the camp, earlier than expected. Dark Moon was not with them. Wind gave instructions to some of his hunting partners on how to get the new people accommodated. Then, he asked one of the men he trusted to make sure that his wife's mother was comfortable.

Walker brought two horses for them to ride. Cricket and Shadow Cat would ride on one, and Wind would lead on the other. One of the new arrivals told Wind that Dark Moon could not have gone far because he was up often during the night to help the old ones. He did not get much rest.

Wind was told that Dark Moon left for the northwest. So, he and the two women set out to find Dark Moon's trail. It would be fairly easy to do for an experienced hunter like Wind. Dark Moon was tired and not in search of a prey, so he traveled on foot without concern about the path he left behind.

After about an hour, Wind turned to both women who were on the horse behind his and said, "I think we will be near to him in a short time."

Cricket who was, by now, an experienced rider, urged the horse to trot faster to keep up with Wind as he traveled ahead. Suddenly, he stopped and put his finger to his lips as he faced them. He dismounted and helped Shadow Cat dismount. He pointed into the forest, off the trail that they were traveling.

"He will be just ahead of where we are now. It is not far, especially for the elk dog to carry you. I'm sure he is resting. Do not startle him, Cricket. And call out, especially if you see him raise his arrow toward you."

Shadow Cat reached up as Cricket bent over to her and kissed her. She said, "You know what you must say to him. I hope that the Manitou blesses you both, and you return to us together as husband and wife, as you were always meant to be."

———◆·▶◀·◆———

Cricket rode about a hundred yards toward the point where she smelled smoke. Then, she dismounted and tied the horse to a tree and quietly walked toward the fire smell that she sensed was ahead.

Dark Moon was sleeping soundly, but he had learned over a lifetime of hunting to react to any unusual sound or smell or movement, even in his sleep. And though he slept, the small crackling sound of something walking toward him instantly made him awake. In a few minutes, he saw her. At first, he thought he could only be dreaming to see Cricket coming toward him.

"What is wrong?" he said to her, almost frightened by what she would answer.

"There is nothing wrong," she said. "Except that you did not return as you said you would."

"I said that I would return the black knife to you, and I did."

"Why did you give it to Wind to return it, and not do so yourself?"

"Because I did not want to see you."

"Were you afraid? Or was it because you hated to look at me?"

He snorted. "What are you doing here?"

"I told you," Cricket said. "I want to know why you did not bring me the black knife."

"You know why!"

"I do not. In seventeen winters, you have never been afraid of me. Why could you not face me today?"

"Because I am tired...and have no more need of punishing myself."

"Seeing me punishes you?"

Dark Moon huffed in frustration. "Why would I continue to see someone who hates me?"

"Are you certain that is true?"

He shook his head. "Why else would you come, except to cause me misery?"

Cricket took a deep breath. "I have come to tell you that I am sorry... for all the things I have done to you—blaming you for desiring Calling Dove and forgetting how much you gave meaning to my life. I have never known true happiness until you came to me as a victim of the bear."

"I implore you," Dark Moon said softly. "Say nothing more if you do not mean every word I hear."

"I mean all of it and should have said it to you long ago," she said. "I should never have blamed you for the grief that I felt at Snake's loss. I had no one else to blame, so I let it be you...to my everlasting sorrow."

He just looked at her. "Please do not say these things if you do not wish to spend your life with me. I miss you more than the air I breathe and the water I drink. I will not live if I know that you are mocking me with these words."

Cricket walked over to him and stood closely before him, looking up into his eyes. "I want you to come back to me...to forgive me for my lack of faith in you. I want you to know, even though it does not seem so, that I have never stopped loving you. And in the winters that we have left in our lives, I want, every day, to waken and reach out and touch you as you lie beside me. Have you ever stopped loving me?"

Dark Moon huffed and smiled. "Can one love and hate someone at the same time?"

"Do you still hate me?" she asked anxiously.

He snorted and shook his head. "I have never hated you, even though you drive me mad sometimes."

"No woman wants a mad husband," Cricket said, smiling playfully for the first time. "So, will you let me try to keep you from growing insane, Crooked Leg?"

He smiled. "Will you love me, even in front of all these new people in our lives?"

"I will love you as I always have…since I found you under the bear."

"You have met Wind and Shadow Cat, then?"

"Yes. They brought me to you. They are together, waiting for us now." She pointed. "Over there."

When they arrived, Wind and Shadow Cat knew they had saved two people in love from the abyss of loneliness. Shadow Cat ran to Dark Moon and kissed him, while Wind kissed Cricket.

"Let us go make our camp a home for happy memories," said Dark Moon.

About the Author

 DONALD GRECO grew up in Youngstown, Ohio, and has lived in Ohio all his life, fulfilling a career as a fifth-grade schoolteacher, a high school geometry teacher, and later as a professor of mathematics. He always dreamed of writing stories, so quietly, in his spare time, he wrote novels throughout his adult life. The only one who knew of his secret passion was his beloved wife, Angie, who sadly passed away several years ago. He is still a resident of Ohio and is the father of three sons and five grandchildren. He published his first children's book, *What Ever Happened to the Smooth-Tongued Cats?* in 2022. The first novel in his *Youngstown Quintet Series*, *Abramo's Gift*, was originally published in 2008. The entire *Youngstown Quintet* is coming soon, with the first four novels republished to match the long-awaited final installment, *The Ghost Hawk*.

greconovels.com
dongreconovels@gmail.com

www.ingramcontent.com/pod-product-compliance
Lightning Source LLC
Chambersburg PA
CBHW030650020726
47493CB00006B/1960